A VOCATION

A VOCATION

David Wheldon

THE BODLEY HEAD
LONDON

British Library Cataloguing
In Publication Data
Wheldon, David
A vocation.
I. Title
823'.914[F]   PR6073.H436
ISBN 0-370-30720-8

© David Wheldon 1986
Printed in Great Britain for
The Bodley Head Ltd
30 Bedford Square, London WC1B 3RP
by St Edmundsbury Press,
Bury St Edmunds, Suffolk

Photoset in Linotron Ehrhardt by
Rowland Phototypesetting Ltd
Bury St Edmunds, Suffolk
First published 1986

PART ONE

I

The traveller's gaze traversed the scars of the mountain. He had been hastening on his journey but the measured sound of the bell caused him initially to stop and then to lay down his pack. The sound of the tolling bell, carried on the hot and unstable air, ebbed and flowed, raising echoes which concealed the direction of the distant source. The day was more than half gone. The traveller sat on a block of lichenless limestone. Sweat dripped from his face. He passed his tongue over his lips. He made no attempt to brush the flies from his body.

Even before the bell had sounded the mountain-side had been a place of waterless isolation. The sounds of his own progress had been uppermost: his breathing, his own footfall, the internal and certain sensation of the beating of his own heart. Beyond these things the mountain had been silent.

The bell still tolled when he reached the irregular plateau of the mountain's summit. The track which he had been following was soon lost amongst the spikes and pavements of eroded limestone and the irregular and fern-fronded mouths of swallets long ago abandoned by water. The karst landscape provided no landmark: the change in perspective brought about by the progress of a hundred yards robbed successive views of any continuity. As the shadows of the rocks lengthened so they merged with the darknesses of the shafts and the swallet-holes.

He reached the further edge of the plateau a little time before the sunset: he looked down and saw below him a building which at first sight he was unable either to identify or never to describe accurately. This first view was unexpected and contradictory: he could not, for those first few seconds, believe that he had after all reached the further edge of the plateau: he found it difficult to believe that he was not looking down at a small building on the side of a slope within the irregular confines of the high ground: it was only while he contemplated the structure that he saw that he was looking down and across a great void of clear air at an immense collection of roofed buildings which, buttressed by rock, lay upon a shoulder of the mountain at a vast distance from him, and itself precipitately above a wide valley, the depth of which was impossible to perceive, for the valley bottom was half-hidden in a blanket of mist.

The walls were, even at this distance, seen as being made of the local stone: they were disproportionately high; the only structure which, by its height as well as by its massiveness, could at first be clearly identified within them was the bell-tower, its tapering walls pierced by sounding windows louvred with stone. He held a hand across his face to shut out the horizontal rays of the sun. Apart from the illusion of movement given by the fluctuations of the hot atmosphere, there was a certainty that the claustral square was empty. The gaze of the eye was unable to penetrate the darkness which lay within the arches of the colonnades; although the arches were wide, the contrast between the white stone and the shadow made any detail impossible to perceive.

As he stared down at the building, filled at last with a sense of his own exhaustion, he felt as though at his back the presence of the dangerous terrain which he had so recently crossed. He saw, for the first time, though in retrospect it should have been obvious long ago, that the path he had taken over the plateau had at its every step been directed by the sound of the bell which tolled with an unwavering regularity. On the other hand, was this not perhaps an explanation too simple to be true? He recalled that, when he had first heard it, the sound of the bell had been quite directionless: he had neither known nor been told about even the existence of the monastery. The first view of the monastery had come upon him unexpectedly, and when he had first seen it, enframed within the walls of a defile, he had glanced at it and had taken it to be no more than a small building, perhaps a shepherd's hut, seen at no great distance. During the instant of his first glance he had certainly not associated it in any way with the tolling bell, for the sound, though distant, must surely take its origins from within a massive campanile. Now he saw that the building was vast; a certainty without any basis in proof; there was no means of telling the height either of its tower or of its walls; there was nothing in the landscape with which to compare it. Viewed as he was in a position to view it, the building was alone on the shoulder of the mountain. The fact of its remoteness was shown by the purple cast given to its walls by the haze of distance. In a certain sense it was only the calibre of the sound of the bell which gave an indication of the size and nature of the building. This lack of any sure yardstick emphasized the loneliness of the bare landscape which surrounded it. The building was isolated: it was incongruous in its arid surroundings. The mountain was drained dry by caverns: by what deep well did this monastery draw its water, or was it necessary to bring water up from the plain below, or from the valley, by pack animal?

How erratic his progress must have seemed to anyone looking down at him from above! Caution had been necessary; the elongating shadows hid holes where a dislodged stone would fall silently for ten seconds or more before bounding into further depths.

He looked up from his feet to the monastery and saw, in the vacillation of the heated air, an unsteadiness about the walls.

When at last he approached the gatehouse, the sense of the instability of the walls grew stronger: he found himself holding his hands over his face as though by this stance he might protect his head and push back the feeling that the walls might collapse. As he stood beneath the gatehouse arch and faced the heavy, weather-bleached timber doors, he could not remove the thought of this instability from his head. Seen from a distance, the building had appeared to be insubstantial, as a building might appear when seen in an evening's haze: now it was perceived as being real indeed, and of its true size and in a dangerous state. He raised his face to look up at the summit of the arch. The keystone, which rested some ten feet above his head, was a weathered block of masonry. It was without apparent support. He saw how precarious its position had become with time: wind had pulled the mortar from the joints around it, leaving the visible sky. He began to fear that the unremitting regularity of the bell (which, now that he was so close to its source, seemed to make the ground tremble) might precipitate its fall. It did not matter that this fear was unreasonable.

When at last he stood under the arch of the gatehouse, and when he sat on the ground beneath its lengthening shadows, his back against the doors, he saw how obliquely he had approached the building. He could not with certainty tell the direction from which he had come. Perhaps a certain rock, now at the edge of sight, was the rock against which he had stood leaning for support, looking at the place in the shadow of which he now sat, uncertain of whether he would ever reach it. He shivered. Perhaps there was the disorder of fatigue in his thinking. As he remained beneath the wall he knew that he was exhausted beyond the tiredness of travel. He looked down at his hands and saw the fever of an approaching illness as though it were an object which could, like water, be held for a little while in the cupped hands.

How should he find the temerity to knock at this door? The sound of the bell, heard through the air of the archway rather than through the timber of the door, seemed to have no communicative purpose; for one moment he had the idea that the sound of the bell was only a corollary of its prime purpose.

II

The traveller's recovery was accompanied by a grey lethargy
as ordered memory returned, bringing with it something of
the sense of stress which had brought about his original leave
of absence and which had become a journey. His fever had
been vivid; it had been filled with recurring but real events,
forgotten until the fever reproduced them. These events were
recalled with an accuracy and a visual brilliance as though
experienced for the first time: now they had gone: even their
memory was elusive. He had witnessed scenes from his past
in a manner in which he had never seen them before, as
though they had been unimportant and unperceived in waking
life, their purpose being the maintenance of the steadiness of
the flow of those things which would be perceived. These
visions were stylized and geometric and as encompassed as
stained glass within a framing arch. Now, at his recovery, this
glass had been broken, giving a wider and a more certain
outlook but on to a greyer and more formless world.

In his fever he had been able to do no more than to submit
himself to all that was done for him. Now, after the fever, he
found that he was lying in someone else's bed in a room which
he had never seen before: there was a sense of shame about
what he might have done or undergone. Voices, often loud,
came up from the room below, but they were unintelligible;
the anatomy of the building distorted the sound of the voices:
not only did the speakers' voices rise directly through the bare
floorboards from the room below, but also they sounded up
the stairwell with a wooden resonance, and there was an

asynchrony in these two ways in which the sound was propagated upwards.

Once, late at night, when the incomplete images of the fever returned, the room was filled with listening people. On another night there was a single person in the room. When he had seen this solitary person, in the half-darkness, he had pointed to a shadow in another corner of the room, imagining it to be his coat hanging on the back of a chair. The figure in the room, real or imagined, had followed the pointing of the sick man's hand without herself making any remark or gesturing in any way. The sick man had continued to point, until his hand grew cold and tremulous, and he had cried out: 'I must pay for what has been done!' The gesture had been refused: perhaps it had not been understood. Later, during the first light of the dawn of the next morning, he knew that, under other circumstances, such an offer of payment would certainly have been construed as an insult: as it was, it had been disregarded because his words and his actions had been irrational. The two sides of the situation were clear: on the one hand, hospitality was a duty which could not be paid for: on the other, hospitality had to be accepted, without payment, as a recognition of that duty. What would happen in the future was unclear. The traveller had lost count of days, an inevitability which could do nothing but add to the uncertainty of what might happen in the days ahead: when he looked through the pockets of his coat, he found neither diary nor passport, and this fact in itself seemed to have a bad prognostic significance, as though in the sum of the losses of these books he had lost a single thing of great importance.

One morning when he awoke he was aware that a bell had rung, a deep bell of ponderous and reverberant sonority, as it might be a tenor bell of a cathedral: its ringing had awoken him. At first, during the instant of wakening, he had thought that the sound had been a part of a dream, an inward recollection, the ending of which had been interrupted by a chance wakening. The bell ceased its tolling as he woke. He had thought it to be imaginary until he had heard the echoes returning from the more distant mountains at the head of the valley: he was certain only then that the deep and pleasing sound had been an event which had occurred in the outside world. There had been a solidity to the echoes which reflected the solidity of the original sound. He saw in his mind's eye the mass of the great bell, stationary now and hanging from its bearings, its down-facing mouth still murmuring in the confines of the tower.

A mist lay in the valley and only the outlines of the nearer trees were visible. Some distance away a dog barked behind a building.

He was aware—and this apprisal came to him slowly, for he could not at first believe it—that he was not after all within the monastery, but in the upper room of a house in the village on the valley's floor.

In this awareness of where he was, or might be, he became more certain of the noises of the valley, though they must always have been there, ready for the hearing. A dog (not the animal which had just barked) howled, wolflike, as though it were dusk and not early morning. There were men and women in the street, talking together, their low voices full of a pleasing equanimity. The sick man heard the sound of cows being driven through a path in the woods, although the path itself was hidden by the mists. He heard the shout of the cowman. He heard the sound of his slender stick—the faint whistling noise as it cut the air, and the crack as it struck the hide of some wandering beast. Nothing apart from the nearer trees could be seen.

He brought the bentwood chair up to the window, leaning on it intermittently; he was still weak and the chair was heavier than it had looked. The effort of moving it brought a sweat to his forehead as though the air were humid.

He slowly opened the window. The casement was in bad order, and the glass was loose in the frame; the unpainted woodwork was wet, and moisture, condensing from the drizzling mist, dripped from its lower edge. The tranquil air outside was warm.

He slept after the effort, leaning on the wooden sill; when

he lifted his head the mists had vanished and the sunlight fell obliquely into the room.

How different was the valley from the conception he had formed of it! He had never seen it before: when he had looked down from the plateau, when he had looked down upon the gatehouse of the monastery, he had been unable to see the valley-floor. Even now, although the mists had gone, he saw only as much of the valley as was enframed by the open casement of the window.

From downstairs he heard the sound of the shutters being closed against the brilliant light. He looked down at his wrist, feeling a movement on the back of one of his hands, and he saw that a fly had settled there. This fly was larger and less agile than a housefly, and when he shook it off, it was reluctant to do more than to crawl away; its wings, brushed momentarily by the fingers of his other hand, felt as dry as charred paper.

Beyond the window he saw the dusty street which wound round the houses and he saw that the potholed surface of the narrow street was covered with mud carried from the fields by the wheels of farm carts. He saw, almost in the shade of the oak-wood, the rubbish-fire which smouldered without flame, its smoke rising vertically upwards, thin and blue against the background of the trees and grey in the upper air above the foliage. The trees themselves, though unmistakably oak trees, were thorn-like in their appearance, with sparse foliage and slender twisted boles; the light fell easily between their branches to dapple the ground which had been churned by the driven farm animals. From further in the wood he heard the sound of someone breaking sticks.

The window faced the wood; to either side the house-fronts revealed extremes of upkeep and disrepair. Most of the windows were shuttered.

Above the oak trees he saw the mountains.

He looked up and followed the outline of the high irregular plateau, which, seen from the valley-floor, had a deceptively even appearance. The monastery stood on a rocky saddle between two peaks. From the plateau the monastery had had the appearance of being situated on the shoulder of a single mountain: from below, where the serrations of the mountain summits were accentuated by the upward angle necessary to gain a view of them, the monastery appeared to be situated amongst many peaks. It had the appearance of being much higher than it probably was; its altitude was exaggerated by the bare peaks which surrounded it. The traveller, looking up, did not realize that he was looking at an artificial structure: the wall which faced the valley was, with the exception of the arch of the gatehouse, windowless, and the stonework itself had a cracked and hachured appearance which gave it a superficial similarity to the planes of bedding and vertical joints of the limestone scars. It was certain that this building, unlike many another high structure, had never been built with any idea of proclaiming itself: the reverse was true: the cursory glance of a stranger could hardly have told that there was in fact any building in the mountains. Nonetheless, even when the building was recognized, one was filled with doubt because of the massive scale of its construction; it was impossible to see the full length of the wall without craning out of the window.

He could see the gatehouse clearly; the shadows within its arch were darkly defined: it was this which assured him that, after all, the building was neither as distant nor as elevated as he had supposed. It was even possible for him to make out the shape of the keystone at the top of the arch. How had he ever imagined it to have been unsupported? This was a massive stone, of a different colour from those which supported it; it was still held rigidly in the place where the builder had envisaged it. Its very irregularity indicated that it had not been cut to shape. The square campanile, viewed as the traveller viewed it, rose up into the air immediately behind the stone-work of the gatehouse. The louvres of the sounding windows sloped downwards; they were seen end-on from the valley floor: it was possible to seek an impression of the dark chamber within. It was even possible—though there might have been the elements of imagination in this—to see the shapes of the nearer of the hanging bells.

He looked back at the valley, surprised again by the limited view allowed by the window. While he had been on the plateau he had formed the certain impression that the valley was broad and wide. Now, looking from the window, he was surprised by its narrowness. In mid winter the sun would never reach the valley-floor.

With the peculiar fixity of aimless concentration sometimes seen in the convalescent he examined piecemeal as much of the wall of the monastery as could been seen from the window. He stared outward and into the darkness of the bellchamber, between the downward facing louvres, until his gaze was unsteady, and the image of the slatted arch remained at the back of his eye.

Something had begun to move silently within the bell-chamber; at first he thought it to be an imagined movement brought about by the fixity of his gaze, an impression of movement to be dispelled by a shake of the head or an aversion of the eye. Within a second he saw that this was untrue: the fact was there: he had seen one of the dark shapes, now in motion, and gathering speed; a bell was about to sound.

He had seen the precursor of the event; now it was impossible to avoid an anticipation of the sound. He remembered, with distinctness, the deep sonority of the bell which had drawn him across the dangerous terrain of the upland plateau, and which had guided his eye towards his first sight of the monastery itself. He recalled the bell which had sounded this morning, arbitrarily waking him from sleep, perceptible by the solid echoes which it had woken from the mountain. What bell would sound now? How many bells were there within the tower? There was no means of telling this with any certainty.

The bell tolled once, and the dark shape within the chamber rose again for a repetition of the sound.

He withdrew his head into the room. There was an involuntary expression of disgust on his face. The sound of the bell had been foreign to any expectation. He pulled the casement of the window, shutting and latching it, as if he wished nothing more than the shutting out of the sound, though it was impossible to shut out such a sound: it penetrated the air of the room as though the window had been glassless. The second stroke of the bell was yet more unpleasant. The bell continued to toll. It took him some time to surmise that the bell might be half-muffled, that its tolling was made up of alternate strokes; both were surprisingly soft. Once dusty and muffled: once sharp, with a waspish harmonic heard for only a fraction of a second before it was quenched. There were no echoes from the mountain: that, and the fact that the shut window had failed to reduce the noise by any degree whatsoever gave rise to the impression that the alternation had had its origins within the head: only the fact of the disturbed birds, wheeling about the summit of the tower, spoke out against this fact. Between the alternating strokes there was a rational silence in which everyday sounds could be heard. The bell sounded perhaps three dozen times (he found it difficult to count them with any accuracy) and then the sound vanished, as though it had been drawn back into the tower. It was only after it had stopped ringing that one wondered how the ringer could have borne the sound of the noise above him, and how, in the presence of that noise, he could have maintained his steady precision in the pulling of the rope.

In the silence that followed the ringing of the bell he opened the window again and looked up at the tower. 'First impressions are no guide,' he said to himself, looking at the monastery, which to all external appearances had undergone no change. The disturbed birds were returning to their nests.

He lowered his gaze to the street and saw that many people stood silently, far more than there had been before the bell had begun to toll: some of them were looking up at the monastery: some were talking amongst themselves, their voices too low to be overheard. He could hear the banging of inside doors within an adjacent house. One or two faces, like his own, were leaning out of open casements.

III

The man who stood at the open door of the room showed open surprise at the sick man's first words, 'How can I repay them?', as though he had expected to find the sick man preoccupied with his own illness. 'There is nothing exceptional for you to be thankful for,' he said, his surprise causing him to speak in a sudden voice. He stood in the open doorway as if reluctant to enter the room. He reached up one of his hands to grasp the lintel of the door-frame. 'You can't repay them. There would be no use making any attempt.' He looked above the sick man, out of the window, as though for some reason embarrassed at the sight of him. 'My name is Thibault. I was here on the night you were brought into the inn: I frequently pass through the village.'

The traveller sat forward in his chair, his posture one of enervation. His face was expressionless, and the lids of his eyes were heavy and dark. He had the appearance of one who has just woken from a heavy sleep; his voice had been unsteady. Now that he had been told the room was that of an inn he wondered whether the proprietor had been dosing him with alcohol; it was quite likely. Perhaps this man, Thibault, had been surprised at seeing so sick a man sitting out of bed. Who had carried the heavy chair from its place against the wall to the window?

'Are you married?' asked Thibault.

'Yes,' said the traveller. He paused for a moment as though the train of his thoughts had been interrupted. 'How does one begin to learn their language? I can neither speak to them nor understand what they say.' He gave no impression of having paid any attention to anything which Thibault had said.

'I follow you entirely,' said Thibault, seeing the marks on the traveller's arms: these shocked him: a few days ago they had been darkish bruises on the surface of the skin: they had given the traveller the appearance of having been cruelly beaten by an assailant who had not spared him: some of these bruises had a resemblance to those made by staves and fists. As though quite unaware of this the traveller had lifted up his right hand to support the weight of his head and the marks were now obvious: a stranger in the room, unfamiliar with the circumstances, would have put his arms out to support him, crying out: 'Who attacked you, and why?'

When Thibault took a step into the room, the sick man put out a hand to keep him away. 'I'm not going back to that bed until night!' he said.

'Whoever said that you should,' said Thibault, making a statement of the question, looking down at the sick man, perhaps wondering whether the marks on the skin, despite all the appearances to the contrary, were evidence of healing. He resumed his stance at the door—for he had taken a few steps into the room on seeing the extent of the sick man's injuries —and again grasped the lintel of the frame. 'You've only been here a few days: eight at the most: possibly you've had a false idea of the passing of time. They say it happens.

'As far as learning their language, here in the village, you might as well forget all possibility of that. What do you want from them? What would you expect to gain by reciting some phrase or other?

'The proprietor and his wife stand nothing to gain. If you judge by local standards they certainly are not poor.' He looked down at the sick man. 'There was some difficulty in deciding which house should take you. It was a strange night for that alone. I've never seen the market square in such confusion at night. The magistrate's wife (the proprietor thought he should call the magistrate) was certain that you were of some official importance: she was in two minds as to what she might do: she wanted you to be taken to the magis-

17

trate's house, and that would have been an honour enough; on the other hand, you were said to be infectious. No-one knew whether the doctor had given the right answer over the telephone that night: "those are never the marks of typhoid", so I overheard the magistrate say. As it was, you were taken here: I could say that you were brought here. The proprietor and his wife made no fuss about it. This place was an inn; now it's a bar of sorts; there are six bars in this village. This no longer gives accommodation under ordinary circumstances.

'You're making your recovery. That will be enough thanks for them. It would have stretched their hospitality to have given them the responsibility of paying an undertaker.' He still remained at the threshold of the room. 'I think I told you that they had the doctor over here to see you.'

'I don't remember a doctor.'

'He came here twice.' Thibault paused. 'He came from the town; they had to ask the telephone exchange repeatedly to put the village line through to him: apparently he had given them instructions as to the sort of incoming calls which they were to put through to him. It took the magistrate himself to make a call, not to the doctor: the exchange wouldn't believe that the magistrate was not making a pretence of his title: the magistrate had to telephone an administrator in the town hall who was himself an acquaintance of the doctor's for the gravity of the situation to be understood. The magistrate himself was certainly aware of the necessity of urgency: it's his wife you have to be careful of in this kind of situation.' He took his hand from the lintel of the door, and smiled. 'She thought that you were a visitor of some importance; she thought that this village was, after all, your destination, and that it was an accident of chance that you happened to be brought down to the place.'

'I never knew that this village existed,' said the sick man, who had given the impression that he had only heard the latter part of Thibault's speech.

'The doctor hasn't sent his bill. What do you think of that? He has never struck me as being a man likely to be easy in his demands.'

'I shall certainly pay him.'

Thibault looked at him. He said, without committing himself, 'You could, I suppose, though he has asked nothing of you. The proprietor knows his address. On the other hand, perhaps he has a purpose in sending no bill. Perhaps he has no wish to be paid: if it were not so, one would have expected that he would have sent his bill by now, particularly as you are a traveller, and as likely as not to be off as soon as you have the strength. I don't know the facts of the situation. He may believe you have no account with him. Perhaps he shared the same views as the magistrate's wife. I don't suppose you remember the night when the magistrate's wife came up here. I think it was on the second night.' Thibault had entered the room. He stood in front of a framed mirror which hung, by a piece of braided wire, from a prominent hook in the plaster of the wall. The glass was old, and had the ability to distort his image; the reflection of his face was sallow and elongated. He raised a hand and touched the varnished wood of the frame.

The sick man for the first time mentioned his illness, laying no emphasis on it, as though it were a fact of no importance in comparison with anything which might happen in the future. The manner in which he talked about his illness caused Thibault to wonder whether he had in fact refused to accept the presence of the obvious and disfiguring sores on his skin, or whether he had, because of the relative slowness of their evolution, grown used to them, so that perhaps they no longer struck him as being as unpleasant and things to be hidden.

'Yes,' said Thibault, looking out of the window above the traveller's head, as though searching for something to say, 'The doctor said that it was typhoid, but that was before the bruises appeared. The doctor's the doctor, and the magistrate's the magistrate. Under the magistrate's orders, the proprietor opened your pack, and gave your coat to the magistrate's bailiff. They could see, so they said, no sign of any immunization certificates.'

'I was told a long time ago that typhoid was not endemic in this area.'

19

'What comment can be passed on the kind of advice given to a traveller?' said Thibault. He looked into the glass and saw his own distorted reflection. He stood in silence. Perhaps he wondered why, earlier, he had been so talkative: it was surely unlike him: perhaps he had been at a loss to know what to say. He turned to the sick man but said nothing; he might have said: 'this talk is of no importance,' but he did not, as though he saw the extent of the man's illness. Moved to an uncomfortable pity if not to compassion it would have been difficult for him to have said anything which was not trivial: what else could one say at such short notice, and in such unexpected and fixed circumstances? Had the traveller, finding himself in a situation foreign to him and beyond his control, shown this concern for his benefactors in order to elicit concern for himself? The traveller had said very little: 'How can I repay them.' 'You must instruct me how to thank them' and, of the doctor, 'I must repay him.' Only then had he spoken, and then in certain but circumspect terms, of his own illness. Now he was looking at his own forearms.

Thibault, when he had arrived at the inn that afternoon, could have had no idea that the sick man might be capable of holding a conversation; he had, it appeared come straight from the street and up the stairs and had not met anyone downstairs; the sick man had heard him walking across the floor of the room below. No-one could have told him of the change in the sick man's condition. Now he looked into the room from the door as though he had the irrational certainty that the traveller, by reason of his six or eight days' confinement in this upper room, knew it intimately, as though the bedstead, the washstand, the chair and the mirror were his own possessions; that this room was his room; that he had lived in this house for as long as he could remember, a long while, and had become familiar with everything which might be seen through the window. Thibault, now looking out of the window above the traveller's head, saw to the side of the oak wood a stone wall with the red valerian growing in the coping; there was no doubt that this view was familiar to the traveller, as though he in some way owned it. He found difficulty in remembering that the traveller had been in this room for only a few days and had been sitting at the window for only an hour or so: this idea that the sick man had certain rights within the room was a spurious one; any appeal that the sick man might make to his past would be a spurious appeal.

Thibault, immediately he had opened the door to look into the room, had found that he was reluctant to speak at all; he had prepared nothing to say; he would have had nothing to say even if he had known in advance that the sick man was conscious. On the night when the sick man had been taken to the inn he had followed the villagers up the narrow staircase, and into this same upper room. When he had seen him in his fever, his face pale and sweating, his eyes staring at imaginary objects, he had half thought that he might be about to witness something profound: the man had shouted phrases, meaningless in themselves, but which (perhaps because of the fact that it had been a dark night, and because the room itself had been restless with the coming and going of the villagers, the magistrate and his wife and the bailiffs) had seemed to have taken on a certain appropriate salience. Thibault had found a curious interest, to which he certainly would not have admitted, in watching this process known as delirium, as though the unconscious words, half heard and half understood and often inarticulate, had origins beyond the man who had uttered them. It had been evident that Thibault had not been alone in thinking this: so many of the men and women from the village had made their way into the room so that there had been hardly enough space in which one might move, either towards the bedstead, or towards the stairwell. The people in the room had striven to gain a vantage point from which they might observe and examine the sick man's face. The very number of people in the room had made it hot. For all the solidity of the stonework of its front, the house itself was badly built, and one could feel the vibrations running through the floorboards as people ran up and down the stairs, brushing past each other under the window on the little landing. The proprietor had insisted that the windows be shut and the shutters drawn to, giving no reason for his insistence, but perhaps feeling in some way that this confinement and enclosure would benefit the sick man in his illness; indeed, he could not be shaken from this belief. The exclamations from the villagers and the results of their sudden movements had made the room noisy: the noise was accentuated because the room itself, though larger than one might have thought from the narrowness of the stairwell and the confined space of the landing, was almost bare of furnishings: there were no curtains over the windows, and no curtains across the door: the walls were of bare plaster, limewashed and unpapered, and there was no carpet on the wide black-stained floorboards. The smell, at first not an unpleasant compound smell, had later become overpowering, as though the people in the room had just arrived from their various tasks, smelling of domestic and wild animals. The air had become rank. There was a sense of continuing commotion, and the restless lack of peace, over which the sound of the bells had presided, heightened the agitation of delirium. For some reason all within the room had been very much aware of the sounding of the bells; the reactions of the villagers were very directly communicable. Indeed, more than once, Thibault, from the corner in which he had established himself, had been sure that some of the older of the villagers had been muttering short phrases, perhaps questions (though not asked interrogatively), into the sick man's ear, and then had stood back in silence, not so much in order to listen to any reply, but to observe any change of expression on the face. What had they been tryng to do by these actions? Had it been done, this muttering, in order to provoke a shouted response? If this were so, then there had been no trace of cruelty in the attempt: the faces of the old people had been reservedly pitying. On the other hand, there had been nothing in their manner of the meaningless phrases spoken by a doctor into the ear of an unconscious man in an attempt to discover the degree of his unconsciousness. All the same, what would a man out of his mind with fever make of mutterings given in his ear in a language of which he had no understanding? And, equally, how might the questioners

22

interpret the inarticulate replies? Had it been only a search? If that were so, the fact of such a search was infectious: at that moment, in that hot room, during that night, the shout of fever had seemed more profound than any statement given in answer to a question.

This train of events had been repeated on the following two nights. When the crisis was past those who stood in the room were content to stand against the walls, and the only noises in the room were those sounds which chanced to come from the outside. By the fifth day nobody except the proprietor's wife came up the staircase to the room.

The washstand by the window stood flat against the wall: above it there hung a brass crucifix: the juxtaposition of these two objects surely indicated that their relative positions had been directly influenced by the juxtaposition of objects in the side-chapel of a church. The bentwood chair had been taken back to the corner in a dark angle of the room where the sun rarely penetrated, and the mirror, which was now in the line of a narrow beam of sunlight, cast an elongated lozenge of light across the wall above the head of the bedstead. The day was hot, and, although the shutters outside the window were partially closed, the heat penetrated the room through the sloping ceiling, which, as it was immediately below the tiled roof, radiated heat. The smell of the birds' nests in the roof filled the hot and umoving air within the room.

The traveller crossed the bare floor to the washstand, and stood in front of it, clasping the marble edges with his hands. The zinc ewer in the porcelain basin was filled with fresh water. Without pausing to consider whether or not he was acting only out of unnecessary habit he poured a little of the water from the ewer into the basin and began to wash himself. His hands were unsteady. He had not noticed this before: he noticed it now only because the water in the basin trembled as he immersed his fingers. His nails had grown. The purple marks, the haemorrhages beneath the skin, on his arms and his body, were turning a brownish colour: one or two of the largest, on the more exposed parts of his limbs, which had

23

broken down into shallow ulcers with poorly demarcated edges, were showing signs of healing. The yellowness of his skin was more obvious on looking in the mirror than on direct examination; perhaps he was still jaundiced. He did not recall having gone to any water-closet while he had been in this house.

He put his hands in the water, which was the hard limestone water from the mountains. The gritty soap (which had the appearance of laundry-soap) made no appreciable lather. As he washed himself he listened to the voices which came up from the room below, through the floor of the room and up the stairwell. He paused in his washing, leaving his hands motionless in the water in order to listen. There were two people talking; of this he was certain; he could hear the regular alternation of their voices, one following another. He found it difficult to avoid an attempt at guessing the meaning of their talk. Listening for a further moment he knew that he had been quite wrong in thinking that there had been only two voices: a third now spoke a single interrogative word, a single monosyllable, but that one word had been enough to prove the fact of the presence of this third speaker. In this way the traveller found that his impressions of what was even now happening in the room below were quite wrong: he had formed a mental picture of two people talking in a room, a man and a woman, for one of the voices had been that of a man, and the other, that of a woman: he had even imagined the circumstances of their meeting in the room below, and even the nature and shape of that room, about which, of course, he knew nothing, save that it presumably had the same plan as the room he was now in, a little different perhaps because the bulky wooden carcase of the stairwell did not protrude into it. He saw that his knowledge of everything in the room below was a product of an imagination which had at its root not a plan of a room but the hearing of voices speaking in an unknown language. There was no certainty of the number of speakers. The third speaker, the man or woman who had spoken that interrogative monosyllable, might have been the only other person in the room: alternatively, there might have been within the room a number of people who, until the third person had happened to speak, had contented themselves by listening in silence to that dialogue. The traveller, at certain moments, on hearing certain inflections, could not help but make the assumption that he was the subject of that talk; that was certainly probable; it was not an unnatural supposition under the circumstances; if his predicament were to be the subject of discussion, what did that matter? Does it matter (so he thought) whether I am being discussed, in my absence, in my own language, or whether I am being discussed in a language which I overhear but cannot understand?

Listening at one moment, the traveller found it easy to imagine that the most neutral of conversations was going on in the room beneath his feet: listening the next, he was certain that he was the subject of discussion, and that that discussion was centred upon his faults and the fact that they had caused his illness, that his illness had been visited on him for past errors, which he himself had forgotten, but which, in the semblances of the voices from downstairs, were being revived. It was quite impossible for him to put aside these unverifiable interpretations: there were cadences, certain sibilant word-endings which bore a superficial resemblance to words which might have given a thorough and dispassionate rendition of his own character, a kind of assessment of himself. At the same time, and recognizing that he was thinking in an irrational manner, he saw that after all he had only himself for a reference point: he had been aware—and he thought this in all truth—that during his fever, and particularly at night he had shouted, as though into an imaginary ear which had the power to listen but not the will to repeat what it heard, confidences of such privacy that he could no longer recall them to the waking mind. At this point he found that he had reached a certain truth in that those who regard themselves as being bluff and uncomplicated are usually liars or people who talk too much about things which are not their concern. At that moment he knew the importance of privacy, and the incursions which illness makes into it. 'I am in danger of attempting to put all things in the context of myself,' he said.

25

He was surprised to find that he had spoken out loud, and that he had spoken in a loud voice: the conversation in the room below him stopped. He looked down, past the moulded lip of the marble surface of the washstand, at the floor. He saw, for the first time, that there were wide cracks between the floorboards, which, being ancient, had warped and twisted with time, springing apart. One crack in particular was wider than the rest, its width augmented by a knothole the knot of which had long gone: this crack drew his attention. Through this crack, and the knothole adjacent to it, it was possible to see the room below. He knelt, first placing the zinc ewer (which he happened to be holding) on the floor beside him; then he lay on his stomach, his forehead resting on his hands as though he had become exhausted. The room below, which he had not seen before, and which he was now seeing from the most unusual perspective possible, was disposed to the viewing of his eye. The room below him was an exceptionally high-ceilinged room for the front room of a village inn. At his first glance he was forced to ask himself whether this building once had a different purpose. He looked down. He saw the bottles and the glasses which stood on the wooden surfaces of the tables. He saw the long darkwood counter with the trays of fruit at one end: the shelves where the tinned and packaged goods were stored, behind the counter, which was seen as a series of foreshortened tiers; the vegetables, the sacks of potatoes and the nets of onions, the knives and the reels of sisal rope, tarred and untarred. He saw the brass yard-measure let into the wood of the counter, the pair of scissors, the rolls of fine-meshed chicken-wire, the sharpening stones, the box of cabbages, and the baker's tray, empty now but still with its tissue-paper lining. All these things were far below him. He saw the heads of the talkers. There were five people in the room below, four men and one woman: the woman was not the proprietor's wife; she was much younger; one wondered why she had stayed talking in the bar, when surely her purpose had been to buy some domestic item or other. Perhaps she was a relative of the proprietor or his wife; she had, even though viewed from above, the same rounded head and the same plump shoulders as the proprietor's wife, and her hair was the same colour as one might have imagined that of the proprietor's wife to have been some years ago. There was an ease and an assurance in the way she stood, her arms crossed, looking from the face of the man who had last spoken to the curtained doorway of the private quarters of the inn, behind the counter: the traveller, lying on the floor of the room above, could only assume that her arms were crossed, her hands tucked into her elbows, because they were hidden by her breasts. Of the other people in the bar below, those who sat in half-darkness beyond the range of the light from the half-shuttered window, he saw only the lighter, uncovered hands, the forearms, the brows, the faces in downward-looking profile.

They had stopped in their talk. The pause in their conversation had occurred, not because of the sick man's almost involuntary exclamation, as he had initially supposed, but because a single bell had sounded.

This bell, not heard before, gave the impression that it would never be heard again: its fleeting assonance with the sound which, in retrospect, one might have expected of it, changed the course of the sick man's thinking, and, while it sounded its single stroke, the pattern of thought itself. When it and its faint echoes had died away, it left, to the sick man's eye, a change in the view of the room below him, though he had no idea whether the sound had changed the course of events in the room below or his perception of them. Why should the sound of a bell have this power? Why should it be capable of causing an interruption any more profound than that which might equally have been brought about by some more commonplace sound? Had the sound of the bell been imagined? Was he still unwell? Had the sound of the bell been imagined, not only by himself, but also by the men and the woman who stood in the room below, or had they ignored or been unaware of the sound of the bell, stopping in their conversation coincidentally, arriving at a natural pause, or had they after all heard the sudden exclamation from the room above their heads?

27

The sick man, lying on the floor with his head in his hands, was now asleep. The zinc jug was by his side, standing half empty, as though in his thirst he had drunk deeply from its encrusted brim. The basin on the washstand contained a little dirty water and the bar of laundering-soap. As for the sound of the bell: that might as well have been an anomaly of perception experienced in childhood, during the night-fevers, at the transition of wakefulness and sleep.

The sleeper was naked. His clothes lay over the seat of the bentwood chair which stood in the darkest corner of the room. These clothes had the appearance of having been vigorously laundered (perhaps they had been boiled) and they had been heavily starched before they had been ironed. The elution of their colour gave them the odd appearance of institutional clothing or a uniform of some kind. His boots, which rested under the chair, were greaseless and stiff.

When he awoke, and began to dress, the noise of his activity was apparently heard in the room below. He was not aware that he made much more noise with his clothes on than while he had been naked. The talkers raised their heads, he could see this through the floor, though they must have known that they would have been able to see nothing beyond the dark-varnished underside of the boards or the joists from which the hardware hung.

The traveller opened the door of the upstairs room, and saw for the first time the landing, which was lit by a single square window high in the wall of the stairwell. The landing was narrow and floored by bare boards. The window above the stairs was recessed in a ledge with a sharply sloping sill; being high in the wall, and directly over the stairs, this window would have been impossible to clean unless a ladder were to be placed over the stairwell. The panes were opalescent with dust: spiders had spun webs across the window from the latch to the hinges, and the cocooned flies were uncountable. The glass was milkily white, and it was impossible to make out anything but vague shapes beyond it. The downward-leading staircase was steep, its risers tall and its treads narrow; the sick man was forced to clutch the rails which were screwed into the boarding at either side of the stairway.

Two of the men who stood in the room, on seeing the traveller's unsteadiness, began to stand. Having stood they waited at the bottom of the stairwell looking at each other as though it was clear in their minds that at some time in the future they must support his weight. They grasped his upper arms. These two men who supported his weight might have been agricultural workers who had been resting during the heat of the afternoon. Their hands were white with dust: this dust, which clung to their clothes, had the smell of old plaster and masonry about it: perhaps they had been demolishing a building. There was experience in the way in which they held the traveller's arms to support him, as though in the past they had had dealings with sick animals, and saw in the sick man's behaviour something not very different. They guided him across the uneven grey flagstones to a wooden bench with a back to it, and took his weight again as he, seeing the seat, made as if to sit. The table, which had been drawn aside to allow these two men to half-carry him to the settle, was now put back in front of him, as though he might require it for some purpose: had the proprietor placed pen and ink and papers on the table it would not have seemed out of order. Those in the room had pulled the furniture aside for the sick man's convenience in the same way that they might have moved it to allow the passage of someone of authority: perhaps they had been told of the magistrate's wife's surmise that he was a visitor of importance: there was an orderliness in which they moved the tables and chairs aside and then back again. It was surprising how much room the two men required. The proprietor poured out a glass of red wine, a generous measure in a tumbler, and placed it at the place on the surface of the table at which the traveller's gaze happened to rest.

Even after the traveller had been sitting in silence for some time he had difficulty in making out how many people were in the room: he had counted five at first, but then he saw that he had counted the two agricultural workers, or demolition men, as being the same person, for they had shifted their positions, and indeed they were very much alike, perhaps brothers. Now he saw that behind them other people from the village sat at further tables; they had been taking no part in the earlier conversation but had been sitting in their own company, some of them reading newspapers or looking at their own hands: some of these further villagers were only seen for the first time when they stood as the two workers had guided the sick man across the room, though it was not clear whether they had stood because of a feeling of deference for the sick man or because they wished to show their willingness in helping the two demolition workers in what little way they could. The only thing that was certain was that they had not stood in order to see the sick man more clearly: because of the commotion which had been caused by the moving of the furniture, he could be seen from every part of the room.

The shape of this room was as irregular as that of the room above. A wide chimney breast protruded into this room, as it did into the room above: perhaps on the other side of the wall was the kitchen-range in its corresponding alcove. The interior was darker than might have been expected. The inward-opening windows were wide open, but the blank wooden shutters, supported on heavy iron hinges let into the outer masonry of the thick wall, were closed against the sun; the door was also closed, and the only light in the room was that which descended the stairwell from the dusty square window.

The parish priest, on his arrival, did not purposefully wake the traveller directly, but, as he drew the chair away from the other side of the table he laid his hand sharply on its surface. He began to speak while he still held the back of the chair. 'They told me that I might find you downstairs,' he said, speaking slowly, as though he had not used the language for some time. 'What can I say?'

His back was to the door, and he was seen in silhouette. Neither his face nor his expression were distinct, but they were imaginable because of the slow and heavy way in which he had entered and then surveyed the room, at last drawing out the chair, holding the upper rail of its back in his hands: he had behaved as though he had no wish to disturb either those at the bar or those who might be sitting down: he had approached the table as though he had expected the traveller to be asleep; perhaps he had intended to gauge whether the sick man was truly asleep or sitting with his eyes closed.

The priest sat opposite the traveller. Had the sick man been asleep, the priest would, in all probability, have continued to sit opposite him, saying nothing but perhaps content to remain silent in the darkened and shuttered room, independent of purpose, but prepared either to stand and to leave at the moment of his choice, or to remain as he was until the traveller awoke.

Evidently he recognized that the traveller, though his eyes were closed, was awake. He said: 'I see from the documents shown to me by the magistrate that your name—' He paused as though he had forgotten it '—is Thomas Colver.'

'I am called Thomas Colver.' He opened his eyes and the priest immediately saw the uniform yellowness of the sclera of his eyes.

'You are still jaundiced!' The priest uttered this phrase as though shocked into saying it. He paused before he said, 'I was with you during the first days. You had typhus very badly. On the third night I wondered whether you would survive it. You were given the two sacraments: one Christ's and the other the Church's.'

Colver rested his arms on the table. 'Wherever I turn I find myself in debt!' he said. 'What do you know of me?'

'Yes,' said the priest, responding immediately, as though recognizing the question as being the first words the sick man had uttered, apart from the statement of his name, but at the same time paying no attention to its meaning. 'In an extremity one has to take certain truths on trust.'

Colver looked at the silhouette of the priest's massive shoulders; he could still make out nothing of his face. 'Typhus? I was told that it was typhoid.'

The priest seemed to be pleased to hear him speak. He stood up, as though he had been given something to think about, and walked to the window, his attitude that of a man preparing himself to listen to the things which another has to say. He pushed one of the shutters open by a few inches; a narrow bar of direct sunlight fell obliquely upon the jamb of the window, and the room was suffused with reflected light. The priest himself had his back to the window and it was still difficult to see his face with any degree of clarity. 'No, not typhoid. There is no typhoid here: there never has been: the water comes straight from the mountain. The same is true on the other side of the hills. You have had the mountain-fever, typhus; one hears sporadic reports of it from the pine-forests at the other side of the range, towards the coast. It's not the true epidemic typhus, but even so, it's a world apart from typhoid. Whoever told you that you had typhoid?' He looked at Colver, as though examining his face in the new light which he himself had admitted to the room. 'The doctor was with you for only a few moments of each of his visits; I've seen you more constantly. I've seen all this before. One becomes used to recognizing these things. Typhoid has a more gradual onset.' He turned to look towards the window, as though about to stare through the narrow crack between the leaves of the shutters. His face was seen for the first time: his profile had a sharpness which contrasted with his massive body.

He looked back at the traveller. He appeared to have become suddenly angry, though it was difficult to know why this might have been so. He might have said: 'Pass no comment on me! You are the stranger here!' He had certainly opened his mouth as if he had been about to speak, but the traveller was uncertain whether or not he had spoken; perhaps he had merely resented being stared at. He folded his hands so that they were hidden; the traveller had noticed, while the priest had been holding the back of the chair, only a moment ago, that his hands were broad, and calloused as though by heavy work. There was no means of telling why he should have appeared to have been ashamed of the appearance of his face or his hands.

Colver looked down at the table, inconsequentially tracing the grain with his gaze, finding an abstract world in its convolutions: at the centre of an eye within the grain there was a knot, and on that knot rested the tumbler of wine: the proprietor had rested the tumbler, an hour or so earlier, when he had brought it from the counter. He saw now that the table was veneered with a burred hardwood which suggested that the table itself had at some time been of some value; perhaps it had come from a house of some importance in the locality. In one place, near a corner, the veneer had lifted, exposing the softwood beneath it. Colver, not realizing at first that the table was veneered, had run his hand along the underside of the table top, as though he might feel the other side of the prominent knot beneath the glass. He had forgotten the priest's look of anger; he was now sure that his words had been imagined and not spoken. 'How can I repay the landlord for his hospitality?'

The priest searched in the pocket of his cassock, taking out a black, cloth-bound book with the word 'diary' printed on the front cover. Although he held this book in his hands he did not look at it. 'You can only be thankful for your recovery,' he said. 'There's no need for demonstrative excess about it.' He paused, tracing the letters of the word on the front of the diary with a broad forefinger. 'You're not recovered yet. My own past experience would suggest to me that typhus leaves a long period of debilitation behind it,' he gave the appearance of choosing his words with care, 'though that is something which one does not generally labour. It doesn't do to under-estimate the power of suggestion over those with an illness such as typhus. It is difficult to generalize about these things. It is difficult to tell what will happen.'

'I am in debt. You must recognize that.'

'Well, you are in debt; that is quite true, but only in a certain sense. The inn is owned by the building on the mountain, which is in some people's eyes seen as being a monastery, as I am sure you will have been told. When I first arrived here I discovered that, in earlier years, when there were more travellers, and when the parish was the parish, it was maintained as a guest-house. There is nothing more to be said than that. The only thanks you can give to the landlord,

33

as you choose to call him, is such thanks as you think he deserves. You might, if it would improve you, choose to regard your illness and your arrival here, and the care which you have received and will receive, as being no more than an opportunity for him to gain merit in the eyes of his masters by proving the extent of his duty.' He said this seriously, but there was a sense of private irony in the formal way he had chosen to speak. 'Thus far, he has, quite probably, gained a greater satisfaction than anything he might gain by any reward you might offer him.' He said this as though he had suspected, in Colver's protestation of his own debt, that the sick man might by this means be attempting to draw further sympathy to his own predicament. He might have said: 'Who are you to praise the assiduity of others? Look at the predicament you are in, and that of your own making! There is no need for you to exacerbate the circumstances which gave rise to it!'

Colver, again imagining that he had heard the priest speak, and again imputing words to fit the meaning of his expression, looked round the room. He found it hard to see it as being anything other than the bar of a village inn. He saw again the ochre-coloured walls where the long shelves were stacked with tins and packages, some of them discoloured by time and dust, and, as he had seen through the crack in the floorboards from the room above, the empty baker's tray, and the iron-mongery; the scythe-blades, the whetting stones, the reels of wire and the tarred hawser-laid rope on wooden drums. The trays of local vegetables were propped outward on the counter to catch the eye. In the dark space under the stairs was the ribbed shape of a forty-gallon paraffin-drum. This inn was no different from any other in the neighbourhood, and the things which were seen showed the ambitions of the proprietor were no different from any other man in a similar position. 'This inn is owned by the monastery,' said Colver in a voice of unbelief. 'Naturally it is.'

The priest followed Colver's gaze. 'It is not altered by what you choose to believe.' He turned to Colver. 'Why is it that commonsense is the first casualty of tradition? Why does the proprietor keep the paraffin under the stairs? Did you ever

34

imagine the danger you were in when you were asleep upstairs? Always we are in peril! As for the inn, the man given charge of it takes it upon himself to suppose that he has the licence to run it as he wishes. It's practical enough, as things stand at the moment. Why should a man in his position be expected to remember the principal duties of his appointment?'

Colver, who still had difficulty in the idea of reconciling this inn with the concept of a monastic hospice, said: 'Shall I see any representative of the monastery in order to pay my debt and to give what thanks I can, if, as you say, the proprietor is only a tenant?'

'I think you know as well as I do from what you see about you that you will see no-one from that particular building.' The priest put his diary back in his pocket.

'The monastery belongs to a closed order, then?'

'The order to which it belongs is, I imagine, closed. The matter of the hospitality which it has extended to you is, similarly, closed.' His manner was not secretive; the reverse was true. He was affable and at his ease, as though, after an initial uncertainty, he had found the sick man to be asking such expected questions as might come naturally to him. 'I make no secret of it,' he said. If he held anything a secret (so one thought) it was because he had no wish to put it into words. 'One grows used to the building when one lives here. There is no more to be said than that. The bells—which you can hear as well as I—are the only communication between the building and the village. If previous experience is anything to go by, then I don't believe that the gates will be opened to you, no matter how deeply you state your sense of debt.' He smiled, as though in his thinking he had broached a new vein of tolerance. 'Debt isn't such an unusual thing.'

The traveller, who was somewhat cold despite the heat of the room, remembered, while he had stood on the upland ridge of the plateau, that sense of the desolate precariousness of the walls. 'You, as a priest, must have been inside the monastery.'

'I have never been inside it,' said the priest. 'When you are sent to work here you can do no more than accept its presence.

35

With time one takes it for granted. What else is possible?'
Perhaps he found his own words unsatisfactory, for he suddenly stood up, and, walking to the window, he pushed the
shutter still further open, and he looked out through the crack.
One could tell by the elevation of his glance that he was
looking at the high walls of the distant building. He put his two
hands together, allowing his fingers to become interlocked. 'I
can do no more than to admit that when I first came here I
found it a perplexity. That is certainly a fact. After a time one
grows tired of the old speculations: one learns that, for peace
of mind, one cannot suffer the old arguments as gladly as one
might once have done. The old words come more unhappily
to the tongue, the old explanations more tediously to the
mind.' His words were slow, as though they had required
more thought in their formulation than their sense indicated.
'In a certain sense it has been a long time since I gave it any
particular consideration.'

'But you, as a priest, must know something of the working
of the monastery; its daily life, its rule, its order.'

'Why should I be expected to have the ability to understand
that order more clearly than those others who are forced
by circumstances to live here? As I have said, there is no
communication other than the sound of the building's bells.'
As he spoke the traveller, who had been listening to him with
some attention, was aware of the metrical intonation of his
voice, so much at variation with the flat and unemphatic voices
of those others who were in the room: no doubt this was a
question of habit. 'A moment ago,' said the priest, 'I told you
that it had been some long time since I had given that building
any particular consideration.' On saying this he fell silent, as
if waiting for comment, but Colver had quite honestly forgotten to what he was referring. He recognized his own loss
of memory in a detached manner, without any sense of alarm.
He looked up from the table's surface and saw the priest's
face as though through a yellow haze; the crack of light
between the shutters had itself assumed a yellow colour.
Although it must have been present since the moment of his
entering the room, this yellow view, it had only now become

apparent: perhaps until his present lifting of his eyes he had accepted it without the need to comment to himself: perhaps this yellowness had only become evident on the opening of the shutter, when the room was filled with direct sunlight, as though previously there had been hardly enough light in the room to distinguish objects and persons. 'This must be what they call a jaundiced view,' he said. He was in no pain: he felt, in fact, healthy and pleasurably fatigued and neither hungry nor thirsty. This sense of his own health gave him the idea that he had not after all been unwell. He looked at the faces of those in the inn, the talkers and the card-players, wondering if any of them were at this moment concealing pain or warding off pity. 'This is a jaundiced view,' he said, with apparent clarity, but his words were indistinct.

The priest said: 'There is no rule; there is no order; there is no routine of daily life. The sound of the building's bells obtrudes into one's life. I would be lying if I said otherwise.' He paused to stare round the room, which, as far as he was concerned, despite the presence of the people who were talking at the bar or sitting at the tables, might have been empty except for himself and the traveller. 'The bells ring at uncanonical hours. There is no reason to them.' He released his interlocked fingers. 'The lack of order, the arbitrariness of their sounding, used to make me physically ill when I first arrived here. Not so much now. One is far more adaptable than one might once have imagined. I am not a native of this region.

'Perhaps it is inevitable that someone who has been brought up in the shadows of those walls should see them in a very different light. The native-born allow nothing a significance unless it bears on their lives or unless a reason can be brought out to explain the circumstances under which it might in the future come to bear upon their lives.'

Colver looked beyond him, further into the room; he saw the faces of those villagers whom he had not seen before; he began to wonder why they were all here in this hot, southward-facing room while the heat of the day was at its greatest. During the time he had been upstairs he had thought

37

that there had been no more than two people in the room: now he saw that the room was crowded. Even though this was true, only three people in the room (apart from the traveller and the priest) were talking: they were those whom Colver had heard earlier, three people, talking together, two of them alternating in the sentences, the third contributing a single word from time to time. By closing his eyes he could imagine that he was still upstairs, in an empty room, and that below him was a room in which two people were talking, a man and a woman, while a third person made these intermittent remarks or asked these intermittent questions. Opening his eyes, lifting his gaze from the surface of the table, he saw that one man, the elder of the two demolition workers, who had been sitting alone at a table in the corner, was now folding his newspaper as though he were about to leave. Colver, for all his present sense of wellbeing, was taken aback by the rapidity with which he had assigned, in his illness, arbitrary identities to those who had surrounded him: he had assumed for no good reason that the two men who had helped him were at first agricultural labourers and then demolition workers: he had marked down the proprietor as being the proprietor even while he had looked down through the boards of the room above, though the man he had taken to be the proprietor might as easily have been a trustworthy man who at some time in the past had been given standing permission to go behind the counter: the same pre-emptory recognition had also been true of the room in which he had awoken: he had thought himself, during the first few moments of his awakening, that the room was a room in the topmost storey—the floor beneath the roof—of an institution: he had, at the moment of his awakening, pictured the nature of the room in which he lay, and who would waken him, with a bell, or a shout, or a rap at the door, perhaps waiting for the reply, perhaps not, and what might be said to him, and which list of duties, compiled before dawn, might be read to him: he had imagined his own rising from the bed, easily, to examine, while washing at the washstand which stood in the space of the dormer under the round-arched lead-roofed window, a familiar landscape of

38

parkland with stands of oaks in broad meadows, beyond which was a flat and fertile plain where monotonous fields of black and furrowed earth were interrupted by thick hedges and dense coverts, parkland becoming arable miles, flat tracts foreshortened at the horizon's edge. It was uncertain as to whom this landscape belonged. When one has access to scant, fragmented and irrelevant information, one's interpretations are necessarily incorrect. 'I am in danger of rushing into misunderstandings,' he said, aloud, facing the villagers rather than the priest. Now he saw that the elder of the two demolition workers had, on standing, looked at the clock which hung from the wall above the curtained doorway behind the counter, and then at his own watch, not perhaps to tell the time so much as to examine any discrepancy between the times indicated by the clock and the watch: he looked first at the priest and then at Colver, and then made his way to the door, allowing, in opening it, an access of further light, far brighter than the light which had been admitted earlier by the priest's pushing the shutter open. The elder demolition worker paid no further attention to the sick man: the sick man's intention, in coming down the stairs, had been voluntary: the two men had risen instinctively to their feet to help him, grasping his arms at the moment at which his hands had left the rails at either side of the stairway, his hands still casting about for the nonexistent prolongation of those rails. They had involuntarily risen to help him, stirred into action by the sight of seeing someone about to stand without support and, unsupported, on the edge of falling: the sick man's action alone had been voluntary. Having folded his newspaper without expressing anything about its contents, as though while reading it he had followed the print automatically with his eye while he had heard with his open ears more local news of greater importance, the elder man left the inn. The other man, not looking at his departing brother, continued in his conversation with the young woman whose voice had been one of the two voices first heard by the sick man when he had been washing himself earlier in the room upstairs, and when he had felt the certainty that he had been the sole occupant of the upper room, and

39

the owners of the two voices, the only occupants of the lower.

The priest, who had been disregarding the movement in the room behind him, said: 'The villagers do not see the building as we see it; to them the meaning of the bells is greater than the sound. A custom has grown up by which names are given to the bells: these names become as fast as fact; within a generation it is no longer known whether the names are descriptive or arbitrary. To someone sent to the village there is only the single fact that the gatehouse is not opened.' He looked down at Colver, as though he had expected him to ask, reasonably enough, how he had become certain of that single fact: Colver, however, said nothing, but continued to stare woodenly downward at the surface of the table, breathing rapidly as though he found deep inspiration and expiration painful. 'Since my arrival I have fought against the custom of naming the bells (it used to be held in the church porch, this naming: now it takes place in some location beyond my jurisdiction); I have learned to anticipate no help from the magistrate; indeed, he will hardly spare the time to listen to me. When I talk to him about the superstitious practices in the village I can see his eyes begin to wander about, looking at various objects which happen to catch his glance, or to gaze out through the window, as though he had no interest at all in the matter immediately before him. Although he says: "Something must certainly be done about these things," one feels that expediency governs his every action. Now, I admit, I have had second thoughts about striving against this superstitious custom. Why should I be so convinced of the correctness of my own point of view? Because the gatehouse is closed, it does not mean that it has always been closed: the fact that it is closed to me does not mean that it is closed to every man who knocks at its doors. I am far less certain of myself when I condemn the villagers' rituals in naming the bells than ever I was during my first years here.

'There is a ritual obscurity behind this custom,' he said, holding out his hands and looking up, as though he had just thrown something in the air. 'Do you remember the bell which

40

you heard when you were on the mountain, before you had ever seen the building, when the existence of the building was made clear to you only by the sounding of the bell?'

'I remember it very well,' said Colver, his voice surprisingly clear, even in his own ears, for he had been thinking of the sonority of that same bell only a few moments before the priest had mentioned it.

'That particular bell is known, because of its deep sonority, as "the passing bell". Usually it sounds out between sixty and eighty strokes before its tolling stops. Occasionally its strokes number less: once, not long ago, it rang out eighteen times. At its cessation there was mourning in the village. It was as though the bell had sounded at the death of an unknown virgin within the building, who, having died in her minority, had died without achievement. Their grief, unfeigned, was as that expressed at a village death. Their sincerity was in their very restraint; a travelling stranger would have been unaware of the village's mourning. There was no call for the viewing of a body: the body was as it were laid out within the building. The proprietor's wife had her husband shut this inn that day. They are not far short of impoverishment. Those eighteen strokes reiterated themselves in my head as I sat in the presbytery garden and I thought of my own past loss.

'I was given to understand that my predecessor would open the church on the ringing of the passing bell, though whether or not this is true I do not know: one must sort out truth from falsehood in any tale of one's predecessor: so often some supposed action of a predecessor is used by others as a lever to shift the foundation of one's own principles.'

Colver looked up. 'When I heard that bell it tolled for several hours. There is no more to be said. It's a pointless argument.'

'Now you are beginning to understand me,' said the priest, spreading out the fingers of his right hand and smiling in the manner of a man who in the course of making one point has shed light on quite another. 'When a bell, for any reason, fails to conform to the expectation engendered by the name, then it is renamed for the duration of its discrepancy.'

41

Colver, who seemed not to have heard him, looked down to the elbow of his left arm and saw a brass alarm clock resting on the table's surface by its two brass legs and its bezel. He could not remember having seen it before; possibly the proprietor had, for some reason known only to himself, put it there only a few moments ago; perhaps he had thought that it might with its rapid ticking give the sick man a sense of companionship. This clock, which was ticking noisily, had lost its back. Colver, without picking it up, tilted it in his hands and looked at the mechanism inside. The wheels of the train lay in a line between the plates. The last of these wheels was moving forward with a tense jerking motion while the first had the appearance of being stationary. The intermediate wheels revolved at various seen or imagined paces. His attention was absorbed by the motion of the wheels. He stared at them fixedly until there was no longer any impression of movement. He raised the clock to his face, surprised at its weight, and lifted it to the level of his eyes: he seemed to be looking at a series of great, dusty arches, dimly lit, receding along the line of a direct perspective from him: the sensation of movement was due to the recession of his own viewpoint: the arch nearest him moved away from him the fastest. He looked down at the clock, feeling its silent weight in his hands. The line of wheels had stopped moving. The clock itself was no longer ticking. The stopped mechanism was too heavy for him in his weakness to hold. He laid the clock on the table, where it stood exactly as it had before it had been picked up, except that it was no longer working. The traveller had the most unpleasant feeling that he had, on seeing the clock, imagined the tick, and, on looking inside it, had imagined the movement of the gear-train. 'Was this clock working when I picked it up?' He lifted his head, his hands still touching the case of the clock.

'It stopped the moment you examined it.'

The priest glanced down contemptuously at the clock as though it were familiar to him. 'Some old clocks only go if allowed to stand in a certain position.' When he next spoke it was with some rapidity, as though he were voicing something

42

which he had had in his mind for some time: the careful enunciation, which had been so noticeable when he had first spoken, had gone; now he spoke indistinctly and it was difficult for the traveller to catch the sense of all he said. 'You've seen the blatancy with which the bells are sounded. You have seen for yourself the self-assurance of those who ring them. You have seen what sort of respect they give us. You have heard for yourself the bells which ring in the night, making no concession to the necessity of sleep or the needs of illness.

'I was twenty-three when I was first sent here. I remember the afternoon of my arrival very well. I arrived in this valley as a stranger.

'After being woken at night, week after week, I was not so much curious as angry. I had tried all kinds of remedies to help me sleep: not one of them was of any use. One can't keep on taking medicines. Once the sound has put your mind in a turmoil, then there is nothing that can be done about it.

'This is what happens! One lies in bed, late in a hot night in summer, unable to sleep because of the heat, and it is easy to imagine that a bell has sounded. One instantly becomes fully awake, as one would have been awakened had that prolonged ringing occurred in reality. Further sleep is impossible. One can only lie and watch the dawn. The doctor's medicines do no good: one becomes used to them, and, as one lies awake the effects of the night-draught one has taken only give ambiguity to the uncertainty as to whether a bell has rung or not. Perhaps you think that I am making my point by exaggeration: perhaps I am. I dislike things which have neither explanation nor explainable cause; no man of integrity adopts superstitions in order that he might gain peace of mind: that's the fool's way.

'How different it is for the villagers! They have lived with the arbitrary sounding of the bells all their lives. The sound has become part of them: their superstition is based on event and circumstance. Watch them. A bell rings: they listen to the sound as though they find in it a source of comfort; events familiar from childhood are strengthened; old beliefs are justified. There is no recourse to argument: only the certainty

43

that in the silence a bell has just stopped ringing or is about
to ring again.

'The outsider tries to dismiss the building from his mind.
That is about the only discovery I have made over the years:
you are welcome to reject it. If you can bring yourself to be
thankful to that particular institution for anything you might
have received in this guesthouse, then you are a better man
than I.' He looked round the room at the open door. 'I would
do anything to be able to disregard the noise, particularly the
soundings at night. If I could plug the sounding-windows of
that tower with straw, then I would gladly do it. Then those
within the building could ring their bells as often as it suited
them.' He glanced at Colver's untouched glass of wine. 'What
does it gain by its intrusion into people's lives?'

The priest, when he had spoken again, after a long silence
during which he had consulted various entries in his diary,
shuffling through the pages with an evident lack of purpose,
had resumed with the initial care which had been such a
feature of his speaking voice. Perhaps his cursory glancing
through the pages of his diary had been an automatic and
calming gesture. 'Those stories in the village which concern
the naming of the bells have taught me a certain amount about
my parish; far more so than ever I would have expected during
my first years here.' He spoke judiciously, in the manner of
one who states an unbelievable conclusion of a long study,
but who knows that he will be able to counter disbelief, at
least to his own satisfaction, by stating innumerable examples,
one after another, each one countering uncertainties in the
one before it. 'My impression is that although the rumours
are universally believed (as far as one can tell), they originate
in the minds of those who are more ignorant than the rest,
those who would see significance in coincidence, the idle,
those who as children might have been praised for what, in
adult life, became nothing more than a quick and worldly
shrewdness. The fact that such as these (and they are amongst
the most respected, because they are, in a certain sense, the
most successful and best remembered) were the ones who

saw an immediate significance in the sound of the bells gave me an insight into the village itself.

'The power of superstition is generally at its greatest when its source has been forgotten or made cloudy by the passing of time. It is easy for someone in my position, a parish priest, someone who happens to come from outside and who has the ear of everybody, to find an interest in the generation of these things. I take an interest (in an unprofitable kind of way) in finding which superstition will survive and which will vanish without leaving a trace to disturb the memory. I have grown into the habit of recording these things; I write this in a diary.' He held it up in one hand. 'For many years I have recorded the prevailing names of the bells and the prevailing reasons given for their sounding. The results are as you might expect; there is nothing extraordinary about them: most of the portents have to do with husbandry, the cycle of the seasons, births and deaths, illness, and, of greatest importance in this enclosed valley, flood. "This is the preoccupation of the foreigner," said the magistrate when I told him about this. Perhaps he was right. What would you have said?' He looked at Colver, as if expecting an answer, though he had put the question as though he had intended a polite and self-deprecating comment; it was difficult to know what kind of answer he expected.

Colver was looking down at the stopped clock which stood on the table. What a useless object it had become! 'I can well imagine how the sounding of the bells might give rise to endless speculation.'

'I daresay you would naturally think that,' said the priest. 'If one were given to the invention of maxims one might say that the experience of the crowd is present in the head of the individual, might one not: but who wishes to epitomize other people's statements?

'The one belief is that the sounding of the bells has meaning. The meaning itself is worked out in a stereotyped fashion; the pattern is much the same in each case; the only major differences occur when the meaning concerns the animate or the inanimate.

'The bell sounds. The rumour is started off by chance

conversations, gossipings, if you wish. This first rumour is passed round the village, tentatively at first, but later becoming consolidated into a statement. The statement is then condensed into a pithy aphorism, often alliterative or rhyming as though the better to stick it fast in the memory. When that occurs there is no shaking off the belief that that statement is true. How long that statement is believed is a different matter: the length of its life depends on the periodicity, frequency and duration of the soundings of the same bell, and whether the nature of its subsequent sounding reinforces or contradicts the reason originally assigned to it.

'How can I best explain myself?' he asked. 'Would an example allow you an insight into my position? Or would I be presumptuous in drawing on whatever example seems best to fit my case? Have you had enough of examples?' He looked at the traveller speculatively, as though by a simple demonstration he might be able to make him believe something against his will. 'Let me, after all, take an example.' He opened his hands as if to demonstrate that they contained nothing. 'Which would I most profitably choose? A little time ago I spoke to you of the passing bell. I saw from your expression that you had heard not only of it, but had heard the sound itself.'

'I had heard only the sound,' said Colver, 'and nothing more. I am surprised that you, who live here, have not found the meaning of the sound to be diminished by the interpretations put upon it.'

'I have no time to indulge myself in empty speculations,' said the priest, 'I'm talking about facts.' He put the flat of his hand on the table. 'I have told you that the subsequent sounding of a bell reinforces or contradicts the purpose imputed to it at its first sounding. This is not the whole truth. I admit that to you now. The subsequent sounding of any bell only mitigates the purpose ascribed to the original. Do I make myself clear or am I speaking to myself?'

'I have only closed my eyes,' said Colver.

'Let me take as an example the bell they call the passing bell. Listen to me: its nature bears out what I say. When that

46

bell tolls less than twenty-one times, an arbitrary enough figure in all truth, there is the mourning in the village as at a death in the innocence of minority. Perhaps you may witness this in the future: if so, you will recall what I am now saying to you.

'Should that same bell happen to toll, perhaps, fifty times, then in the silence which follows the tolling there is the sadness as at death in the prime of life (an expression not ordinarily of my using, and one for which I do not care). What is the purpose of this mourning? The next day the bell is forgotten, and so is the mourning, and all that is left is the familiar geography of the valley. Who has not been close to someone who has died in the prime of his life? What alteration is brought about by their death? The bell is forgotten; only the reason which has been ascribed to it remains.

'There is a muted gladness, a sense of the appropriate, when that same bell tolls eighty times; the belief is that it has rung as a sign of the journeying soul which has died in fitting circumstances, and which is, even as the bell tolls, permitted to glance towards a goal of eternal felicity. What of that? Why are all these assumptions made? The soul and its creator are too close for the wedge of intercession to be interposed. As for the sounding of the bells; it is, one might say, too unimportant a thing to be worth any attempt to discourage. On the other hand, what use is my opinion? The results of today's freedoms are the cornerstone of the future's superstitious restrictions. The circumstances of this village are very well as they are. The bell rings eighty times, and beyond the sadness as at a death there is the resignation as of the contemplation of a complete life.

'The marking-point of the falsity of the superstition is this: should the bell continue to sound and toll beyond what must be regarded as a normal span, then it ceases to be the passing bell, and is called by another name: in translation, the nearest I can render it is "the summoning bell", but this is only a prosaic name for what is regarded as being an unexplained event. Another name for it might well be "the bell of vocation", though this again is hardly a complete translation of what is,

47

in all truth, a word-of-mouth metaphysic. The bell has, so to speak, one meaning at one moment, and another meaning the next: each beat alters the meaning of the ones which have preceded it.' He placed his fist against his own breast. 'I say to you: when that bell begins to sound, look at an established woman of the village. Watch her face! Her expression will be full of sorrow while the first few strokes toll: this is true: there is nothing feigned. Watch her expression change as she sees, in the continued ringing, the death of the marriageable young; the death of the parent of a young family; the death of her own parents; then the death of her contemporaries. How long will the bell sound before her face assumes that expression of empty tranquillity? There is nothing artificial or contrived about the change in her expression: it has only expressed in a few minutes the expressions she might have undergone in the span of her years. There is nothing mechanical about it. The name of the bell and its invented purpose have become the subject of an unwavering belief. I, here constantly, have difficulty in entering these things. The villagers themselves make no effort to persuade a stranger of their beliefs.'

The traveller disliked the examination of the beliefs of others: perhaps he considered that, belief being beyond communication, the examiner could learn only the shadows of those things unimportant and general enough to be allowed to stand beside his own beliefs, while, of all the sounds that he hears during his examination, he might see significance only in those which, half-recognized by reason of a deep internal longing which though unadmitted guides his inquiry, are thus heightened even as he first hears them: as for the important things: the examiner is quick to dismiss his piecemeal gleanings of those overheard sounds and overseen sights the sense of which have been denied him, important matters perhaps rarely being put into words, language making at most only an indirect allusion to them, the believing hearer knowing within himself the substance of the believing speaker's message: the examiner makes his own results according to the rules of the various theories currently flitting through his head: he is not embarrassed for an answer, though he has with caution

48

avoided too close an approach to the thing he studies lest he lose his status as an examiner and gain instead an uncertainty of the truth of his own beliefs: there is, said the sick man, though he did not articulate these thoughts into words, no examiner. Privacy, like freedom, is defended by cooperation, said the sick man, who, for the first time since his arrival, no longer felt an unease on hearing his own name spoken aloud by another.

'As for the building you call a monastery,' said the priest, 'I have told you that there is nothing to be gained by speculation.'

'You have made that very clear,' said the traveller. He had taken the silent clock into his hands as though to feel again its weight. 'You must have been tempted yourself to make surmises about the monastery, no less now than when you first arrived.' He felt that the priest's comments, despite the air of sincerity with which they had been given, were untruthful. Perhaps he had found a need to speak to the traveller, who was after all someone who spoke his native language. Had he, out of a need for simplification, abbreviated what he had initially intended to say to the point where it had become false? What had he compressed for the traveller's sake? The traveller wondered what the man had undergone in his past. Did the priest and himself have nothing in common? Did they speak the same language or similar languages? Had there been a similarity between his viewpoint of the institution and the place of his own education? Colver himself, perhaps because of his illness, found that he was astonished by the ignorant way in which he had previously taken the examples of others for granted. A little while ago he might have appreciated the statements which the priest had voiced, agreeing with them, seeing in them a general correctness. Now he found that he could not accede to them: he turned over in his mind phrases and sentences recalled one after another. Although the priest's words when placed together had a sense to them, the sum of the whole was untrue: each phrase, each answer, each question, each statement contained the same slant towards a pre-existing supposition or imaginary conclusion, each phrase preordaining the bias of the next and ratifying the bias of the one which had gone before it. 'You must have been tempted to make surmises about the monastery when you first arrived here,' said Colver, speaking as though out loud.

The priest considered the repeated question. 'Of course I have made surmises. Why do you ask me that question again? If I knew the answer I would have told you. It is a strange and an unusual place which, for all I know, may have its counterpart in every habitation. I know no more about it than I did on the first day of my arrival. Truth to tell I know less about it now than I did on that day: when I first arrived I had no preconceptions about its nature.

'Within the first few days of my arrival I was certain that the villagers were hiding something from me. That was an easy conclusion to arrive at. The truth is that most of the villagers have no curiosity at all about the nature of the building which lies above them. It's an odd thing to ask a stranger to believe, this incuriosity; you are a traveller; perhaps in your journeys you have grown to understand the fact that to the native-born nothing local is unusual. It was this very incuriosity which caused me to fear that they were hiding things from me. One can look at it from their point of view: they were born here, under its shadow, as it were; they have heard the sound of the bells from the first day of their lives: who knows; perhaps the sounds are mingled with those other sounds first heard through the walls of the mother's womb. They have been given reasons for what they hear from child-hood. Perhaps, in later life, they may grow to discard those reasons and to invent their own. Who knows? Who, after all, decides whether these reasons are right or wrong? They all serve as explanations. The fact is that nothing of it matters much. The only thing I dislike is the noise. As for the building itself: to them it is no more than a rock formation, a geological phenomenon, or a part of the mountains. I don't suppose they need to consider who populates the place (if it is a monastery). They live their lives in accordance with the evolving principles of superstition, while maintaining an indifference to the existence of the source of their superstition.'

'They cannot all be indifferent to it,' said the traveller. He

50

looked down at the brass clock again, which, now that it was levelly placed on the surface of the table, had resumed its ticking. The traveller felt suddenly very tired; his weariness seemed to be exacerbated by the renewal of the rhythmical sound. He felt an urge to tilt the clock until it stopped again. His hearing had become very acute, particularly in the higher frequencies; he could hear the whispering of the uneven hairspring as two adjacent coils touched one another at one point in its rapid windings and unwindings, while the loudness of the tick of the escapement itself suggested that the clock was more an instrument for making noise at regular intervals, a metronome, and less a mechanism for indicating the passage of time.

The room had darkened considerably in the last few moments. The sun had dimmed, as though a mist had gathered in the higher air of the valley; a breath of wind had pushed the leaves of the shutter together, while, coincidentally, someone (who, a second ago, had been heard walking across the gravel of the yard) stood in the doorway, obscuring the incoming light.

'There is a mill-worker in the village,' said the priest. 'Retired through ill-health. I shall take you to meet him. He is a respiratory cripple: winters and the wet weather are bad seasons for him. In the summer one would hardly know that he is as ill as he is. Chest disease is uncommon here.

'I shall take you to see him when you are a little better.' The priest looked up at the traveller's face.

'Why should he want to see me?' asked the sick man.

'Someone must have told him that you were in the village. That is not surprising.' He paused. 'During the first few nights after you were brought here, while you were delirious, the sound of the bells affected you. That in itself is reasonable enough: they can be loud, and, particularly at night they are unexpected, most of all those rapid bells which beat like an alarm, when one doesn't know what to do, or what to put over the ears. One would expect such noises to echo within the mind of a sick person. Who can say of what they reminded you? Those villagers who happened to be in the room (I couldn't keep them out for any length of time; they returned, I am sure of it, the moment I left) listened to you and watched the sense in which you cried out on hearing each of the bells which happened to sound. I don't know what they expected to hear. The rumour went round the village: "The sick man has a vocation!" You must forgive my inexact translation, but it was quite clear: you were dying, that was a medical fact. Your predictive ability was regarded as a death-sign. Your recovery, unexpected though it was, is now a fact. What do the superstitions say about you now? Do you have the ability to tell which of the bells are about to sound?'

Again the traveller found that he had listened to each of the little phrases which the priest had spoken, and again he found each of them influenced by an internal bias.

'No, of course not,' said the priest. 'I was using your own case as an example of how superstitions arise and how easily and quickly they can assume the status of fact.

'Now you see something of what met me when I first arrived to take up my post in this valley. You can understand the regard I hold for the building. Its communications are arbitrary, and its noise hinders the work I have been set to do. There is no order from it; no sense to its messages; nothing that it states is enough to base a single fact upon.

'When I am in church, during a service, a bell may unexpectedly ring out. There is no indication of how long it will continue to ring. When I hear the first stroke I know that I might as well stop in what I am doing, and put down what I am holding, and save my breath, pausing in mid-sentence until the sound has finished. In the past I have been forced by a prolonged tolling first to wait and then, after waiting, to abandon a service.

'When I first arrived I used to try to shout over the noise of the sound: that I stopped when I happened to see, on chancing one morning to look down between the metal arms of the reading-lamp, the faces of those who were in the church. It is true that those faces were looking at me: it is equally true that their attention was elsewhere, as though there were nothing to listen to but the sound of the bell. It was clear to me that they were drugged with the sound and able to think of nothing but the meaning which they themselves had given it.'

'What order is it?' asked the sick man suddenly.

'There is no order.'

'I should have asked: to which order does it belong?'

'How is that to be answered? There is no communication.' He stood rapidly, aware of the passing time: he had looked at the face of the clock which the traveller had stopped.

IV

Until he stood at the arch in the yard wall and saw the extent of the valley, every prospect had been enframed by the windows of the inn. Beyond these limits he had imagined the valley to be closely confined.

A single glance told him a greater truth. The valley took its origin at the foot of a cliff beneath the outlet of a hanging cwm in the mountains. A series of wet-weather waterfalls, now dry, hung from the lip of the cwm and fell by precipitous limestone steps to a densely wooded basin, over-shadowed, dark and murmurous with underground water. The trees, seen from afar, were tall-stemmed and their foliage was in shadow and black against the limestone cliffs. Swifts coursed in the air above the trees, flying to and from their nests beneath the stone overhangs in a curving flight: the speed and the purposeful direction of their wide acrobatic flight emphasized the height of the cliffs behind them. The weathering of the rock enhanced the clear view of the planes of bedding of the rock. Verdure hung from the fissured blocks at the edge of the dry waterfalls. In flood, in wet weather, this head of the valley must be a watery and an isolated place.

The dry river bed below this upland basin, marked only by its course of rounded stones, led down to the resurgences where the river took its origins. The river, collected from its several resurgence-caves, ran in slow meanders along the alluvial floor of the valley. The valley itself turned an almost complete right angle to a plain bounded by mountains deprived of prominence by the haze of the heated air.

The village itself lay on a terrace of land raised above the river within the dog-leg of the valley. It had the appearance of having been forced to this higher ground in the past by floods. The wood of thornlike oak trees enclosed the shelving ground between the village and the river.

The inn faced the wood. Its windows allowed no complete view of the valley. The inn was a stone building; its walls were bare and unplastered. The builders had incorporated many oddly shaped stones, smooth and water-worn, in the courses of masonry. The houses to either side were built of any materials which had come to hand, porous brick and pieces of calcited stone showing where the thin plaster had fallen away. The houses were built as though for a hotter climate: here, in the hills, the shallow pitch of their roofs and the fabric of their walls must be unsuited to the continual night mists and the heavy relief rains. The school, the towerless church, the presbytery; these interconnected buildings formed a peninsula which was partly immersed in the thorn-oak wood where fowls kicked at the layers of leaves beneath the trees. Through the boles of the trees the rapid movement of silver reflections marked the resurgences of the river: the walls of a ruined mill rose up from the further bank; the stones were large and water-worn, by their size chosen to withstand high water: perhaps they had been lifted, ready for the building, directly from the river bed. The lower branches of the trees and the stone sills of the windows of the mill were draped with the desiccated vegetation left by the last flood. The village itself lay on higher ground behind the inn. The magistrate's house stood above both the river and the upper end of the village, a solid-fronted building with round arched windows: the walls were of limestone and blue brick and the roof was slated with dark grey imported slates. Colver looked up at the house, marvelling at its dominance and its solidity, while contemplating the opportunities which must lie open to the magistrate of a village such as this.

His walk round the village took him a quarter of an hour. He looked down the back streets where the house-fronts leaned outwards, seeing their plasterless walls of friable and porous tile-brick and local stone, the courses built unlevelled, the materials reused from earlier and now forgotten buildings, reclaimed and rebuilt. The broad gutters in the centre of even the narrowest of alleys was evidence of heavy winter rain. The carriageways were made of pulverized stone and broken tile, sharp edges of which pointed upward from the compacted surface.

When Colver arrived back at the inn the sun was behind the mountains. He stood in the yard, looking down at the broad outlet of the valley. The air was cooling rapidly. The mists had begun to rise rom the flat ground by the river. Although the sun had gone, and the valley had taken on the aspect of a tranquil twilight, the sky above was still the sky of a summer afternoon.

His brief walk round the village and down by the river had exhausted him far more than he would have thought possible. He sat heavily on the wooden bench (the same one on to which he had yesterday been lowered). The proprietor, hearing him, put his head round the curtained door which led from the counter to the private quarters. He had recognized the travel-ler before he had seen him: his glance was only confirmatory. He grinned with an unconscious exaggeration which was out of character: in his dealings with the villagers he was quiet and his face was shrewdly expressionless. Perhaps he grinned at the traveller because he thought that a more subtle ex-pression might well be misinterpreted by him. He withdrew to the kitchen, behind the curtain, where he talked, in a flat conversational voice, to his wife, who returned no audible answer. He returned after ten minutes with a tray; he walked down the length of the room and placed the tray on the surface of the traveller's table. When he was thanked he only shrugged his shoulders in a watchful lack of understanding; he stood at the end of the table, looking down at the traveller. He shifted his weight from one foot to another in silence; then he put his hand out, in a fist with one finger extended, pointing to the food, two plates, one of steamed fish and the other of cut bread, an invalid's meal, and he spoke a few words in his habitual quick voice (which was the same voice in which he spoke to his customers and to his family: a loud voice for all its rapidity), something which might have meant: 'do not let it cool', or something of the kind; perhaps he had said: 'do you know how much that costs?' Perhaps he had not been talking about the food at all; perhaps through a back window he had seen the traveller staring enviously at the solid walls of the magistrate's house, and was commenting on that, saying: 'Yes, I saw you looking at that house: how solid it appears!' He had the look of a man who speaks without thinking (one had difficulty in imagining that his words were manufactured in his head before they were spoken) and who sees everything in the light of his own possible advantage. That was his look: his words might have signified something else. The sick man, not understanding the language, found that he had to restrain himself from imputing some meaning of his own into the proprietor's expression and indeed into his words. Very possibly he had mentioned both the food and the magistrate's house in the same breath. The proprietor stood at the end of the table and watched him while he ate; his arms were folded and he held a glass-cloth in one hand. His apron was not as clean as it had been yesterday.

Despite his walk Colver was not at all hungry. Since his illness hunger had been replaced by a sensation of emptiness which, at the thought of food, particularly fatty food, brought a taste of bile to the back of his tongue: by a kind of contrariness he kept on thinking of the smell and the taste of rich food, particularly fried food, as though he fully recognized that he was responsible for his own nausea. He disliked eating this meal under the direct gaze of the proprietor, who maintained his attitude of silent observation as though he had little else to do. He found it doubly difficult to eat; in the past, a phrase or two might have sufficed to combine gratitude with good humour: here it was difficult to express either. The proprietor's wife had come into the room through the curtained doorway, as though she wished either to say something to her husband or to judge for herself the extent of the sick man's appetite.

*   *   *

57

The traveller, asleep after this large meal, woke to the sound of the clock which stood in its accustomed place at the end of the table by his elbow. The magistrate, who had just entered the room, darkening it as he stood at the doorway, sat opposite him; he would have been recognizable as the magistrate had he not worn the usual coat of a provincial magistrate. The proprietor of the inn, standing behind the magistrate as if ready to answer any request or to carry out any duty, had begun to light the hanging lamps. This silent task, in which he became absorbed earlier and earlier each evening now the nights were drawing in, had been started earlier still tonight with the unexpected arrival of the magistrate.

'My family have been a support to me here,' said the magistrate. He looked across the table at the traveller. The tone of his voice, rather than the sense of his words, had shown an inner intensity. He sat with his back to the lamps, and his head was seen in outline only, rather as the priest's head had earlier been silhouetted against the line of daylight entering between the shutters. 'I saw that you were a representative of the civil authorities: that was evident in your manner, even during the worst of your illness. Education shows through even at the height of illness. I would have come to see you immediately had I known that you were out of bed and downstairs. I have been wishing to speak to you for some time.' He paused. 'My wife was certain that you were a visitor of some importance the moment that she first set eyes on you that first night.'

This vicarious claim to importance disturbed the traveller. Why should anyone have thought him to be of any importance at all? He searched his mind: had he boasted of anything or drawn attention to himself in any way? All that came back to him was a series of half-obliterated impressions of objects, noises, smells and touches, each a single part in a falsely continuous series, each perceived as it had been under a different state of mind. 'That's a very false impression,' said the traveller. 'I am of no importance: I can't understand why your wife should have come to that conclusion.'

'She was emphatic about it,' said the magistrate, somewhat

indulgently; as though willing to overlook the fact that he had been contradicted almost at the moment of his arrival. 'Not that it matters at all: you are who you are: and you know your own place in the state of things; if you don't, you will have a sharp lesson coming to you at some time or another.'

'I hope that I was not misrepresenting myself in any way!' said Colver. He saw in his mind's eye a memory of a sight of faces, a muttering, a smell of fever, and the touch of the heated air. He could not remember having exalted himself.

'The use of a phrase such as "I hope that I was not misrepresenting myself in any way" implies something, does it not?' said the magistrate as though making a studious observation. 'Or perhaps it does not. I do not know why my wife came to the conclusion she did. Quite possibly she is mistaken. Very likely you are of no importance at all. Does that suit you better? Can we start off again on a more informal footing? Are you honest with yourself?' He said this without any attempt at humour. Although he was sitting he put his hands behind his back. 'My wife likes to maintain a presence in the village. When she heard you were ill and had been taken to this inn she made it her business to visit you and to find out something of your circumstances. The decision to call the doctor was hers. The only telephone is in my house, in my office: perhaps it wasn't surprising that the bailiffs, who were somewhere in the vicinity, overheard her say: "Please connect me to Dr Hartshorne," and, after a delay of some minutes: "An important visitor to the village has arrived. He has typhoid! You must connect me to Dr Hartshorne!" One has to shout into provincial telephones in order to be sure of being heard. That's the cause of your importance; an exaggerated shouting used to call the doctor.' He looked at the sick man with a frank stare. 'I have the more important of your belongings in the office-safe. They were put into the hands of one of the bailiffs by the proprietor, the day after your arrival: he was unwilling to keep them. Perhaps he was afraid that something might happen to them, and that he might be blamed for any consequences; he hasn't any secure place in this inn; sometimes he gives me letters and packets for safekeeping. You have only to call in to collect your belongings. That's the only reason for my being here now.'

'I have not seen you in here before,' said the traveller.

'I come here infrequently,' said the magistrate. 'Only when necessary. Tonight there was the matter of certain tenures. I had to do one or two other things, none of them of any importance, and I had to come and see you. As for your documents: I had them fumigated before bringing them into the house: the process has dimmed some of the inks on the passport particularly; they are still in the fumigation-box at the moment; one has to do what one can when these eventualities arise.'

'When may I collect them?'

'You are free to collect them at any time during the working day.' The magistrate looked across the table at him. 'How long do you expect to remain here?'

'I had hardly thought of that: the whole situation is unsatisfactory: I have been told various conflicting things, and I am not sure what to believe,' said Colver, though not with any degree of conviction, as though ashamed at his own improvidence.

The magistrate, as though noting a lack of conviction with an air of shrewdness, perhaps mistaking it for insincerity, stood up with an air of finality. 'The whole situation is unsatisfactory, I agree. I had hoped for a chance of conversation. I have few people to speak to, not that that is a matter of any great concern; I've never found any pressing need to look for any company beyond that of my family.'

'The priest,' said Colver, speaking for the sake of doing so and looking past the magistrate, 'struck me as being an intelligent man.'

The magistrate did not sit down; he grasped the back of the chair rather as the priest himself had done earlier, and said: 'Well, yes, naturally on the surface you would think that,' without any stiffness in his manner but at the same time leaving as a certainty the impression that he had no wish to discuss anything that the priest might have said. 'One can usually bear to hear a thing repeated only a limited number of times after one has heard it stated once,' he said.

The traveller, not unnaturally, found himself unwilling to

become a party to local opinion. 'Do you know Mr Thibault?' he asked.

'Certainly I do,' said the magistrate, sitting down again at the table opposite the traveller. 'He is an ironmonger's assistant in the town. He comes here whenever he can. He is often here at weekends. Perhaps it's a case of his wanting to get as far away as possible from work; he thinks of himself as an honorary villager; he is one of those who have become fascinated with reports they have heard of the monastery.' He said this disparagingly. 'I couldn't fail to see that he was with you for some time when you were at your most ill. I hope that he did not thrust his queries on you.'

The traveller was surprised to hear the magistrate speak of Thibault as though he found him contemptible, for, on first seeing the magistrate he had assumed that the magistrate and Thibault were related, perhaps uncle and nephew or even father and son. There was no doubt that they shared a number of facial similarities; their gestures and use of phrases had something in common. The idea that they were related had been reinforced by the fact that Thibault, when he had referred to the magistrate, had appeared to be embarrassed and even defensive, in much the same way that a school-master's son may be embarrassed when circumstances call on him to refer to his father by his title in front of his peers. Evidently all this had been erroneous. 'I recall him saying nothing much of importance,' said Colver.

'Do you enjoy talking about mundane and prosaic things?' asked the magistrate.

'When I first recovered it was above all pleasing to hear someone speak my own language,' said Colver, looking up for the first time as if to see the magistrate's face. 'I did not know of this valley or this village. That's a fact. I can withhold no information from you. How can I explain myself except by saying that I believed that I was in a familiar building which had undergone a change? I had looked for certain people I expected to see and called out their names. The sounding of the bell caused me to look again at my surroundings and to see that the room and the people were unfamiliar.' He paused.

61

'As for Thibault, as far as I can remember he talked of material things of no importance at the time but which when I was alone were a proof that the world had altered little enough. Until that time I might as well have been within the monastery. That is what I at first believed.'

'So everything that is has undergone an alteration because you have woken from a fever,' said the magistrate. 'That's an easy course; perhaps you are always thinking of the easiest course; it's not unexpected; perhaps, were I in your circumstances, I would take the easiest of courses.'

Colver, although he had spoken with every intention of being truthful in the presence of the magistrate, saw now his own insincerity as though he had neither lied nor told the truth: he had said that the unfamiliarity of his surroundings had been at last mitigated by the presence of things familiar to him: he had admitted that his course had been the easiest he could have undertaken. The truth was that during his fever there had been nothing familiar in the room. His clothes had been removed and returned to him—altered—only when he was past the worst of the fevers. His documents had been in the safekeeping of the magistrate. Only when he had learned that he had never been within the walls of the monastery had Thibault, the ironmonger's assistant from the town, spoken to him in a language in which he might correspond. He was certain of one thing above all else: he had been more distressed by the presence of his own familiar belongings than by their absence: the change in their very substance had caused him more anxiety than the comfort lent by their familiarity. He had many times held in his hand one of his own belongings as though its nature, its purpose and its history had become inseparable: one example, the example to come to mind for the moment; once, when he had awoken in the dawn, prostrated by the night's fever, he had found a traveller's knife stuck deep into the bed-head with such force that the wood had split and the blade had become embedded. While he held the handle of the knife the action had been imperative. He had not thought himself delirious then: he had thought, and he remembered this clearly, that the difference between actions carried out in a delirium and actions carried out in waking life differed only in that the reasons for the actions of the former are later forgotten. What had given rise to this state? Even now, sitting at the table opposite the magistrate, he knew that were he to call to mind any object having significance as a token—during his fever he had held out a bank note to the light of the lamp as if in recompense—he would have difficulty in distinguishing between the object as a token and the object as an engraving with a portrait of the monarch to its right and a perspective of a causeway, an obelisk, a triumphal arch or a representation of an orb to the left, as though these engravings in their own right were vested with the power to determine the systems of any transaction. His perception had certainly been changed by what he had undergone. Everything that he had heard, from Thibault, from the priest, from what he had been able to make out of the proprietor's disposition, and now, it seemed, from the magistrate, had had an inward-looking confinedness to it, as though these people lived their lives unaware of the broad and unusual landscape which comprised the valley: perhaps it had been this confinedness which had given him the earlier illusion, before he had seen the valley for himself, that it was a narrow and isolated place, almost overarched by the mountains' sides.

'Did Thibault, in his conversation with you, mention me?' asked the magistrate.

'Why do you ask that?'

The magistrate leaned across the table as though about to say something which he did not wish to be overheard. He gripped the edge of the table with his hands as he leaned over its surface, and the sleeves of his coat (black silk cuffs, black braiding and buttons) rode up above his wrists to show the soiled cuffs of his shirt sleeves. He did not seem to be aware of this. 'His fascination with the monastery has made him intrusive.' He looked down at his hands, giving no appearance of seeing the incongruity of the new coat over the dirty shirt. 'I cannot continue to put up with interference into areas of my jurisdiction,' he said. 'It makes my own work difficult. I can no longer accept that.

'A few years ago I would have had him removed: I am more tolerant than that now. Even so, one can only stand a certain amount of interference with one's view of one's duties. I have a broad back: without it I would not be where I am in this valley.

'I can tolerate anything which Thibault might have to say to me, but it has become known to me that he discusses my work with anyone whom he happens to meet, not only here, but also in the town, making implications, imputing motives where they cannot be defended. I thought it likely that he might attempt to envenom you with his dislike for me, particularly as he will have heard that my wife said, rather indiscreetly perhaps, that she thought you to be a visitor of some importance.'

The traveller searched for a way to distance himself from this parochial dispute. 'I am of no importance,' he said, then, 'Thibault told me nothing about you: I can't remember him mentioning you, except in an oblique way, saying that you had put various of my belongings in a safe in your office.'

'Well, if that is so,' said the magistrate, without any alteration in the tone of his voice, 'I am pleased to hear it.' He looked away as though to indicate that the matter was closed, but then he said, 'I only mentioned Thibault because it was quite possible that he might have tried to have put you against me; it is a poor thing to do, to slander someone in front of a stranger. Perhaps you think that I am doing the same thing by him, now, but that isn't the case: I am not concerned with disparaging him; it would do me no good if I did. One only lowers other people's opinion of oneself by slandering strangers in front of strangers. Besides, I know nothing about you; I have no idea what your influence is.'

Colver was embarrassed because of his own mixed feelings: the magistrate had certainly been unaware that his own words could only serve to lower the traveller's opinion of him, and that by speaking as he had he only made himself appear to be unable to communicate anything except a sense of his own lack of authority. This unease (so the traveller felt) was without direction; he had said nothing specifically against the parish priest, and for that matter he had said nothing about Thibault,

64

except to accuse him of maligning his character; even then his manner had been quite sincere, as though in the past he had found by inquiry of reliable sources that the slanders were true. He had spoken with a verbal clumsiness, his phrases often having an unusual pattern. Occasionally he made an unusual choice of word which did not fit into the context of his speech; perhaps he was not a natural speaker; perhaps he had not spoken nor even thought in the language for some time. The traveller, on looking at him now, was unsure as to whether or not this unease was in fact due only to a minor incoordination of his larynx. The magistrate had spoken of his jurisdiction and of his authority as though these were self-evident qualities which everyone might possess to a greater or a lesser extent. He had made the accusation of character-maligning only a few moments after he had met the traveller; despite his leaning over the table (as though to ensure secrecy) he had spoken loudly, almost explosively, so that one might even have thought that he had been joking: if so, then perhaps he had been speaking ironically when he had talked of his jurisdiction and the authority he held. The traveller, who even now did not know for certain whether the magistrate had been joking or not, had detected a slight stutter in the magistrate's speaking voice; this stutter, only perceptible because the magistrate sat opposite the traveller, showed itself as a tightening of the throat preparatory to speech. Colver, on seeing it, was aware that he had been on the verge of misjudging the man entirely. This premonitory tightening of the throat, this stutter, seemed to be of the kind which must be followed by spoken words, even arbitrary but habitual words which have no direct accordance with what the utterer wishes to say. One sees stutterers who end their sentences with a set pattern of such habitual phrases, said Colver to himself; he would normally have striven to disregard such things: now he was unable to do so: on the contrary, he found it difficult to follow the sense of the magistrate's words because of them.

'When I first saw you,' said the magistrate, 'I thought I saw an unfriendly judgment in your eyes, and I wondered what tales you had heard.'

'I was exhausted. You must have taken my exhaustion for the unfriendly judgment you mention.'

The magistrate sat back in his chair. He appeared to be in some way relieved. 'When I first arrived here I used to stammer very badly,' he said, aware that his difficulty in speech had been noticed by the traveller.

'I had the impression,' said Colver, wishing to save the magistrate the further embarrassment of talking about his stutter, 'that Thibault was frequently in the room.'

'He is, as I say,' said the magistrate after a few seconds' hesitation, 'wide-eyed over anything that anyone has to say about the monastery. I have been told that he was in the upper room on many occasions, standing in the corner, saying nothing. He was, I suppose, as curious as the villagers as to what in your delirium you would make of the sounding of the bells. This is nothing particularly new. He's often here, in the village, trying to find out what he can about the monastery. He's always trying to find out new facts about it: facts, incidentally, which I could have told him if only he had asked. He thinks me a fool, probably because of the hesitant way in which I speak; one develops an eye for these things. Had he asked me I could have told him that there is nothing mysterious about the monastery if only one takes the trouble to understand it. Perhaps he doesn't want that: perhaps he wishes to make his own enigma. For myself, I have no time for invented enigmas.'

'Do you know the working of the monastery?'

'Of course I do,' said the magistrate, 'as much as is necessary: as much as I know about anything: how could I fail to understand it? How could any man in my position fail to understand it?

'Soon after I was appointed magistrate here, I was given the authority of secular agent to the monastery. That is an unpaid burden which I never knew existed until my arrival here.

'I have authority over the monastery's property: a statutory control held on its behalf. I would be lying if I were to say that the administration of the monastery's lands is an easy

66

task: when I first arrived here I found that the agency was in a state not far short of disorder. I do not exaggerate. It would be difficult for me to explain the work necessary in the re-establishment of communications which had been allowed to slide: tenancies had expired, rents had been long un-collected: boundaries were in dispute or were unmarked: local people had assumed proprietorship of various of the monastery's lands, and had in some cases let them out in badly demarcated subtenancies: roads and tracks belonging to the monastery had been taken up, the stone used for building, and the land ploughed: landmarks had been re-moved: mileposts had been bodily dug up and used as lintels and gateposts.' He held out his right hand, with his fingers stretched out, shaking it to accentuate his words. 'I believe that, were it more accessible, the very road to the gatehouse would have been mined as a quarry for its stone. I'm only telling you the beginnings of it. Some acres of woodland at the head of the valley have been for so long taken for granted as common land that those who use it have forgotten to whom it belongs. All this will make you ask: what sort of man was my predecessor?

'I never met him. There was a vacancy in the tenure of several years between his death and my accession, but I believe on good authority that even when he was a fit man he had allowed the agency of the monastery's lands to slide downhill. "Consigned to history," one might say of documents which pertain to ownerships and tenancies where origins and rights are lost beyond retrieval. It is difficult to speak ill of a man never met, known only by repute, now dead, consigned, as it were, to history. He was in a state of ill-health towards the end of his life (it was his sick-room which became my office) but even as he saw his own decline lying uncertainly ahead of him he failed to appoint a manager who might have carried his authority: it is as if he wished to maintain the substance of his position until the last hour of his life. He made no attempt to delegate his responsibilities. He did not wish per-haps to arouse in others an enthusiasm for the thought. On the other hand it does not do to be critical of others: what might be one's own failings under other circumstances? Even I can see, with hindsight, the temptation which forced him to adopt the standards which surrounded him.' He had raised his voice. 'The villagers have no respect for or loyalty towards the monastery!' He looked steadily at Colver. 'And, because the situation is, perhaps, finely balanced—you are following what I am saying?—the last thing I wish for, the last thing that any man in a post such as mine would wish for, is outside interference. Thibault, by his presence, has done nothing but interfere, however unconsciously or thoughtlessly, with the working of the secular agency.'

The traveller, surprised to hear the magistrate speak of Thibault again, remarked that from what little he had seen of the man he would have thought him unlikely to interfere with someone else's work.

The magistrate looked at him with a glance which conveyed a misunderstood anger and a willingness to appease: a strange mixture, surely, perhaps due to unfamiliarity, perhaps due to a wish to retain the traveller in conversation. 'Sometimes,' said the magistrate, 'I find that the idea of someone looking over my shoulder amounts to interference.' He looked round the room, and beyond it, as it were, to the valley, as though he had the power of seeing through both masonry and plaster. One wondered how long he had been here. 'Seen from the point of view of a casual traveller,' he said, 'the day to day work must appear pleasant and easy. Indeed, such a person could hardly perceive it in any other way.' He looked down at his hands which lay in a position of rest on the table. 'My brother-in-law and his wife visited us shortly after they were married. One evening, the day after they had arrived, my brother-in-law remarked: "How can any work undertaken here be laborious?" In a certain sense he was being truthful: he was certainly speaking his mind. The fact is, however, that the work is difficult because of the very fact of this rural utopia (another phrase of his, and probably of the travel agency also); there are many things to distract one, to lead one from the path which has been set; and, too, one has to accept that, were one to tell the truth, much of it would never be believed. I do not believe that it would be possible for me to convey the exact nature of the monastery to anyone who does not already know something of its nature.' His voice had lost much of its hesitancy: indeed it resonated in the rafters. 'I have never had sympathy for those who make hard work of their tasks and complain about them to others; I can only sympathize with them over the dissatisfaction which they must feel at the end of each day. At the same time it is painful to be misunderstood. The two phrases come at you from all visitors: "You say you are the secular agent to the monastery." You answer to the effect that that is so. The next phrase comes as a statement, as a step in a path of logic: "You say that there is no communication between the village and the monastery." In answer to this you reply that that is true; it is widely acknowledged that there is no communication between the monastery and the outside world. Then the *non sequitur* follows: "If there is no communication between the monastery and the world beneath it, then how can you occupy one of the monastery's official posts?" When this question is asked, one can only reply that the word "communication" has no meaning in this context. The post by definition is temporal. At the same time, this secular appointment is granted by a body which has no worldly concerns other than the single fact of the ownership of its property. This is clarity itself to me. Perhaps that in itself is the only thing of importance.' He paused in thought. When he spoke again his voice was lively, as though he had rediscovered an amusing memory. 'My superiors in my previous post, when they knew the name of the place where I was to be sent, gave me a fishing-rod.'

'Are you a keen fisherman?'

'I have never enjoyed the sport. The purchase of the rod was a joke. Its aim was to demonstrate the fact that my superiors knew and appreciated the intricacies and the difficulties of the post I now hold.'

'Have you no time for fishing?'

'I have time enough,' said the magistrate. 'No-one who wishes to be believed makes out that he is forever working. One can find time for anything one must do.

'My colleagues did not know the geography of the place. The valley is a closed depression. The river rises in percolation water in the body of the mountains, and flows for only a short distance before it is swallowed by underground cave systems. The river is only the brief surfacing of an underground stream. It dries in the summer. There are no fish.'

This seemed to be so tangential to what he had been saying that Colver did not attempt to reply. He sat in silence, his eyes closed. The day was exceptionally humid, and he was aware that his face was wet with sweat. At his elbow the brass alarm clock ticked in a halting, irregular way as though its mainspring were nearly unwound.

The magistrate seemed to be quite content to remain sitting opposite him. Occasionally Colver heard the stretching of the fibres of the cloth of his coat as he leaned forwards to pick up the glass of wine which stood on the table in front of him. Colver heard him swallow, but did not look up; the lashes of his eyes seemed to be woven together, the eyelids themselves unduly heavy, and his cheeks also, as though his face had become oedematous and weighty. 'I have never known such a long and continuous illness,' he said to himself, but speaking aloud, for he heard the slight sound of the magistrate's coat as he leaned forward to listen.

'Have you a family?' asked Colver, abruptly, opening his eyes.

'Yes,' said the magistrate, surprised, as though he had made the assumption that the traveller had fallen asleep.

The magistrate looked at his hands. 'My wife and my eldest came to join me here only after I had been a year in post,' he said. 'I called them only when I was assured in my own mind that my position was settled. I wished a certain stability. You will perhaps know how it is with these domestic moves: I was reluctant for them to join me before I knew my environs; I wished to have this life organized in a straightforward pattern. I remember the pleasure with which I set the date of their arrival: I can recall the particular calendar now, even to the advertisements on the board which held its pages. The days seemed very long in passing. The house was made ready for them. I had inherited a good set of servants who themselves could not hide their pleasure in seeing it in occupation after so long a vacancy, my predecessor, as I have said, neglecting it and confining himself, within a single room, to a pallet on the floor. I took a pride in showing my wife the sights of the valley. We enjoyed a good social life in those first few years. My youngest child was born here. The doctor came from the town: he hardly needed to be asked to attend: he was a frequent social visitor then.' He paused in reflection for a moment. Colver opened his eyes to look at him. 'Yes, it is strange,' said the magistrate. 'When I first arrived here I was reluctant to ask my wife and child to be with me, at least until I had set the pattern of order upon affairs. Now I find that my family are a support against any disruption of that order. My children in their innocence accept the circumstances under which they have been brought up as fact. As for myself: I am not as confident in my quick judgments as perhaps I once was. All the time I see in my work exigencies of which I was once ignorant. I know that whatever happens I have the assurance of my family. It's good, very good, to be able to go home and to be quiet.' He looked up at the traveller, almost as though the latter had been sitting above him. He seemed to be wondering how much of what he had said had been taken in by the other man. 'Are you married?'

'Yes.'

'I understood from Thibault that you were.'

The traveller sought to remember what he had told Thibault, but the magistrate interrupted his thoughts by saying, in his somewhat explosive original manner, 'Marriage is a good state to be in. There is always a time when the disorder of your surroundings becomes too much to be considered rationally. One tires of decisions. It is at these times that you can look to the order—which you have been instrumental in creating—of your own family. Perhaps this is a platitude: if so, then it is a truthful platitude, and one that will bear restating from time to time.' Unexpectedly he said: 'I have altered during my time here. I have, I think, become less reliant on my own judgments as well as those of others.

Situations and occurrences which I would once have thought to be of great complexity now have a simpler look to them, and I cannot understand how others can see such difficulties in them: I cannot understand how I once saw difficulties in them myself. On the other hand,' he said, weighing his words, holding up both of his hands with palms cupped, 'things which I would once have passed by without looking at, accepting them as they appeared, my eye being set on some further goal, have now assumed circumstances which I would now find difficulty in glossing over or taking for granted. A few moments ago I told you the two statements which were invariably put to me when I talk of my position as secular agent to the monastery. Visitors cannot accept that one may act with the authority of a body which claims nothing but ownership. I can only act as I feel it my duty to act: I cannot be doing with their arguments. I have heard them before. I can only assume an attitude of welcome; at the same time I find myself inwardly rehearsing the answers to the questions which they will ask.'

'You like order.'

The magistrate stood up suddenly. 'Do you appeal to me to fabricate order?' He shook his head slowly. 'I dislike disorder.'

The traveller looked up at him: had he misheard him? 'Why do you speak to me? Why do you confide in me? You came in here this evening, seeking me, cautioning me against Thibault and the priest and yet quoting one and voicing the thoughts of the other. I am uncertain. I am a chance traveller: tomorrow I shall be gone. I don't even know the name of the organism which has caused my illness.'

'Typhoid,' said the magistrate. 'It's common enough.' He paused. 'Why confide in you, as you say.' The magistrate let out his breath slowly. 'I did not ask you about your illness. I made a point of avoiding that. Would solicitude have helped you?' His voice was hesitant; his stutter had worsened. 'Why confide in you? A chance traveller, as you say? I have no confidences to give. I felt curiosity enough to wish to talk; after seeing you fevered and delirious in the upstairs room it is only natural that I should feel a sense of curiosity as to who

72

you are. As it is, you are a chance traveller; perhaps that allows me to speak less guardedly.'

'I am a chance traveller.' Colver looked down at the brass clock. He would have wound it had he the will to have done so. 'How do you communicate with the monastery?'

'By letter.'

This answer surprised Colver, and for some reason agitated him.

'I am forced to type my correspondence myself. I have no secretarial assistance. That finished with my predecessor.'

'Excuse me, please,' said Colver, beginning to stand, putting his hands out to the table to support himself. A sudden feeling of sickness had welled up inside his ribs. He felt in the pockets of his coat for a handkerchief. He clasped it immediately; it had been the only thing in any of his pockets: it had been laundered and ironed: it was so heavily starched that he had difficulty in unfolding it: his mouth had filled with bile.

'Where are you going?'

'Outside. I want to breathe.'

The magistrate looked up at him. 'What is the matter?'

'This room is airless!' The open door before him enframed an openness which seemed wider than the openness of the valley itself: the entering light lay on the flagstones of the floor in a broad lozenge.

On looking up, immediately outside the door, he saw with a renewed surprise that no religious symbols ornamented the gatehouse arch, or the gables of the roofs, or the corners of the bell-tower. He had made the same observation many times before: only now did he see how unexpected it was.

The magistrate, the proprietor and the proprietor's wife had followed him out of the door, the proprietor's wife first, then her husband, the magistrate standing behind them and looking over their shoulders. The traveller looked away from them: he wished in his sickness to be alone.

V

One evening the traveller, sitting on the block in the yard of the inn, looking at the ground just beyond his feet, heard a voice calling out to attract his attention, though on first hearing it had seemed to him as though it were an involuntary shout, either for help or of warning: he lifted his head and looked up and down the road. He could see no-one but the priest.

'They've got you outside now,' said the priest, dismounting from his bicycle. 'How much longer will you remain here?'

'Two more days only.'

The white cliff faces in the mountains flung back the day's heat into the valley.

'The doctor came out again, then.'

'Yes, they called him out for the last time. I was told that the magistrate's wife considered it wise. I shall be gone in two days.'

'What report will carry of your findings?' asked the priest, in the manner of one asking about the outcome of an amateurish project which from the moment of its setting up could never have been of any importance. On seeing the traveller make ready to stand he shook his head. 'I am only quoting to you what one of the bailiffs is saying in the village,' he said.

'It's a myth of the village to think of the traveller as being blind,' said the priest. 'It's true, I suppose, to an extent. His experiences are compressed; it's in his nature to misuse the freedom of travel, which allows him to see or to ignore anything he wishes.' The priest, looking at the open door of the inn, had all the appearances of sincerity as he said this. 'I have seen travellers stand where you are standing now, having been in the valley for a few hours: they have been given food and drink, they have bathed their feet: they have slept: they have taken what the proprietor chooses to give them, then they say: "which road to the pass?" and look up and down the valley as though they had been familiar with it since the day of their birth. "How far is such and such a town?" they ask, with rags of maps in ther hands: the accuracy of these guides is never questioned: it is unclear whether they are speaking to you or to themselves. They always stare past you. One does not know whether they require an answer; anything one might say would be seen in such a light as might be used to impel them on their journey.' The priest leaned the cycle against the wall of the inn. 'One makes generalizations! I see you sitting apparently asleep in the courtyard, but the minute I mention the notions of the villagers you are suddenly alert.' He took his watch out of his pocket but already it was too dark to see its face clearly.

'You make it clear that you can't generalize,' said the traveller.

Down by the river a dog barked, and the close echoes, when they had gone, emphasized the stillness of the valley. 'I told you about the parishioner with an interest in the bells,' said the priest. 'I will take you to see him if you wish it.' He paused, listening to the sounds of the valley. Within the inn the lamps were being lit. He put his watch back into his pocket.

'Where does he live?'

'Only a short walk distant.'

Colver saw there there was a small case strapped to the rack above the back wheel of the cycle. Perhaps the priest had returned from visiting a sick person somewhere in the village.

'Now you will ask me: why should you wish to meet him, and why should he wish to meet you? What, to put it in another way, have you in common? I can say very little, except perhaps to explain the way in which you might see him. He will try to maintain your first assumption that you have a language in common. It's a point of pride with him. The truth is that you have hardly a word in common.' He turned to face the oak-wood, and stared between the thin boles of the trees as though expecting to see someone he recognized standing in the darkness. 'You have very little in common except appearance; were he your age you might look somewhat similar.' His manner had altered. He now seemed displeased with himself for having asked the traveller to go with him to see the parishioner: perhaps he was asking himself why he had dismounted in the inn yard instead of merely giving a cursory greeting to the traveller as he passed; even that would have been unnecessary for the traveller had been asleep, or, if not asleep, looking down at the ground. It was certain now that he regretted that he had, a moment ago and in a lighthearted manner, suggested the visit.

'What are you looking at?' asked Colver, following his gaze and looking with him into the wood.

'No-one,' said the priest, 'I see no-one.'

They were walking down a narrow street when the priest looked across to the traveller and paused. 'They call you "the sick man".' The priest paused at the mouth of a narrower alley. There were no lights, not even a glimmer from a window, and the only evidence of the alley's existence was the echo and the thin ribbon of starlight which spread downwards along the gap between the houses. Some distance down this alley the priest stopped beneath the lintel of an ill-fitting door which allowed light to escape from under the rotten ends of the boards. A number of people gathered round them as the priest searched with his hand for the latch of the door. He lifted the latch with a brisk clacking sound and pushed the door open, kicking the bottom of the door as though he knew it to be prone to sticking.

'Why did you suggest this?' asked the traveller. 'And why did you then change your mind?' He had no wish to enter the house; he felt that his own presence would be an intrusion, that he would be called upon to witness some event, that the priest would make an example of the occupant or the occupants, who at this moment were surely sitting inside their own house and leading their own lives. Surely the parishioner of whom the priest had spoken was a man with natural wishes for a right to his own privacy? It might have been the case—the thought crossed his mind—that the priest wished to make an example of himself before whoever was in the room. 'Why did you suggest this?' he said again.

'I thought it possible you might be interested.' The priest, having opened the door, took hold of the sleeve of the sick man's coat as though to pull him into the room against his will. No sooner were they over the threshold than a man, one of those who had been standing unnoticed in the darkness of the street outside, followed them into the room before they could close the door, and, himself followed by others, stood within the shadows. An uncertain number of people had been in the room before the priest had opened the door and an uncertain number had entered after he had let go its handle. The room was dark, almost as dark as the alley outside; the one lamp shed little light; it was difficult to see how the eyes would ever become accustomed to the darkness of the interior. The air was stale, as though until the door had opened there had been no ventilation and the atmosphere had been breathed and rebreathed. This room, like a hutch, was constantly lived in, day and night. There was no other door in the room apart from the one through which they had entered: there was no staircase; the room was unconnected with the rest of the terrace except by way of the alley: the room above must belong to one of the adjacent houses or perhaps it was approached by a flight of exterior stone steps which had been invisible in the darkness. The traveller could make out the shape of a bed which had been slept in and which was now a bundle of blankets, the bedclothes being creased and tangled by restlessness and the turmoil of sleeplessness. Someone could be heard walking about in the room above; the traveller thought to himself: how difficult it must be to sleep in such a place. The gap under the door was a portal for the entry of the rats which themselves endured their lives in the drain which ran along the middle of the alley. As he turned to look further into the room he was pushed against the bed by the inward crowding villagers, and he was unwillingly forced to put down a hand to the bed in order to keep his balance: he found that what he had taken to be crumpled bedclothes were sheets of crumpled paper which crackled as he touched them. At the far end of the room another lamp was being lit. The man who was lighting it was hidden by the shape of the priest, and the sick man saw only the hand which held a match between its fingers; there was a sense of purpose in the way that the match, the lamp having been lit, was extinguished by a pinch of finger and thumb and then thrown to the floor. 'Why are there so many in the room?' asked the traveller, speaking into the priest's ear.

'We contribute: they are always inquisitive,' said the priest, as though he found the confusion which filled the room a commonplace event and unworthy of notice.

Colver saw the old man who sat at the table at the end of the room. He seemed distant, but this was an illusion due to the press of people in the room, standing without speaking but not silent. The old man who sat at the table looked up; his eyes were staring: his pupils extraordinarily black. Certainly, until a moment ago he had been sitting asleep or awake in the near-darkness of his own room. The traveller's first thoughts on seeing him were 'How does this man sleep?'; this question must have been apparent in his expression, for the old man's face held a look of shamed embarrassment. 'How can you bring yourself to intrude like this!' said Colver to the priest.

'It is necessary to visit every room in the parish.' The priest pointed down to the table, on the surface of which were a number of books, their bindings dirty with constant handling, pencils, pens, and bottles of inks of different colours, a set of three tuning forks with the plating worn down to the underlying brass, a magnifying glass and a yard rule of dark boxwood. A pair of spectacles lay in the fold of the open book which rested on top of the pile of closed books. The old man reached out his two hands to these glasses, bringing them up to his face and resting them on the bridge of his nose. That action altered his face; the traveller felt a sudden pity as he looked at the parishioner's face, one grave brown eye staring at him

78

through the lensless frame while the other eye lay behind the cataract of dust which covered the remaining lens.

'Is this—' The traveller spoke to the priest (his voice on the edge of laughter) but pointed towards the old man '—your idea of humour?' His own pointing had made him angry and he put his hand behind his back.

'You cannot judge things by their appearances,' said the priest in a slow, authoritative voice. 'You can only ask yourself the question, "What forms and what procedures are being mimicked here?"'

The old man began to speak. The priest, as though contemptuous of anything he might say, stood in silence, his arms folded, not looking at him but rather at a pattern made by the outline of a stain on the wall above his head. His mouth was closed, his lips tightly pressed together; he made no attempt to translate the parishioner's words, but stood in a weighty silence nodding his head to a gentle beat of his own making. The old man was speaking rapidly, barely giving himself enough time to draw breath; while he spoke he turned the yellowing pages of the book in front of him, his eye traversing the lines of his own writing, though it was certain, from the way he spoke, that he spoke from memory.

Seeing that he was not understood he began patiently to reiterate what he had said, looking beyond the priest at the traveller.

The priest, shifting his stance, at last interposed a dry translation, flatly laying down the errors and the generalities in his interpretation. Colver, looking from the speaker to the translator, was aware after a moment—indeed it was shown by his manner—that the priest was translating only those few uttered phrases which caught his ear: perhaps he was selecting what he should or should not translate; perhaps he had a fixed idea what the traveller should or should not hear: within a moment, Colver saw that he had made an untruthful surmise; it became clear not only that the priest was translating only generalities with which he himself was familiar, but also that the speaker and the translator were reciting a sequence familiar to them both; the former muttering those phrases which he knew would be translated, laying expressive emphasis only on those which he knew from experience would not be deemed worthy of translation; the latter giving a translation of those phrases which he had heard in the past and which he could no longer be bothered to listen to, recognizing them only from the sound of the voice. The traveller, when he had reached this conclusion, found himself looking backwards and forwards from one man to the other, wondering which phrase would be muttered and translated, and which would be shouted and ignored. He looked at the speaker and the translator in a different light: it was difficult to know which of them was right and which was wrong: he had no idea what was being said, or who was to be believed. The varied conclusions were that the priest and the old man had been through this rigmarole before, or that the priest in fact understood but poorly the language of the village in which he had served for so many years, or that the old man was speaking complexities which were beyond the translator's interest, which indeed seemed to be very limited, for in between the phrases of his translation the priest had begun to hum a tune of his own, in part a copy of a little song that must have been unknown to him before he had been sent to this locality, which rose and fell with the same cadences as the old man's voice. For all this, the translation, rattled off intermittently, had the general coherence of an everyday matter. 'A bell, an E flat bell, sounded ten years ago. Then it had sounded eleven times. Perhaps it is the same bell which sounded this year, in February, but how can this be proved? The latter bell had only sounded once, and that softly: it sounded then while I had been on the edge of sleep. It is difficult to know the pitch of a bell which rings only once. It is difficult to know the pitch of a muffled bell. As well as being ready with the tuning forks, one has to carry the pitch of the bell in one's own head: sometimes, in a search for the correct pitch with the forks, the original sound will be lost. The echoes of the mountain are a confusing influence: had a lightly-struck bell sounded twice or three times? The rapidity of the striking confuses the knowledge one has of the echoes. The echoes of the mountain can be a trap, even when one thinks one has these echoes fully understood. Sometimes one can hear a bell, and smile as one hears the echoes, thinking to oneself, "I have them understood". Sometimes the echoes bear no resemblance to echoes one has heard before. It's an effect of the mountains. The mountains sometimes cause a double-echo, as though the basin at the head of the valley had the power to magnify sound. I have an assistant. Sometimes he stations himself at one of many places in the valley. The loudness of an echo varies with the pitch: then the study of what the assistant has heard is helpful. Certain echoes of the more rarely-heard deeper bells will, in certain weathers, be louder than the prime source. Mist, fog, wind, rain, snow, storm, flood: all causes of inaccuracy. Bells of a certain pitch may appear to sound from any part of the valley: in these circumstances even the most willing assistant is no use, even if he can be trusted: I have no money; I have to rely on the goodwill of such an assistant, and though he may have enthusiasm he may have less integrity than one would wish for. Sometimes a bell gives in its sounding out, during a winter's night, the sense that it sounds out directly overhead.'

The traveller, listening, aware of the generality of the translation (and aware too of a certain gloss consistent with the priest's own manner of thinking), saw in this translation a description only of events; there had been nothing in it of prediction or of divination. He had heard, untranslated, from the parishioner's lips, a few words and phrases in his own language; the priest had not translated these phrases: they were, after all, made up of words borrowed from the language into which he was translating; perhaps he did not consider the phrases of sufficient importance to be brought to the attention of the traveller. These phrases, though they were in his language, were too short to be by themselves comprehensible; they were grains of familiarity in a foreign matrix. Their sense lay in the unfamiliar. When he asked the priest the context in which one of these phrases had occurred he was told that the phrase was quite meaningless, and had only been spoken for effect; the old man had picked up a number of words and phrases not only from a demographic team who had come to study the villagers some years ago, but also from those who had come to examine the exterior dimensions of the monastery. The traveller, though he was unable to prove it, was sure that this was not so; he had become increasingly certain that the translator understood neither the meaning nor the context of the parishioner's words. The traveller's own state had been altered by a chain of simple facts about the things he saw: the powerful concentration of the old man's brown eye with its wide pupil: the odd appeal to understanding brought about by the wearing of those spectacles: the appeal of a pitiful dignity: the dim lamp which cast a near-formless shadow of the speaker on to the uneven ochre wall behind his chair.

'Look behind you,' said the priest.

The traveller looked back at the rear of the room and saw the rapt faces, the gaze of each resting on the old man's face.

'The gist of what he says does not alter very much. There is nothing in his manner or his speech that alters very much.'

Colver remained silent.

'He would try to make us believe him if he could. Perhaps he has repeated his words so many times that he now believes them himself.' He looked at the walls of the room as if looking for a clock. 'Do you wish to stay here?'

'No,' said Colver. He had expected a return of his sickness in this low-ceilinged room, where the air was foetid because of the number of people who had crowded into it, but he did not feel in the least unwell: the opposite was true: he had an inappropriate sense of his own wellbeing. He looked back at the old man and caught his glance. 'Ask him how he first found an interest in the sounding of the bells.'

The priest tolerantly repeated the question, as though finding a necessity in verifying its accuracy before translating it. Then he said: 'No, I cannot translate it. Not now. Not after all that he has said and all that I have translated. One must have some compassion.' He turned away from the parishioner and began to walk away from the table. 'The woman next door cooks his meals and washes for him.'

When they had reached the door, the priest pushing his way, they stood outside the open door for a moment. Above their heads the line of stars between the roofs showed the orientation of the alley.

The priest led the way along the alley, feeling for the walls with his hands. It was necessary to walk with care to avoid the central gutter. 'You have a kindly nature! I have hardly met a more innocent man! I have known him for a long time. I know something about these things; I see that he sensed your initial doubt and altered what he would have said. He chose to talk about the general nature of his life. He's an accomplished speaker. He can suit his talk to his hearers. He is adaptable. Were you to go back now you would be able to judge that for yourself.'

Colver, who thought it natural that one should speak according to the nature of one's hearers, said, 'Why does he wish to make his views known?'

'I don't know the answer to that.'

'Has he altered with the years?'

The priest, having reached the end of the alley, paused in the darkness; his familiarity with the nature of the roadway between the walls of the alley had allowed him to walk quickly, whereas the visitor, familiar only with the darkness and forced to walk more slowly, feeling his way along the uneven walls; with his eyes wide open in the manner of someone finding his way along in pitch-blackness, could do no more than follow the direction of his voice as best he could. In order to induce the priest to speak he therefore asked him questions, the answers to which were of little importance except to act as guides to direction: the echoes showed the alley to have a number of oblique corners and re-entrant walls. Small snickets and passageways led from it into the maze of houses. 'Has he altered with the years?'

The priest paused to consider this. 'I don't think he has.'

'Where does he come from?'

'I don't know.' The priest seemed surprised; not so much by the question as by the direction from which it came. 'I have never asked him that: I have always avoided asking that question. I don't want to encourage any claim he might have to recognition. I know nothing about him except that he was once a mill-worker, so they say.'

Colver found that he was lost and unwilling to move; he had seen an open well-shaft somewhere here; he remembered remarking to himself how dangerous it was, particularly for the children of the families who lived in the neighbourhood: perhaps the iron cover of the well was normally kept closed. He took a step forward and trod upon the iron cover which sounded hollowly beneath his feet. He stood still, not knowing whether the cover lay over the well or lay to one side of its open shaft. He stared at the darkness in front of his feet, no longer listening to the priest's voice. He stretched out his hands and found that he was in a covered passageway: when he looked up he could no longer see the stars, but instead only lines of light which came through gaps in the floorboards of a ceiling above. He had entered through an open door and had become a trespasser in this passageway. He looked up and down the passage and found that his eyes were sufficiently adapted to the darkness to see his way forward to a small courtyard, or backward to the alley.

At that moment a door opened in the courtyard, allowing an irregular prism of yellow light to fall on to the stone slabs which made up the floor. Two girls came out through the door of the half-concealed house: they had been talking to each other and to someone else within the house; their voices were blithe and carefree and he found it a pleasure to listen to them. As they came out they both looked back at the door of the house: the door was still open: he could see the shadowy outline of the person to whom they were saying their farewells, but no more than an outline; the mist was growing more dense by the moment, and now even the outline of the open door was ill-defined. The two girls were dressed for walking, with shawls round their shoulders; they carried lanterns, holding them well out from their bodies so that their clothes should not become tainted with the smell of the oil. As they walked out into the courtyard the light of their lamps illuminated fragments of a domestic scene; a washing-tub was upturned on the flagstones, and on its upturned bottom were a number of scrubbing brushes. The light of the lanterns briefly shone into the interior of the copper-house, showing for a second the square brick boiler, its firehole and flue outlined against the shadows within the room. As the girls walked towards the passage, the light cast a long and magnified shadow of the cast-iron pump across one of the walls of the house.

Colver, standing in the courtyard, had followed them with his gaze. He remembered the sight of the girls coming out of the house for a long time. The simplicity of the recollection was pleasant.

As he made his way up the alley, feeling along the walls again, a recollection of his first feelings of compassion for the old man passed through his mind. What was the family he had lost? Did he come from this village? Was he a foreigner here? It was difficult to think back to the courtyard where the two girls had talked together, saying their farewells, the light from their lamps magnifying the shadows of objects in the alley, without feeling that the pleasure of witnessing small events such as this might once have been a part of the old man's life.

As for the girls, they went their way down the alley, the traveller watching them as their lamps lit up the walls. Windows and doors, which a moment ago he had touched in an effort to discover his way, were now seen for the first time.

VI

During the next forenoon the traveller retraced his steps of the previous night. He was impelled to return to the mill-worker's room from a sense of shame; last night he had been misrepresented not only by the priest, but also by himself, as an unknown person with a blank face who had acted as though he were demonstrably a foreigner, his manner that of any touring visitor conducted from a public place to a private room with such speed that he stares round himself hardly seeing the difference between the two. As he stood in the alley, near the open well, someone who was walking from one end of the alley to the other but who had been following his movements in passing with interest, pointed to the latch of the door as though it were not evident, and seized it just as his own hand was about to grasp it, flinging it, roughly, as though it were an entrance door to any common yard, so that it banged against the wall, striking it with such force that plaster rattled down the wall.

Those who had followed him down the alley and who had waited behind him at the door followed him into the room and crowded behind him. He looked at them from the darkness of the room and saw their answering expressions, each with the marks of forthrightness or secrecy, of shrewdness or guilelessness: it was difficult in the light within the room to know how far their expressions represented the nature which lay behind them or to what extent shrewdness was affected and guilelessness counterfeit.

He had gone to the room to make his apology and to

demonstrate that his presence the night before had not been inspired by the priest's scepticism. He remembered that he had on more than one occasion stood with the pointing finger of a spectator who, in a distant place where he has no particular interest in what he hears or sees, or in what he does, must continue to comment on the events which are taking place before him in order to placate his guide.

In the daylight the room was an ordinary downstairs room. The one window faced the lightless alley. The outer surface of the window-glass was dirty as though from upward splashing from wheeled vehicles which had travelled at speed through the alley. The plastered walls, remembered as being uneven and a mottled brown colour, were now seen as coloured with a limewash pinkened by a mixture of ochres. A patterned edging paper ran along the top of the walls and round the ends of the ceiling joists: in many places it had been laboriously cut and spliced in an attempt at making it fit the odd angles of the plaster-work. The bed was made with coarse grey blankets, and beside it, on the top of a small chest of drawers, stood a candle in a pot holder and a black bible. Through these things one saw immediately the ordinariness of the old man's life. Had the traveller magnified in his own mind the events of last night? In memory he saw again the embarrassed eye, grave and brown, fixing him with the involuntary stare of conviction. Now he saw that the old man was sitting at a board table; he was wearing his old clothes; he wore a chequered flannelette shirt and a pair of corduroy breeches such as were hung up for sale on the wall of the inn. In the wearing of these clothes the old man made no concession to bodily infirmity: it was clear that he wished to preserve at least the outer appearance of vigour long lost. The uncomfortable chair in which he sat was padded, over its back, with a quilt and a feather bolster, from the striped ticking of which the quills of large feathers stuck. He sat as though fatigued. His expression of discomfort was neither increased nor diminished when he saw the traveller within the room. He leaned forward with a sudden awkwardness: he reached out his hand as though to grasp Colver's for support: when he spoke his words were hardly coherent: no formal translation was necessary: now, Colver heard him saying that the words 'the sick man' were identical in meaning to the words 'the man is dead' and 'the man has a vocation'. The old parishioner pointed to the bruises on Colver's forearms. Colver leaned over the side of the parishioner's chair, supporting the extra-ordinarily heavy weight of the parishioner's head with his hand, enduring as he did so the pressure of the goose-quills which had penetrated the cover of the bolster: he looked away from the parishioner, across the room, towards the window, seeing that the sudden light of the sun had risen to fill the glass. Innumerable unmoving specks were caught in the path of the light. The growing ray touched first the edge of the table and then the books and then, dyeing the bottles of ink with colour, revealing the grain in the wood of the table's scrubbed surface. The glass of the window, dusty and un-cleaned, was now a rectangle of translucent milkiness, broken only by the division of the glazing bars. The light touched the face of the parishioner, causing him to shy from it and making him incline his head in Colver's arm, forcing him to turn his head unconsciously to Colver's chest, unminding of the weeping sores: their embrace, involuntary as it was, revealed as though by a preordained design the illness which they possessed in common, as though it were able to give rise to two outward forms: in the traveller, the sores and cicatrices of sores; in the parishioner, a bodily weakness. The parishioner gave no further attention to the waxing light which momently (as Colver saw on looking down) brought about a change in the emphasis of his expression, deepening the creases in the skin of his face, giving the illusion that his eye was further set in his head than it was, and at the same time firing the colour of his moist iris. The light changed his attitude: one could see for the first time that he was in discomfort; the light caused his finger to point, not at the lesions on Colver's arms, nor at the page of the book which was laid in front of him but which because of the angle at which he lay he could not see, but at the faces of the villagers who were now behind the traveller. What had they expected

88

to see? What had Colver expected to see? With a backward glance, Colver saw the reflections of that light and of that pointing finger in the pupils of the eyes of the men and women who stood behind him. Why were any of them in that room? Nothing unusual had happened. The sun had risen, illuminating the old man and irradiating the items on the table. There was nothing more than that. The parishioner, in an effort to take the weight of his head from Colver's arm, struggled to support himself, gripping the arms of his chair with his hands; Colver, seeing this, removed his arm from its painful position amongst the folds of the quilt. Those in the room above were walking to and fro across their floor, and talking in ordinary conversational voices, but sufficiently loudly that what they said might be understood were one familiar with their language. The old man, who paid no attention to the sound of these voices above, lifted a heavy brass-cased watch to his eye. Once his watch was seen the noisy and irregular sound of its escapement was immediately heard. Perhaps after all the watch had been heard before its face had been seen. The old man lowered his head to study the enamelled face as though he had only partial sight in his one eye. He lifted his other hand across the surface of the table and he raised, momentarily, a tuning-fork: he touched one of its tines, and then touched a stump of a blue pencil, holding it in his fingers. He turned the pages of one of the books. A bell was about to sound. He waited, but the expected moment died. He smiled, quietly, with a lack of any embarrassment which indicated less of a gesture of failure of prediction than a frank admission of the futility at the attempt. He said nothing. He dropped the pencil, with a conscious attempt at releasing his grip on it, into the fold of the open book.

Colver, as though awakening, found that he had gripped the metal edge of the table.

'Nothing ever happens,' said the parishioner, voicing these foreign words as though for the privilege of the traveller.

There was, for all the expectation, pleasure to be gained from the certainty that no bell would sound. The villagers began to leave the room. One or two of them smiled, with a brisk alertness, aware of the passing time and the closeness of the exact hour at which they must begin the working day, which, after all, had started long ago, before the sunlight had ever entered the valley.

The morning was well advanced. The traveller had been in the room for an hour. He looked back through the open door, about to close it. The parishioner was staring back at the book. Despite all that had passed it was clear that he had expected the sounding of a bell. He was now absorbed in the complexity of the pages which he himself had written. He reached for a pencil, as though he knew where the mistake in his prediction lay.

VII

Colver, in his sitting on a step of the inn yard's mounting-block, every morning, soon after dawn, before the coldness of the night had gone (always the same step—sometimes wet and sometimes dry, a matter of habit), followed with his eye the ribbon of the road until it was swallowed by the mists: on some days he could not see his own foot; on others, the road was lost as it reached the river and the wood; once, with an effort, his eye followed it in all its hidden turns up the side of the valley to the summit of the pass itself.

The transition from the hanging dampness of the foot of the pass to the heat of the sun at the summit was momentary and abrupt. Within a few moments of his standing on the road at the summit of the pass his damp clothes were steaming in the heat. He had become resigned to the uncertainty of the position and the identity of any landmark seen through the mists: when he had climbed above the hanging layers he was taken aback by the clarity of the air and by the distances which were opened by the altitude to the eye. Downwards, in the direction from which he had come, the familiar valley was hidden by mists, and downwards, in each of many further directions, their ways unknown to him, range upon range of hills, all of them unknown to him, enclosed other unseen valleys. There was not the slightest perceptible movement of the air. Even the grasses about the bases of the limestone outcrops were unmoving for all that they conformed to the pattern of the turbulences of a past wind. The thorn trees, lying close to the ground, the conformation of their growth laid down by the direction of that wind, were of the shape of the weathered boulders between which they grew. In the present absence of any movement of the air this weathering was the only evidence of the wind which ordinarily dominated the pass.

The mist which lay as a silent and enclosed lake lapped up to the pass in broad and unmoving waves. The shadows of the higher peaks lay across its white surface as though across solid land: to the prospecting eye it seemed possible to walk across this illusory plain, making a monotonous white journey of it.

The monastery's walls, across the valley, were half submerged in a mist which gave them the appearance of being the walls of a harbour or of a solitary coastal fortification. The tower looked out blindly above the walls as though its narrow windows had been constructed with surveillance as their purpose. The sense of the isolation of the building was heightened by the stillness and by the very clarity of the upper air. Its stonework had a look of age as though it was of a natural and not an artificial origin. It was difficult to conceive the idea that it had ever been constructed. The shadows which lay in the angles of the re-entrant walls between the salients were black and sharply defined. From that moment of the first glance to the conclusion of a prolonged examination the building by its white walls and their black shadows gave rise to the immediate judgment: it is a ruin.

A bell began to sound, slowly at first but gaining as though by familiarity an uneven and a hesitant momentum.

The traveller sat by the side of the road. The sound of the bell so accorded with his feeling that it might have begun its sounding within his own heart. He turned his head to follow with his eye the further ways, in the further valleys within the crumpled land, beyond the pass; but he saw in them avenues of progression untenable to him in his progress, paths of a journey which were denied him whatever the direction of his journeying: the mists which were even now dispersing in the valley were recondensing in the tracts beyond the pass: even now those further prospects were much less distinct than they had been even a few minutes ago.

The bell continued to ring. For all its unusual uncertainty it ceased in its tolling, with an apparent arbitrariness, there being nothing out of the ordinary about the sound or nature of the final stroke, only at the time appointed to it.

'You are free of cares,' said the magistrate, raising his hand to his eye. He held in his hand a passport, which, for some reason, Colver was convinced was his own, an irrational conviction, since the exterior covers of passports are the same, even the information within hardly differing from one to another. The sight of this passport, or book which resembled a passport, whether it was his own or not, made him very much aware of the insecurity of his own position. The passport itself was not his; it belonged to the civil authorities; the magistrate had the power to hold it for as long as he might wish—an insignificant fact: the passport was of itself of no particular importance.

The magistrate turned his head to look at the others in the room. His stutter had worsened since Colver had last spoken to him.

'I am as you say free of cares,' said Colver. 'Talking of one's cares makes for prevarication. I have never wished to lie about myself.'

'Why should you lie about yourself?' The magistrate stared round the walls of the room. He replaced the passport in his breast pocket. 'One does not lie in conversation.' His stutter and the tightness of his throat caused him to speak in an odd metrical fashion, so that he laid stress on certain words for their place in that inner metre rather than for an emphasis of their sense. 'On the other hand,' he said, assisting the evolution of his words by looking down at his hands, which were again clasped together in front of his body, holding the passport, which seemed now to be his own, if one were to judge by the possessive manner in which he held it, 'why should you tell the truth about yourself?' The way in which he said these two contradictory sentences suggested that he had been prompted to speak by his examination of the room.

Colver found himself pitying the magistrate if only for his

93

impediment of speech. On his arrival he had wondered whether the magistrate was drunk; he now saw that he was not: indeed he had the manner of a habitually temperate man; perhaps he had reached an extremity the nature of which was known to himself alone. On seeing Colver his first words were: 'You are behaving as I used to behave. Ah! the heady days when you only play at disbelieving the principles which you have been taught! The days when you can afford to feign an attack on the standards which from childhood have been your backbone!' Having said this the lightheartedness fell from him and he became silent, staring hollowly at the floor. He said, suddenly, lifting his head, 'I shall not be here much longer.' He had attempted to keep his voice low but his stutter had precluded this and the outcome was that the tail of his utterance was sharp and distinct. The proprietor looked down from his evening ritual of lighting the lamps. 'A letter arrived two days ago.'

'You made no mention of it that evening.'

'That is quite true,' said the magistrate, looking across the room again, 'I had no wish to discuss it at the time.' He appeared to be watching the lighting of the lamps. 'I think I intimated that I expected to receive it. That is not the same as saying that I expected it when it came. It does recall me. It is a letter which has been written to humiliate.'

Colver, to whom the magistrate had mentioned on so many occasions (though only in the most abstract of terms) an expectation of receiving such a letter, said nothing, but listened to the magistrate's speaking voice, hearing in it such a metrical emphasis that many of the words were robbed of meaning.

'It is a letter which refers to my duties. The words "certain unspecified neglects" appear in every paragraph, each one a reiteration of the one before it. No mention is made of any effort on my part. No mention is made of the fact that I have spared nothing of myself in the course of my duties.'

'Have you told your wife of the arrival of this letter?'

'No, I have not told my wife. I have not told, as you would say, anyone, of the arrival of this letter. Who is there for me to tell?' The magistrate was not watching the lighting of the

94

lamps but looked past the proprietor, out through the open door into the void of the night. 'I have looked at it for so long that its sense is lost.' He held up a hand with his fingers spread out: one might have expected to see the letter in his hand but his hand was empty. He looked at his hand, knuckle and palm, inspecting his fingers, examining in turn each of his finger-nails: every gesture was filled with empty exasperation. 'A moment ago I said that I did not believe the meaning of this letter.' He said this as though stating an intention to base his words upon a firm foundation. 'It arrived to fulfil an exigency long considered but long dismissed. In the past, my wife and I had talked about the possibility of its arrival so frequently that we had come to believe that its arrival would forever be postponed. Each day with no letter was a day of respite, and each day the sending away, the loss of post, seemed to grow more and more remote.'

'Do you wish me to read it?'

'Sometimes I wish that you would read it and sometimes I think that it would be for the best if you were not to read it, for your sake as well as mine.' He paused. 'That being said, the statement is plain enough: the letter is unambiguous and there is no room for any latitude as to its meaning; I am old enough to understand that there is no possibility of any redress.'

'You said, a moment ago, that you had looked at it for so long that its sense had become lost to you.'

'I was speaking as it were from form. I know its language. When I first saw it I was filled with incredulity: immediately my eye searched for a weak clause, an extenuation allowing an ambiguous reading. There is no such diversity of interpretation. There is no possibility of ambiguity. The letter speaks for itself without any compromise.' The abruptness left his voice. 'I am only surprised, in retrospect, that it had not arrived sooner.

'I had thought that I was doing well here; at first I had no reason to think otherwise. I was reasonably content, then, and very hard-working, and my wife—she was vivacious, then, and ambitious for me—she lived for the social evenings which we used to arrange here every few months. There used to be, in the old days, meetings of varying formality, arranged by local administrators and other men of business. At one time I made a point of setting aside a certain week in June, late June, when work was at an ebb to take leave and to go with my wife to the regatta in the confluence town. In the early years, those we knew in the town came to visit us in the late summer for the sake of the mountain air, to escape the heat of the plain. It became habit. There was no reason why that had to change: there was no change in my surroundings: the change was internal. That is why I said: "the heady days, when you only play at disbelieving the principles which you have been taught".

'My accession to the secular agency to the monastery caused the disjointed awkwardness which militated against the search for a satisfactory life. It was then that things began to go hard for me.'

'I notice that you imply that your accession to the post was a wilful decision on your part.'

'Yes, that is true but apposite only in a certain manner: such an appointment was no more than I might have expected when I first saw the circumstances which surrounded me. I arrived here and I saw my surroundings and I tried to make the best of them. I had been told something of the character of my predecessor: I arrived at the house and I saw the state of the things which had been left me. You might well say that it would have been easy to have had the domestic arrangements put in order: on the other hand, how can one live in such a condition, and yet administer the outer things in the manner which one has been taught? There was no vestige of any system by which the place had been administered.'

'Do you drink much?'

'I do not drink at all.' The magistrate paused and looked at Colver. 'I don't resent that question,' he said, in a low voice with hardly a trace of the stutter.

'What will you do now?'

'I hardly know. The letter has disturbed any confidence which I might once have had in my own capabilities.'

96

'You say that the undertaking of the responsibilities of the secular agency of the monastery increased the difficulty of your standing. Why was that?'

The magistrate smiled as though recognizing, behind the formal phrasing of the question, the fact that the traveller was hardly in a position to question him: that he could hardly know anything about the magistracy except from what he had heard from the magistrate himself. Perhaps he found something second-hand in hearing the words 'the secular agency' used by another. 'Why did those responsibilities increase the difficulty of my own standing? I hardly know the answer to that. The only thing I can say is that it is impossible to work for the civil authorities and for the monastery without compromising one's own honesty and without jeopardizing one's own integrity. One tries to maintain standards. As for the monastery and the civil authorities, it would be too easy to say that the work done for one is inimical to the work done for the other. When I first took the post as agent I did not consider that there would be any difficulty: things were very different then. There was nothing which I could not prosper in to the benefit of myself and my family. It is only with the passing years that one finds that the two forces pull, sometimes concertedly, sometimes in opposition, making any decision a difficult thing.

'Honesty. There is indeed the question of honesty. It is impossible to be honest when one deals with the civil powers and with the monastery. Honesty to one is in a sense dishonesty to the other. There is no possibility of the occupier of this post being impartial. My attempts at impartiality have done nothing but prejudice my own integrity. How can one describe terms such as "honesty", "impartiality" or "deception" without invoking an internal system? How can I make definitions without trusting the feelings which I have towards either of my masters?

'When I began my present work I saw nothing of this. In the beginning I tried to serve the interests first of the civil side, and then of the monastery, but it is impossible to do that while continuing to pretend to keep the eyes uncovered. The

97

fact that I have been administering the monastery's lands for so many years is in itself an indication of the extent to which temptation has been put in my way: all manner of things have threatened to expose the strength or weakness of my will, one thing after another, beginning with the lack of communication: you have seen that for yourself: I cannot communicate with the monastery: now, due to this inability I find I can no longer communicate with the civil authorities. Had you known me five years ago you would not have recognized me: I had become so ingrained in the ways I had undertaken that I believed (or had come to believe) that I was always acting in the right. I could always justify everything I undertook on behalf of the monastery, even if this necessitated an action which was directly contrary to one I had carried out only a little while before. It is easy to see how this happens. It is easy to persuade oneself that there is communication where in reality there is none. It was only after those initial years that I saw myself justifying not actions, but principles which had been arbitrarily acquired.'

'One might have expected your task to have grown easier with time.'

'Would you have thought so? Some express one opinion, others an opinion quite contrary. Indeed so. It was easy to say, at first: "hard work now: in a few years' time and by experience such solutions as are necessary will come naturally": by so saying I did nothing but postpone the consideration of them to a future time. I think that I can see how things began to go wrong for me. Were my successor in front of me, I would give him advice.'

'What would your advice be?'

'I would tell him straightforwardly that one is never dishonest for the good of oneself.

'When I first came here, and later, when I had in my own eyes established myself, it was clear that it would become necessary for me to gain the favour of some of the important people in the district. This was not out of any conceit: conceit of that nature is foreign, I hope, to my character.' The impediment of speech had, imperceptibly at first, returned to his voice, unnoticed at first by the traveller, who had to some extent grown used to the unusual way in which he enunciated his words. The traveller, who might once have thought that the magistrate's mannerisms were due to the isolation which surrounded him, saw that this was not the case; the valley was not as remote as he had thought: the mention of the administrators and magistrates dispelled that idea. These hills, which had at first seemed so remote, were after all as populous as any other part of the country; one imagined, as the magistrate spoke, a town at every valley head and a village with a church and a school at every crossroads.

'It is a mistake to make conciliatory gestures,' said the magistrate. 'I never did any good by being dishonest on other people's behalf: the memory of dishonesty lies longer in the mind than the memory of conciliation.

'It is remarkable, now, that I did not see at once, at the moment of the inception of the thought, the dishonesty implicit in the assumption of responsibility for the external affairs of the monastery. Again and again, shortly after I arrived here, I found myself caught in that familiar cleft. The ability to work for both authorities required a blinkered and directional approach which was beyond me.' He laid his hands on the table, slowly but with an exertion of power, as though trying to push something concealed in his palms into the substance of the solid wood. 'All this nebulous uncertainty is in the past: the letter has arrived.'

The traveller, who might have been expected to feel pity for his predicament, felt no such thing. The magistrate had been speaking with a lack of spontaneity which made his admission of his own dishonesty sound spurious: Colver had no idea whether he regretted his past actions or whether he even regretted the future imposed upon him by the arrival of the letter of recall. Beneath the fact of his difficulty with speech there had been a bland flatness in his manner which had the appearance of being due to a continual appraisal of his own predicament. His stutter did not allow the weighing of the relative importance of his words: Colver, on listening to him, wondered how he might have expressed himself had

99

the stutter not been at the forefront of his mind: the stutter to some extent determined his choice of words: many of his sentences had been bracketed by words, prefixes and suffixes, used with a ritual regularity perhaps because they came easily to utterance; his gestures surely had been made not to emphasize his words but to make his speech easier.

'How long have you had this difficulty with speech?' asked Colver.

'Only for the last year,' said the magistrate. 'I never stutter when I am with my family.'

'Why do you stutter now?'

'It is the subject! You, surely, are not conceited enough to think that your presence makes any difference!' He stood and walked across the room. He remained standing for some time in the open doorway, looking out into the darkness, his elongated shadow stretching across the flagstones of the yard.

'I see that you wish to talk to me about the monastery,' he said abruptly.

Colver, who had been on the verge of falling asleep, looked up and saw that the magistrate sat opposite him in a posture identical to that in which he had been sitting before he had stood to walk away; he still held his hands pressed on to the surface of the table. It did not seem that he had moved: perhaps Colver, in falling asleep, had only imagined that he had walked to the door and had stood in silence looking out at the night. 'It is natural,' said the traveller, 'for anyone in this valley for the first time to be curious about the monastery.' He wished that he had kept his silence; he had no desire to indicate anything other than his own weariness.

'The truth of it is that the place very quickly loses its interest,' said the magistrate, speaking surprisingly fluently and with an articulate ease which had been absent in his previous speaking voice: perhaps, while standing in the doorway, looking out into the night, he had regained a composed attitude never before seen by Colver. 'One might best see it as a landowner: there is no more to it than that. It would have its own method of administering its external lands were it able to find an agent who would give his whole day, his whole life, to act on its behalf. I can only spare a few hours each day to its work: I cannot neglect my other duties; neither do I wish to take on a burden of extra work; my time is hard stretched as it is: I rise,' he said, looking at his watch, 'at five to begin my day.' He shook his head. 'The villagers have never known the rule of the monastery. They have never appreciated the authority which is due to it if only because it is the landowner. They only know that they will never be called to account for any misdemeanour which they might commit against it; the monastery, apart from its title of right, has no mechanism of authority. You will understand their resentment: those who live within earshot of the monastery have no knowledge of its claims and its rights. They do not know the sense of awe which the first sight of the monastery, when it is recognized as such, brings to the uplifted minds of those strangers who pass through the village. Those born here find in the monastery a natural phenomenon; left to themselves they would regard its land as being not the subject of tenancies, nor even common property, but, rather, as lapsed land the ownership of which has been forgotten, and which is there for the taking and the claiming. How could anyone who represents the monastery's temporal interests expect to receive praise? There is a confusion which reigns in the minds of those who live in this valley! There is a confusion: otherwise, how are these people able to deny the monastery its right of authority over its own lands yet to use the sound of its bells as a series of portents?

'When I assumed that authority on behalf of the monastery I was forced to have the lands revalued and to agree new tenancies. In doing this I was constrained to use military surveys and to make tenancy agreements along the lines of those issued by the civil authorities. I thought it important beyond all else to begin as I intended to continue. I said, many times: "Let any standard slide and all will be damaged, even that which has been satisfactorily accomplished in the past." I made it clear from the outset that all the transactions would be conducted with honesty and without regard for position or means. These standards hold now, without compromise, and they will continue to hold until I am removed.' He continued to speak in an irregular manner, his stutter directing the pacing of his words. 'Considerable sums pass through the hands of the secular agent,' he said. 'For safety's sake nothing of worth is kept in the magistrate's house. I make the journey up the track on horseback every week, on Tuesday afternoons, the bailiffs acting as guards, to post both money and copies of the accounts. Perhaps you did not even notice the letterbox in the stonework of the gatehouse to the left of the doors.'

Colver replied that it was true: he had not seen the letterbox, but he after all had not been looking for it; it was the last thing which might have been expected to catch his eye: he had been beneath the unstable keystone which hung so precariously above the arch of the gatehouse: his eyes were on nothing beyond the mass of that hanging stone.

To this the magistrate replied: 'Nothing is stable! Even the most stable object only appears so because of the brevity of the time of viewing! The keystone appears to be unstable only should one happen to look up while standing beneath it. I have stood beneath it many times: I cannot begin to count them: I must stand thus when I deliver the monastery's dues: one can only leave the bailiffs outside, instructing them to keep an eye on the masonry and to shout if any movement is seen in the walls of the arch. I always deliver the messages myself: it is my place to undertake that short journey into a place of danger. It is a task which I will never delegate while I have my health. I stand under the arch, put my hands over my head—as though that would do any good: it is instinctive habit—and feel my way towards the door. On the instant the packages are delivered I lower my gaze, shut my eyes: I leave by what way seems best.'

Colver remarked that an unscrupulous man would have unlimited opportunities for dishonesty.

'So, at last, we come again to questions of dishonesty and integrity,' said the magistrate. 'One might have the power to keep back anything one might choose: there is a certainty, even as one stands beneath it, that the monastery will not break its silence. Indeed, the very danger associated with standing underneath the keystone of the arch tempts one to delay posting the dues until a safer season. One must start as one means to continue: on the very day I obtained my appointment I ordered the bailiffs to act as guards: they were chosen because they were demolition workers and could best amongst others judge the stability of the wall above the gatehouse. They worked at that time for a demolition contractor in the town at the confluence of the rivers; indeed, they still do some work for the same contractor even though they are paid employees of the monastery.

'The monastery maintains its silence. Whatever my actions there would be no rebuke. I have asked myself many times this question: why, under such circumstances, did I retain the honesty which was assumed to be mine at my appointment? I have found no satisfactory answer, except for a certain appeal to personal integrity. It is a fact—I say this to you in confidence—that apart from the obvious temptations, to which I have never given way, there have been times when I have benefited by my association with the monastery. These things I disliked: who wishes to see dishonesty intrude into one's family life? I have benefited. What could I have done? What would you do if you had to finance social evenings which were beyond the means of your saved salary?'

'The monastery's lands are extensive, then?'

'They are extensive.'

Colver, who had for no good reason assumed that the monastery's lands must end with the boundaries of the valley, suddenly said, 'I never knew it was as complicated as that.'

'Most people assume that the monastery's lands are coterminous with either the boundaries of the parish or with the range of one or other of the bells which they happen to have heard. I'm only telling you the beginnings of it, and I'm only speaking in generalities.'

'It must have been difficult, serving two masters!'

'It is difficult,' said the magistrate, laying emphasis on his own use of the present tense. 'What else can I do? In order to uphold the civil standards I serve the monastery.'

'For all that, you imply that your service to the monastery is self-imposed.'

'Viewed in one light that is partly true,' said the magistrate. 'On the other hand these things are not as simple as perhaps they first appear. At the appearance of any unexpected situation critics and experts demand a hearing of their opinion; the less they know, the more the shouting and the more copious the advice.

'It is not possible to take so simple a view of any of the monastery's secular appointments. I was appointed as a magistrate, a provincial official with a certain circumscribed authority. The post is not an important one. I am the first to see my faults; I am provincial; I am not articulate: I have never been ambitious except for my family: I have always wished for as much responsibility as I could bear and no more: I have always wished for nothing more than to keep myself to myself at home when I turn aside from my work: I have never had a further ambition. For all these reasons I was pleased at the appropriate foresight which the civil authorities had shown in matching my character and the requirements of this post: the short-list was, I understand, considerably long and the interview was no light matter.' He looked down at the table. 'When I was in post I immediately became aware, in a moment, of the existence of the monastery. I had not seen it before. I looked up through the rain. I raised my eyes to its grey presence, and saw, in that same moment, that it would oversee my every action, every corner of the extent of my jurisdiction. It was in that same moment, as I stood in the rain, that I was certain I would obtain, at an early stage, a secular appointment.'

Colver, realizing that he was at every minute seeing a new aspect of the monastery, exclaimed, out of surprise, 'There are many such secular appointments!'

'Indeed there are many secular appointments. By what means might such a foundation maintain itself without a comprehensive staff?'

Colver was about to say that if the monastery employed no craftsmen except for the demolition workers, it was no wonder that its fabric was dangerous. He said nothing. His right hand was for some reason beginning to hurt him as though someone were holding it in a tight grip; he was exhausted and he wished to do no more than to sleep. 'A moment ago you talked about the fact of an awareness of the monastery,' he said. 'Does this awareness come to all people?'

'I did not mention "awareness". I dislike the word. I said that one recognizes others who feel the assertion which the monastery is capable of putting into the mind. The monastery is not inert: it asserts itself and on feeling its intrusion one can no longer ignore or disregard it.'

'Has your perception of the monastery altered since your arrival here?'

'It has. One always learns new facts about matters which have been long established in the mind. When I first came here I did not know of its existence. I was a servant of the civil authorities. The question I ask myself is whether events would have proved different had I known of its existence before my arrival—and the answer to it: that must vary with the state of mind which happens to be uppermost when the question is asked: sometimes I think, yes, events might have been different: but always I know that, beneath that answer, the certainty is that below that transient state of mind, independent of it and deeper than it, what little foreknowledge that might have been granted would alter nothing: events could have been no different.

'I arrived,' said the magistrate, 'in winter. There was a storm in the mountains. On our descent from the pass it rained without ceasing. The wind, as I remember the night, was turbulent but prevailed from no one direction. The carrier had been unsure of the way and had followed us: his men waited at the river from afternoon to night in the hope that the rain would stop or at least slacken, though in the end the carrier, taking action at last on seeing that the water would rise further during the night, risked the ford: the unloading was done by lamplight in driving rain: the possessions I valued the most were made worthless. I heard the sound of a bell which drowned the sound of the wind and the water. The

105

sound beat down as though from an invisible heaven. I asked the driver the meaning of the noise; he answered that, as far as he knew or had been told where the matter lay, it was "a bell from the monastery". Such was the turbulence of the air that the sound waxed and waned as though the source was not stationary, but was, in some improbable way, moving from one imagined boundary to another. For one moment I was drawn to the conclusion that the sound came from two buildings and that the ringing was a communication between them, across the space of the valley and I cried out, over the wet cases, one of which had burst; I cried out aloud, over my ruined possessions: "To what place have I been sent?" Working strenuously by lamplight, the driver and the carrier's man had not finished before the bell stopped tolling; I could see them turn and look upwards as though they had taken the sound for granted; it was only then that I saw how they had worked in coordination with the sound: now it had stopped and they stood in the rain, dispirited and cold, looking about themselves into the darkness. I could hear the rivers roaring out of the resurgence caves in the rocks at the valley's end. I was visited by the priest an hour after my arrival.'

'What do you think of the priest's view of the monastery?'

'No doubt,' said the magistrate, perhaps wondering why the question had been asked, 'No doubt he is forced to be dismissive about it. He brought me to this inn. He did not, that night, speak much about the monastery; he said only that it was an inopportune time to begin to talk about such a thing which would, his own words, "in the future become very much part of my life". I took the view then that he was speaking with some degree of irony. It is not, I suspect, the building itself which he holds in contempt; rather, he holds in contempt those who would interpret it for their own purposes. One only has to look at him to see that he attempts to suppress any attempt by his parishioners to regard the sounding of the monastery's bells in a divinatory light. When I first came here I thought his attitude inflexible. There was, I remember, one man—he must be old now: he was old then—who attracted his animosity in some particular way: he had made a system by which the bells might be interpreted. It was not, in my eyes, particularly original: it was, I saw at once, only a kind of peaceful introspection. The priest singled him out as though to make an example of him. Why did he do that? His public show of censure only lent him light by which he might be seen.'

'I have met this man, the parishioner.'

'The priest has already taken you down to see him?'

'Not long ago.'

The magistrate crossed his arms over his chest. 'I am not surprised to hear you say that: the priest takes those new-comers who show an interest in the monastery down to his house to see him. Perhaps his intention is to humiliate. I was taken down the day after my arrival. The old man was an old man then. I have no idea of his age.'

'What connects the two authorities beneath which you work?'

'It has taken you a long time to ask that question: it is almost without exception the first question put to me by a stranger.'

'Well, I have at last asked it,' said the traveller. 'I am not sure that the order of the questions is of any particular significance.'

The magistrate seemed to be amused by his own clear intention of not answering the question as by the question itself. 'It would be an introspective truism to say that the only association between the two is the confusion which fills the minds of those who seek to serve both. The direction of loyalties is not clear. On the one hand I can only say that I am able to hold the view I do without making any statement about it. On the other, I can ask the necessity for describing all circumstances by means of words. An attempt at definition may often alter meaning to the point where the very truth lacks truthfulness. Certain loyalties and beliefs are damaged or irretrievably altered by the bluntness of words.

'The question which is usually put to me is "Might not the monastery represent a spiritual authority, in the same way that the civil powers exert a temporal one?" How one tires of these questions! The question I have myself put implies in its answer

107

a simple way of approaching such a division of authority: it implies a child's answer, the thought of a child who has never been, nor expects to go, beyond its boundaries. The monastery is a building: it has a local jurisdiction in its own matters; it regulates its own affairs. How could it be a spiritual authority? On the other hand—' He smiled as though he were pleased at being able to state a paradox long familiar to him '—how can it be only a building? It is only within the last few years that I have come to know the system by which the monastery works.'

'Are you able to tell me of "the system by which the monastery works"?'

'No; I could talk, but I could not tell you my conclusions.'

'Has the realization (as you imply) of the system by which the monastery works given you cause for any doubt as to your loyalty towards the civil authorities to which you are responsible?'

'When I first came here I made myself a motto—how trifling it seems now: but under some circumstances guiding principles must be invoked—and I made it into a simple rule: "Conduct yourself as those who appointed you would have you conduct yourself." I have no wish to lead a double life. In many ways the growing uncertainty of my position has made me understand how little I know about the powers that appointed me. There is no suggestion of conflict: there is only the necessity to avoid self-deception.'

'I don't follow what you are saying,' said the traveller, who had indeed lost the thread of the magistrate's talk, not so much because of the train of his argument but because of the incoherence of the words. The magistrate's sentences had become disjointed; he gave the impression that he was thinking out loud: this gave rise to the suspicion that the magistrate's idea of the nature of even the civil authorities was different from the traveller's. The traveller began to believe that he would receive only an abstract reply were he to ask the magistrate his understanding of the nature of the civil power which had appointed him. So strong did this belief become that he could see the magistrate's lips begin to form the prefatory ritual words before the stutter: 'What is an appointment such as mine but an expression of conventions which are for the moment recognized as the rule?' and, further: 'What appointed me but an authority where direction is given by those general terms first uttered to me when, in my loneliness and uncertainty, I gratefully looked upwards with beseeching eyes and accepted what was offered and set out before me?' But he did not say this: it would have been against his nature to have given way to such emphasis: the traveller, or, as he had only recently begun to think of himself, for all the extent of his illness, the sick man, had been listening only to an internal voice. He looked up at the magistrate, wondering how far this internal voice had caused him to misunderstand the magistrate's words. The traveller had felt himself to be on the edge of sleep many times and perhaps would have slept but for the crushing pain in his right hand and forearm. How much of what the magistrate had said had been imagined trains of thought in his own mind? How much of this half-articulate talk, so difficult to listen to, had been due to his own tiredness and his own defects in hearing? He remembered, a few years ago, being shown a slide of fixed and stained typhoid bacilli: an imitation of this now passed before his eyes, small reddish rods, sharply defined, parallel sided and evenly stained. For one moment he found himself the victim of an illusion that he had imagined the magistrate's voice and that the magistrate had sat silently opposite him all evening, sitting thus, doing nothing more than to swallow water from time to time and to listen to the words which were being imputed to him. Yet he remembered the magistrate saying, in a very fluent voice: 'Compromise is unstable. When any action is undertaken the degree of compromise resulting from it cannot be foreseen. Look at the compromises I must make in my tenure here! Nevertheless, I am glad that the conflicts which arise in the conduct of my duty are so well defined.' Had the magistrate said that, or had it been a gloss which the traveller (by now being forced by the magistrate's constant reiteration of what he called his duty to re-examine the manner in which he himself understood the word) had put into the substance of the magistrate's utterance? The magistrate's manner was not difficult to parody, and the substance of his words was easy to predict or to imitate. He looked past the magistrate's head at the hanging lamps: had the lamp-chimneys been always so yellow?

'Shall I tell you about the circumstances which led to the arrival of this letter?' The hesitancy in the magistrate's voice as he asked the question recalled the diffidence he had shown when he had first met the traveller.

'I would be grateful if you would,' said Colver, looking down at his own right hand which lay in an attitude of inaction on the surface of the table.

'Two years ago, when my eyes were opened to the fact that matters were noticed to be not as they should be, I received a letter from those in the civil authorities to whom I am responsible. I half expected it, I think, though it is difficult to be certain of this with hindsight. That original letter was so vague that it was difficult to make out its importance. The impression was that I had neglected certain areas of my work; it intimated that in the future I must answer these neglects. There was nothing more specific than that. The letter, as I later discovered, was only the first of a series of letters.'

'Why are you telling me this?' Colver was alarmed, not only by the directness of his confidence, but also by the composure of his manner, as though his own future and that of his family was a matter of indifference to him: against that; perhaps that indifference was not his true feeling at all; perhaps in the last few years he had learned that he was able to speak coherently only if he could manage to control his emotions. Perhaps he was telling lies, or exaggerating something which was by itself of very little importance. Indeed, the traveller's voice, to judge by its echoes was, perhaps because of the pain in his hand, much less calm than that of the magistrate. The traveller repeated his question: 'Why are you telling me this?'

'I would rather tell you myself rather than have you find out an approximation of the facts from some other source.' The magistrate paused. 'I showed that first letter to a man I had regarded as a friend, a doctor, in fact, from the town at the confluence. Indeed, the circumstances of my showing it to him indicated to me the slight importance I had attributed to it: I happened to take something out of my pocket, a ring of keys, I think it was, though why I took that out I do not know—certainly to unlock nothing; it might have been a pen for which I was looking, though with the intention of writing nothing; the letter came out with it, the ring of keys, or the pen, and I found myself holding the letter; the doctor's wife remarked that the paper was unusual (she only spoke, I think, for something to say; she is in the habit of making peremptory remarks—indeed they are almost involuntary—about unexpected things which, before she looks away, catch her eye and happen to startle her). I showed the letter to the doctor and I asked him for his opinion of it; he said, in a low, carefully enunciated voice, "I would rather that you did not show me in my wife's presence." He folded the letter as though the sight of it was abhorrent to his own eye: he folded the printed side of the page away from his sight; he handed it back to me. I could see that, although nothing concerned him greatly, he wished to speak briefly alone to me; his wife, being observant, seeing his expression, said something, a little generality about the town, an observation about the square; she walked a little way down the road; the doctor said: "There is no use in staving off the truth. I must tell you that, in the light of the letter which you have just shown me, I have no alternative but to regard our friendship as being at an end. Painful as this is to say I fear that there must be no more visits of a social nature between yourself and myself and between your wife and mine." I could see that from that moment he regarded our past friendship as never having existed. Perhaps, even at that early stage, he had seen that the machinery of eviction and dismissal was being set in motion, and that he had better keep away: had he been an honest man he might have said: "These things have a habit of firing wide." To be truthful I was not as displeased as might be thought at losing his friendship; my wife and I had wasted enough evenings at his house, talking about the future, playing cards after dinner—I find card-playing a tedious waste of time, dull beyond belief—and my wife never approved of the way the doctor's mother and father used to indulge the children.' He said this with a dry lack of emphasis. 'The other letters began to arrive with regularity.' He took a letter out of the breast pocket of his coat, with difficulty, bringing the passport out with it; he looked at the cover of the passport as though he had forgotten that he had had it in his pocket, and was surprised to see it; he did not replace it, but left it lying on the table where it had fallen. He held the envelope which contained the letter in both hands, feeling the weight of the paper within the envelope; he laid it gently on the passport as though to keep the envelope from being dirtied by any grime or wetness which might be on the surface of the table. 'When you first came into the room I asked you if you would read it, and tell any conclusions you might make from it.'

The traveller looked down at the letter; the paper of the envelope was imbued with the same yellowness which tinged everything else in the room. 'You have not told your wife the substance of the letter?'

'No. How could I have done? I woke in the early morning, thinking about the impossibility of doing that. The thought of the impersonal machinery anonymously firing these letters at me—the thought does not make for rational behaviour.' An unnecessary pleading tone came into his voice. 'I have difficulty in talking about this. My wife can endure no more of it; she wouldn't believe me; she would tell me to have less pity for myself. The priest is sceptical. My colleagues no longer bother to hide their opinion.' He passed a hand over his forehead, and shook his hand as though it were wet with sweat, though the skin of his forehead was dry. 'In the early morning I wrote a few lines of poetry.'

'I would not have thought you a poet,' said Colver.

'I am not a poet.' He pointed to the paper. 'This seemed the best way of stating what I felt to be true.' He reached in his pocket again. 'May I read it to you?' he asked, his manner suggesting that he would be pleased with any comment by way of reply.

'If you wish.'

'Do you think that I am being foolish?' he asked.

'Not at all.'

The magistrate held the piece of notepaper in his two hands. He opened it awkwardly, the movements of his fingers jerky. One wondered how he would find the light to read it; except by walking to the middle of the room, and holding the piece of paper almost under one of the hanging lamps, he could not have hoped to make out the sense of the writing. Perhaps he had the words of the poem memorized, and needed the paper only as a prompt. A studied concentration was uppermost in his expression; all his previous emotions had been subdued to this new one. He laid the paper on the surface of the table, and smoothed it with the palms of his hands. He stared down at it. One might have thought, to judge from his expression, that this piece of paper with his own writing was of more importance than the official letter which intimated, if he were to be believed, at his disgrace. The traveller watched his throat tighten with the effort of intended speech. The magistrate said nothing: although his mouth was open, and he had just taken a deep breath of air, the muscles of his face, his throat and his neck were tautened in immobile rigidity. He shouted with explosive anger: 'Why can't I speak?' He sat again, shaking, wiping the spit from the cuffs of his coat.

'Shall I read it for myself?' Colver, looking down at the paper, was well able to see that the poem was laid out in verses, each of which had six short lines, the fourth and the fifth being the longest.

The magistrate folded the paper and replaced it, together with the letter and the passport, in the pocket from which he had originally taken them. 'Any man who can write his own name is, in a sense, a magistrate: but I cannot read it,' he said.

'Why do you hesitate?'

'That should be obvious to you! I stutter! I don't know where I am at the moment! I don't know who you are. You might have some authority in the civil administration. What an exhibition I have made of myself, not only about the letter, but about everything else I have said!'

'I have told you that I have no particular authority,' said the traveller. 'But, if you will not believe me, then there is nothing more that I can say.'

VIII

Towards the noon of the next day a runner arrived at the inn
with a message: at first Colver, without acknowledging him,
could only look at him with disbelief, though he saw a second
later that the message could only have come from the magistrate: although the magistrate lived no more than a third of a
mile distant the runner was exhausted by the effort of the
journey as though he had taken it round the village by the
most circuitous route. Having laid the message in front of
Colver he stood back, in a corner of the room, as far away as
possible from Colver, panting, regaining his breath, unable to
speak either to the traveller or to the proprietor: the proprietor,
on hearing the messenger entering the yard by a narrow
wicket-gate in the shadow of the stables, a recognized short
cut to the magistrate's house, and on seeing him running
diagonally across the yard, his eyes fixed on the inn door, had
come from behind the curtained doorway behind the counter.
The runner, looking first at the traveller's face and then at
the proprietor's, grinned at them both as though finding
pleasure in his own arrival.

The envelope was edged with black in an indication of
official mourning. A red seal, of a brighter scarlet than the
usual wax, sealed the flap of the envelope. The traveller,
aware of the runner's alternate stares towards himself and the
proprietor, broke the seal and took out the single page.
The paper, also edged with black, was headed by a printed
superscription which included the address and qualifications
of the magistrate himself. Colver had not known that the

magistrate possessed such qualifications; had he not met him he would have wondered why a man with these qualifications was wasting his time out here in the provinces; the letters indicated a childhood and youth straitened by diligent study and crowned by success in the civil examinations. He saw that the magistrate's surname was the same as his own and he felt a curiosity as to why the magistrate had not thought this fact worth commenting upon at their first meeting; perhaps he had been ashamed of his name; if that was the case then he would have expected the traveller to have been ashamed of his name also.

The handwritten message invited the visitor to a picnic which the magistrate and his wife were intending to hold, the weather being fine, that afternoon, in a field at the valley's edge. The tone of this brief letter pointed to the informality of the event. A description of the nature of the preparations was given, as though to whet the visitor's appetite and to make it difficult for him to refuse the invitation: perhaps, as a result of his discussions with the magistrate, his company was after all genuinely required. The letter recommended strong walking shoes and a rain-proof coat lest the weather change; it asked Colver to return a message to the magistrate's house by the runner if for some reason he found himself unable to go; otherwise he would be awaited, at three, outside the inn.

The contrast between the deep black margins and the trivial nature of the message was extraordinary: it was as if the writer, in enframing his brief message in black, had intended either to make an obscure appeal, the sense of which was lost on the traveller, or to exercise a sense of humour. The traveller, seeing the black margins rather than the note enclosed by them, had no idea who had died: perhaps the black edging was an acknowledgment of an official death long ago: it was possible that this black-edged paper (which was heavy and of fine quality) was no longer used for anything of importance. He began to speculate upon the train of events which had culminated in the juxtaposition of words and stationery; perhaps, he said, thinking aloud, an important death had occurred twenty years ago. Perhaps at the time of the death the black edging had had a significance long since leached out: perhaps the death's forgetting had been as sudden and as unexpected as the death itself. Each provincial magistracy must have been long ago allocated a quantity of the mourning stationery. This magistrate, never writing official letters, had never used it, so that when its purpose had been forgotten, the death having become with time the death of a cipher, the paper was fit only for local notes and local communications. If this were so, then quite possibly the magistrate's children would be given sheets of it to draw upon.

The heat stilled any thought of talk beyond the brief greeting, and thanks given for the invitation, and the expression of pleasure that the guest was able to be present. These necessities over, they walked through the village and along a well-used lane which was hedged by ragged hawthorn bushes. The lane out of the village took many curves and sudden bends round the edges of narrow fields, revealing unexpected groups of cottages which faced each other across small squares, many of them with a well or a water-trough under a clump of trees in the centre of the bare ground, from which every blade of grass had been plucked by fowls. The cottages stood with their dusty windows open and the shutters pushed shut sufficiently closely to deny a direct entry to the sunlight. The squares were empty. The dogs lay silently in the dust beneath the farm carts, unmoving, but following every movement with their alert eyes. The magistrate, without a jacket and with his shirt partly unbuttoned as a concession to the heat, carried a striped blanket over one shoulder, perhaps for them all to sit on when they reached the end of their journey; in his right hand he held the rope handles of a plaited raffia basket in which there were a number of wine bottles separated from each other by straw, which he paused to damp at one of the horse-troughs. He walked slowly, methodically setting down his feet in even paces as though he had never throughout his life known any sense of hurry. He was, one saw for the first time, slightly bow-legged, and he walked in the manner of a man who has from youth been accustomed either to working at a stoop or to carrying a heavy load on his back. Because of his stoop and because of his shapeless trousers and his collarless shirt he might easily have been mistaken for a man from the village. His wife, behind him, walked awkwardly as though she found the journey an exhausting ordeal; perhaps this was a matter of temperament; as yet they had not walked very far: perhaps a mile at the most.

The magistrate's wife was younger than the magistrate. Looking at them both as they walked, one would have been surprised on being told that they were married; the differences in their ages, the differences in the manner of their walking, their expressions, and the way their eyes viewed the road ahead would surely indicate to a stranger that these were two people who chanced to take for a mile the same road, who chanced to have the same immediate destination, and who shared only the necessity of travelling together and the forbearance necessary for the undertaking of a journey through the most intense heat of the day. The children, having been this way many times before and knowing full well where they were going, had run on ahead, and shouted in the distance, urging their parents on and calling back to their guest by name.

The traveller walked behind the magistrate and his wife. He carried the basket of food; he had taken it from the magistrate's wife. She had carried the basket from the village, but had changed it from hand to hand with a resigned regularity every few minutes, stopping in her step and lagging behind her husband, though when Colver had suggested that he might carry it for her, indeed, that he would be pleased to carry it, she had smiled and had protested that she enjoyed carrying it. Besides, she said, the women of the village carried heavy loads: why should she be in any respect different? She had said this with feeling, though when she at last relinquished the basket to Colver he could not help thinking (for the basket was very light) what an ill-chosen parallel she had drawn, and, furthermore, what a slender meal they were going to have. He had been pleased that he had kept the black-edged invitation, which he had put in a drawer of the washstand, thinking of how, on some future occasion, he might bring it out in the company of those, who, in the future, he might call his friends, to illustrate his words, drawing out the heavy stationery to illustrate his point.

The magistrate's wife, perhaps seeing his reaction to the weight of the basket in the expression on his face, said that although the basket did not weigh very much there were some very solid meat pies in it; the pies, she said, were local to this area, and very filling; the meat in them was lean; the pies had been, she said, made by the housekeeper herself, a woman of some experience who had worked for her husband's predecessor; she was very capable of calculating the extent of another person's appetite.

There had been a forced quality to all this. Talk of a sort was a necessity, but the effort and the heat removed the sense from the words before they were uttered and even while they were still being formed in the mind; there were other things to occupy the brain; the going was more difficult; the lane had become narrower, its gradient increasingly steep. The track was now rough. Talk had become a series of stilted phrases. The valley floor began to slope up to the mountains; the lane lost its hedges and became a network of animal-tracks which wound about the outcrops of stone in the high fields. The land here had once been cultivated in terraces; now it had been overgrown by briars. A few roofless cottages, their interiors wildernesses of bramble, their yards seas of nettles, only their chimney stacks remaining vertical, marked the edge of the valley. At one point a thick iron water-supply pipe crossed their path as it ran up to a group of derelict houses from a stone shed by the side of a spring; within the shed a hydraulic ram was still working and the iron pipe rung and shook as though struck with a rhythmic hammer. On looking up at that small level site on the side of the mountain it was certain that it had only recently been deserted.

The track steepened rapidly. The gradient and the intensity of the sun brought out a sweat, and exertion precluded speech. They climbed in single file, the magistrate first, each of his steps placed firmly and purposefully. He looked neither down nor ahead of himself. His wife, a hundred yards behind him and looking down at the ground as she climbed, pressed her hands on her thighs with each step. She breathed loudly, through her mouth, as though the sound gave her encouragement. The hem of her long-skirted print dress dragged against the stones and the tussocks of grass. The traveller followed close behind her. He found the pace of their progress too slow for him, and he paused frequently to allow the magistrate and his wife to make headway before he followed them; he had time, while doing this, to look up and to watch the magistrate and his wife as they climbed, their heads each surrounded by a nimbus of flies. Beyond and far above them he saw intermittently the bright clothes and the clear faces of the children as they scrambled about amongst the rocks. Looking at the climbers he saw that the side of the mountain had steepened until it became a dangerous cliff overhung by piles of loose boulders. 'They cannot climb a yard higher!' he exclaimed. Looking above him at the magistrate and his wife he was forced to admit that what he had taken to be slowness had been a necessity in their progress over precipitously steep terrain, one hand over another, searching for firm handholds with deliberate caution. When he stood where they had climbed he saw this for himself; he knew the vertigo which they must have felt; he strove to find and grasp with his hands the handholds which he had seen them use. He began to feel angry that he, as a sick man, had been brought out on this journey without any knowledge of what it might hold: the black-edged letter had said nothing about these dangers. Had the basket been much heavier he would not have been able to carry it. Perhaps before his illness he would have been able to climb this rocky wall with ease, and carrying a heavier load: now he knew the extent of his weakness. His right hand, though no longer as painful as it had been, could not of itself support his weight. 'Who is weak?' he said, looking down and seeing that he had climbed far higher than he had thought. The valley lay below him. The houses of the village were so diminished that the individual roofs could not with ease be distinguished. The village itself lay almost vertically below him.

* * *

The place for the picnic was a narrow tract of grass that lay beneath the cliff and which looked down over the valley.

The magistrate began to walk amongst the tussocks, his head bent down, as though searching within close limits for a place familiar to him. He held the striped blanket loosely in his hands as though about to throw it down. He dropped the blanket suddenly, raising his hands as he did so, and the blanket fell with hardly a crease. He called back, pleasure manifest in his voice, to his wife: 'This is the place.' He pointed downward and, turning from the ground and looking at Colver, who had followed him, he said: 'We marked the place so.' The traveller, sitting on a stone and following his actions, for his was the only movement in the dry stillness, saw four or five corks, still with wine-stains, now bleached, lying on the top of a hummock, at the parting of the grass. 'Excuse me,' said the magistrate, 'you are in the way.' He pulled the blanket across the tract to a position where the grass concealed no stones. 'One has to be careful in searching for a place such as this,' he said. He began to take the wine bottles from the damp straw in the basket. He sat down. He laid the bottles carefully in the shade of a stone. The traveller, watching him, and moving when asked, wondered why the magistrate had fallen into this habit of finding the same place on each visit in which to lay the blanket, but, saying nothing, he sat on a flat rock some distance away from the blanket, which lay almost in the shadow of the overhanging rock, and watched the magistrate's wife as she took the food from the basket and, with an inner absorption, began carefully to lay it out. The children were playing amongst the fallen boulders at the base of the cliff directly beneath the cracked shelf of the overhang; they had found a stream which ran over a broad bed of worn stones, a small gully made and swept free of vegetation by the torrents of winter, and they had already gathered sods of grass and small stones with which to build a dam.

The traveller, still sitting on the rock he had chosen, looked beyond the playing children to the place where the stream emerged from the cliff's base; it ran out from the shadow of a boulder, shaggy with lichen and moss; within this shadow was a cave. The entrance of the cave was a smooth phreatic ellipse, wider than it was tall. From its mouth the stream—hardly more than a rivulet—flowed out through the shadow of the boulder into sunlight. The children played as though oblivious to the draught which blew like a cold exhalation from the mouth of the cave.

'We decided,' said the magistrate, some distance away, his voice abrupt but very clear, 'to come here on the spur of the moment. I ought to have given you more notice, but the weather was good. One has to take advantage of things while one can.' He poured out the light wine, putting down the bottle carefully, and holding out the glasses. 'Come closer,' he said.

'Do you regularly come up here?' asked the traveller, climbing from the flat surface of the rock he had chosen, but reluctant to leave it; the rock on which he had chosen to sit seemed a much safer place than the square of blanket beneath the overhang of the cliff.

'It has become a habit,' said the magistrate. 'When time allows, in the summer and the autumn; not in the winter.' He looked about him. 'I must leave the concerns of the village from time to time.'

'How did you first come upon it?' said Colver, very much aware of the weight of unsupported rocks above his own head now that he was standing close to the blanket on which the magistrate and his wife were sitting. Looking round at the narrow level tract, he saw that a ruinous stone wall still stood not far from him, a vestige of protection from the drop below, a marker of the shelving edge.

'I saw it first on one of my predecessor's maps. There are many such pieces of the monastery's lands untenured; this is one of the more accessible of them; it was, as one can see, enclosed. There are the ruins of a shepherd's hut.' He pointed to an angle of dry-stone walling, all that remained of a building otherwise destroyed, perhaps within the last few years, by falls of rock loosened by the repetition of thaw after frost. 'I came up here four years ago in order to find out the name in which the tenancy was written; as with most of the monastery's property, no rent had been paid on it for many years.' He stared at the base of the tumbled and insecure foot of the cliff, which in its instability might have been the face of a working quarry. 'As you see, it is never used. There is no claim to it. I come up here from need: the place has a peacefulness to it.' He took a drink of wine and stared down into the valley, as though some small moving object had caught his eye. His voice echoed from the rock face behind him. 'I applied for the tenancy last year. It had been my ambition for some time. I waited until I was certain that there would be no dispute.'

Colver looked at the magistrate's shoulders, which were set as though in a flinch.

'Since I first saw it I have had a thought, a consideration,' he said, consciously easing his shoulders, as though very much aware of the weight of stone which overhung his defenceless head. 'I could see in my mind's eye a plan. From that first moment I seized upon the idea of a building—nothing of any size; nothing more than a shelter—for the summer. It is remote from the village and from the roads. No one comes here. I had the idea of securing the tenure for some time. I have set it down thus in the books. The rent, which gives some protection, is no less than the worth.'

'Have you ever been inside the mouth of that cave?'

The magistrate followed his pointing finger. 'I have no liking for confined spaces.' He turned to his wife. 'You know the cave.'

His wife, lying on her side, as though exhausted, her hand touching the basket, interrupted in some private reverie, slowly raised her head and looked at the ground by his feet, but did not speak, as though she had not heard him.

'This stream always flows,' said the magistrate. 'Even in drought it does not dry.'

The magistrate's wife, interrupting the regularity of her own breathing, as one half asleep, called to the children, in a weak voice, as if to them alone.

The traveller looked at the magistrate and his wife. The man was sitting with his eyes closed. His face was tranquil and undisturbed; perhaps he was asleep. His wife, half awake now, preoccupied in dividing the food equally on the plates, did not look up. Her hands were constantly in motion, brushing the flies away from her body, from her hair, from the food and from the basket, from the half-filled glasses in which some of them had already begun to drown, even though the wine had been poured out only five minutes before. There was an irritation in her manner as she brushed away the flies, as if they had been sent to plague her alone, as though she were the only being to hold an attraction for them. Behind her, by the stream, the shouts of the children were reflected from the bare face of the precipitous side of the mountain. Despite the heat of the sun, the grassy level was not warm. The river of cave air flowed coldly outwards from the cave entrance and fanned out in the stillness to cover the grass like a carpet.

The traveller stood inside the cavern at the threshold of perceptible light. He looked back; the entrance was an ellipse of light hardly larger than a bead. The magistrate and his family sat on the sloping ledge, the man looking down at the valley, his wife close beside him, her head turned to avoid the direct glare of the sun, the two children kneeling by the basket.

In the roof there were rounded domes, formed by the erosive turbulence of vanished water, as rounded and as smooth as casts made from an exaggerated female anatomy: one wished immediately to put out a hand to feel the rock. The stream, flowing silently over the sandy floor, cast the incident light upwards; the moving water changed the steady sunlight into a rippling akin to itself. The air of the cave was cold and water-washed; it blew in a steady draught from the darkness of the extremity of the cave: the air had a taste of exceptional purity, as though all traces of organic matter had been removed by its percolation through the cave system; the pure air, in flowing outwards, had preserved the scalloped walls from the dust of the outer world. Only the mouth of the cave was fringed with mosses and ferns, and then only in the higher places inaccessible to the winter torrents.

Colver, standing at the threshold of his dark-accustomed sight, and looking still deeper into the cave, heard a sound behind him, echoing beyond him and returning to him. He had been facing one of the walls with his head turned towards the deeper parts of the cave; on hearing the sound he moved his head to look in the opposite direction. He saw the silhouette of the magistrate's wife against the ellipse of light at the entrance. He remained still: she could not know that he was beyond her; her own eyes must still be blinded by the light outside the cave.

She was a small figure. Her face in silhouette had a distinctness of outline which would have enabled Colver to recognize her had he only glanced towards her. She was examining one of the walls and her upturned face was seen in profile. She looked into the cave and called him formally by name.

He walked slowly back, following the side of the stream, retracing his own footsteps. He asked her how she had known with such certainty that he had been in the cave. She said that in the pure air of the cave she had been able to smell him from the entrance; furthermore, his smell was unmistakable, not that it was unpleasant; it was a smell which she had grown accustomed to, associating it with him, ever since she had known him to be present in the inn on the night of his arrival in the valley; his smell was only perceptible now because of the purity of the outward-flowing air. She said that she had discovered the cave last year when her husband had taken her up to the grassy level; that year the flies had been a plague, arriving in early summer after a warm, wet spring; the insects had been unbearable; she had entered the coolness of the cave to escape them: since that time she had been in the habit of standing inside the entrance whenever she and her husband had come up to the level. The air was always the same, summer or winter, no matter what the season. As for the cave, it was no permanent refuge; it must be inaccessible in flood-time; the water-washed boulders at the entrance showed that it was an active flood resurgence, but apart from this evidence of flood the place was changeless. On coming out of the cave she was, she said, immediately aware of the smells of the valley which in everyday life were unnoticeable. The atmosphere of the valley was always tainted with the smell of the decaying vegetation and the smell of animals and animal dung; the smoke from the rubbish-fires lingered acridly in the air; even the magistrate's house was full of the smells of the village and of the waiting-room of the court, of the coal fires and the lamp-oil, of the servants and even of the magistrate himself. The cave air, cold and changeless in its temperature, had been so unexpected that in the humid heat of the last summer she had welcomed every chance she had of standing in the cave mouth. The effort of the journey was worth the peace and the clean air of the cave.

She asked Colver if he had looked at the recesses of the roof.

He looked up at the cavity which hung above him, following her pointing finger. In the rounded dome, dimly lit by the entrance light, he saw a figure made up of chiselled lines. His first reaction was one of anger at this defacement.

'I came up here on several occasions to draw these figures,' she said, still looking upward: the elevation of her face diminished the resonance of her voice and diverted its echoes into another direction. 'My husband sent the drawings to someone in the museum in the confluence town. We received some opinions on them, but nothing consistent. One reply, from an archaeologist, a man of some local distinction (to whom he had written because of that fact), claimed that such things are not uncommon in the locality; he sent us a paper (of which he was an author) which gave descriptions of figures found in a similar cave, though when one looked at the photograph there was no real resemblance. He sent us, as though as an afterthought, a few days later, a list of references to other of his papers (on diverse subjects: his list might have been a part of his curriculum vitae): some of his papers were published in unobtainable journals. Where, I wonder, did he expect us to find access to a library?' She stood by Colver following his eye and looking in the direction in which he was looking. 'In his letter he gave a name to those who had carved the scratchings and he even named the scratchings themselves, often on quite arbitrary grounds, it seemed to me, so that I could not by looking at his photographs and pencil-sketches even guess the reason for his coming at such and such a name. Out of one shape one might have made a hand with fingers and thumb extended; or a fingerless hand; or a torso without limbs. But he had no such difficulty: his titles were quite clear: "A hand holding a spear." "An animal's antlered head." "A male face with misaligned features."'

The magistrate's wife, looking down from the carving, seemed to be reluctant to leave the cave; indeed, she continually looked at Colver as though she were about to walk towards him and deeper into the darkness. 'On the two occasions when my husband left the house to go down to the inn to see you I could not fail to notice that he had prepared himself carefully,' she said, suddenly, as though saying something which had been at the forefront of her mind for some time. 'Not only in the matter of clothes, though on both occasions he asked for the new coat which, though he had it made when he first heard of his appointment here, he has never had any opportunity to wear, but also with regard to various documents in his office. He was the first to tell me of your arrival in the village. No more than a few minutes elapsed between my first hearing of the runner's footsteps on the road and my husband's coming into my room to tell me of the event. He was up and out of bed for most of that night; he made many attempts to telephone those he knew who might be able to tell him something about you, and where you had come from, and where you had been going before the illness brought you down to the valley. We had a bed prepared for you. My husband asked me to telephone for the doctor to see if he knew anything about you; not the doctor who lives in the next village, but another one, a man we used to know well until recently. I visited you in the inn when the doctor had gone: it was the first time I had ever been within the upper room. Someone has to give the prescribed medicine as it has been ordered. You were delirious with fever. The doctor left only the chloramphenicol tablets, but if one doesn't have faith in medicines what does one have faith in?' She looked again at the carving within the shallow scallop of the roof; then, her gaze directed by the flow of the stone of the walls, she looked first to the entrance and then to the darkness of the deeper cave. 'We considered preparing a room for you in the magistrate's house; it would have been more comfortable than the inn. There's still a room there for you.

'There were factions in the village I did not know existed until they sought my husband's judgment over what should be done. It seems pointless now, looking back on it. You have recovered, and that is possibly the important thing. I watched it all from a corner of the downstairs room of the inn; now I find it astonishing that such a thing could have assumed such proportions. There's an air of unreality about it now.

'My husband came to see you. The first time he prepared himself to visit you (when he had heard that you were downstairs and able to hold a conversation) he seemed to expect that you might be the bearer of a message for him. I remember that he wished to see you, and that he put aside other appointments; at the same time I could see that he fought down his dislike of putting a foot inside the inn door after the arguments he had had there.'

'Why did he dislike going to the inn?' asked Colver. Hearing the magistrate's wife speak now, her voice echoing in the confined space of the cave, and with the echoes adding weight to what she said, he was embarrassed: he had not expected his question 'why did he dislike going to the inn?' to be taken seriously, but the magistrate's wife paused in thought as though it were an important question worthy of a mental struggle. 'He has always regarded the inn as being an obstacle to his work as secular agent to the monastery,' she said. 'The proprietor has always been less than cooperative in these matters. Perhaps you can understand it, the inn being what it is and the secular agency having the authority it has. The same arguments were brought up on the night of your arrival. The proprietor, now he is installed as the proprietor, has for the first time a certain opportunity to raise feeling against my husband. The proprietor is a vindictive man. If you doubt that, you should have heard him talking about the expenses which he has incurred by your staying in the inn: furthermore, I am told that he is confident that you can't understand his language, and that he talks of his own expenses on your behalf in front of you, to his customers, pointing at you as he does so, saying that only because of your circumstances (which necessarily have become his circumstances, so he says), has he been forced to put up with this expense without remonstration. "With whom might I begin to remonstrate?" he asks. Latterly he has done this so frequently that he bores people with his remarks, and they no longer listen to him. In the first few days he was more reticent: he could hardly talk in front of you: he didn't know how much you understood of what he might say.'

'If that's the case, then it's a game of which one would rapidly tire,' said Colver, wondering whether this was so; true or not he felt injured by the allegation; he had grown to respect the proprietor for the ordered placidity by which he conducted his life. 'How often does your husband go to the inn?'

'He goes there as little as possible. He has always made a public point of never trying to compromise his own position: no doubt it would be easy for him to behave in a lax manner. That's what is suspected, I gather, of those who gain the advantage of a post in the country. Both the proprietor and the priest have, in the past, asked my husband to attend the seasonal fêtes in the village. It wasn't so difficult for him to put in an appearance when he was only the village magistrate. Then, he could go out, and enter into the spirit of the occasion; he could stay until the early hours with the best of them. Indeed, one might say that a patronal festival would have been incomplete without his blessing eye. He enjoyed those days: he will tell you that himself: he looks at the photographs still. A change occurred, however, and one must live with that. Since he has been appointed the secular agent to the monastery he has had to be very careful as to what he legitimizes and to what event he can put his name. A magistrate going to a fête such as those which are held in the inn yard or the barn can be there either as a magistrate, in the early part of the night, or, later, he can return and be a magistrate off duty and out of uniform: a secular agent is always a secular agent, and he always personifies a certain institution which carries with it a certain standard of behaviour with which he must always be seen to conform. He is never off duty. He must either condone what he attends or else show his disapproval by his absence. His stance, made from clear-sighted judgment, must be made public.

'Not that this is of any importance,' said the magistrate's wife. 'The only reason that I asked my husband to invite you to his tenancy this afternoon was to give me the opportunity to speak to you.'

'I represent nothing. I have no authority; I am of no importance. I have said that to him many times.'

'So you have said, and so you continue to say: but on both occasions when he came to see you at the inn he took the trouble to ascertain, by circuitous means, that you would be likely to be willing to see him. He changed many of his other plans for the sake of those two visits. He prepared himself for the formality of each occasion well in advance; it was difficult for him to do that; he has, as you will have noticed, an impediment of speech, particularly in the face of a formal interview, whether its outcome is certain or not. You have given him no hope: he says as much himself, when he speaks about it, though he clouds what he says by underemphasis; he only pretends that he doesn't care whether you have the authority to help him or not.'

'How could I be of help to him?'

The magistrate's wife said nothing for a few moments; the sound of the stream, which, while she had been talking had been almost below the threshold of hearing, now reasserted its dominance. 'He must have told you about the arrival of the letters,' she said. 'I don't show too much curiosity about his work: the official side of his life is his own. If he wanted me to know about it, then he would have told me without any need for asking. One has to know only a certain sufficiency in order to run a household. As for him: I only have to look at his face. The regular arrival of these letters has made him weak with continued anxiety.' She began to look towards him, though it was plain that she could not see him clearly, and that she was forced to rely on memory in order to see him at all: perhaps she had not heard him speak for she had ignored what he had said: his own voice seemed even in his own ears to have been drowned in the sound of its own echoes.

'I shouldn't be confiding in you: I don't know why I am doing so,' she said, her voice clear and distinct. 'I knew nothing of you before the day when you arrived in the village. I saw you when you were ill: one cannot help a compassion towards the sick person of character unknown, of origin unknown. You were shouting in your fever. I thought to myself: he is only human like the rest of us; where is his authority now? We expected, as I think has been said, your death; character unknown, origins forgotten, destination no longer to be brought to the front of the mind, the very meaning of the word beyond recall: authority as though it had never been. Later, when the acuteness of the illness was over, and you used to sit at a table in the inn yard, asleep, not looking at anyone, an attitude of habit, I suppose, I would have liked to have talked to you then, before my husband spoke to you, but the word would have quickly got round that I had gone down to the inn yard to ask favours of you; they would have said that the magistrate has sent his wife down to the inn to ask favours of the sick man or to plead for his intercession.'

'None of this has anything to do with me,' said Colver. He was thinking of the letter which the magistrate had held in his hand last night; he saw again, in his mind's eye, his struggle in his silent attempt at speech. 'Why doesn't he tell you what these letters contain?'

'In broad truth it is easy to see what they contain. Originally they were ordinary letters, possibly even circular letters directed to the post rather than the man, some of them containing routine statutory instruments, not even personally directed at him: not personally directed at anybody; they began to arrive from the moment he took his post; doubtless they had arrived and had fallen unopened on the floor during the years of vacancy when the post had been without a tenant. I remember that one was forwarded to him before he had even arrived in this valley; he showed it me; he was proud of it, and, when I

131

saw it, I was pleased that he should by its anonymity see a ratification for the step he was about to take. It was only when he had been in post for some time, when first he grew warm to the ambition of gaining the secular agent's post that he grew dubious over these letters—I remember no one day, no one coming together of circumstances to point to or to refer to. It was only then that he began to regard their arrival with concern, saying, as I remember well, that even the first, the one of which he had once been so proud, had implications in it beyond its meaning. Now he will say, taking up a letter newly arrived by post, holding it unopened in his hands, "This is another of them!" Sometimes he will say that he has never opened any of them; now, as matters stand, either they aren't worth opening or he doesn't wish to know what they contain. He has a pile of letters, kept together with an elastic band, at the side of his desk. What am I to make of it? He says that whatever he has done in the past, there is no point in opening any of them now. Occasionally he describes in detail the state of circumstances which would seem to prevail when a letter arrives. More often I am sure that he is thinking aloud. That's all that I can say.' She paused, and an echo of her voice, as a bodiless whisper, returned from the dark recesses of the passage.

'Do you say that he opened only the first letter?'

'Yes, I believe so. He once told me that he had shown the first of the letters (the one of which he was so proud in his youth, and which he habitually carries with him) to a doctor, an acquaintance of ours, and that after reading it the doctor had given it back to him without making any comment.'

Colver said that the magistrate had mentioned only last night that he had shown the letter to a doctor in the town, and that the doctor had at the time regarded the letter as having a very serious meaning.

'The facts are quite the reverse,' said the magistrate's wife. 'I know the truth of this; I see the doctor and his wife frequently.'

'Is this Dr Hartshorne?'

'No, a different physician altogether. They aren't in the

same practice and though neither of them are from the locality they both come from the provinces. My husband values the doctor who attended you for his skill; the poor especially speak highly of him; this other doctor, the one to whom he had shown the letter, was a social acquaintance; if the truth be known the opinion is that he has a somewhat indifferent professional reputation; some in the town would go as far as to intimate that he is able to keep his practice only because of his social standing. My husband told me twice, at some length on each occasion, about their meeting that morning: he told me the first time immediately after it had taken place: on the second occasion he woke me up at night—dawn broke while he was telling me—to say that the incident, trivial though it had been at the time, had been weighing on his mind and that he had not told me the circumstances of the meeting correctly the day before. He said that he and the doctor had been standing in the market square under the bank's portico. The square was quiet. The doctor had given my husband an invitation for an evening's dinner and cards. My husband told me that the last thing he wished to do was to accept the invitation; he could not see how he could refuse; he could feel an expression of distaste forming on his own face; in order to interrupt (for he could not bring himself to speak) he took the letter from his pocket, held it out to the doctor, and asked him to read it, as though, as he said later, on the second occasion of his telling me of their meeting, it had been a request to be left alone. The doctor stopped talking, looked at my husband as though he had done something astonishing, took the letter, read it and gave it back without making any comment.

'My husband had said, on the first occasion of his telling me of this meeting, that, as he continued to listen to the doctor after showing him the letter, he had become aware that their conversation was a thing of dead form. However, when he woke me up at night, to recount the story again, he stressed that the doctor had been offended, certainly, but by nothing he had read in the letter: only by the brusque manner in which his flight of speech had been stopped.' She paused. 'I

133

remember his expression to this day: it was as though a weight had been taken from his mind: I remember it particularly because otherwise the day was quite normal; it had begun normally enough with his waking before the dawn; a silent breakfast, and, then, the preparations one normally makes before going to the town. He said that after the doctor had read the letter and had returned it, this letter in which after so many years my husband had seen so dreadful an interpretation, seeing it as he said himself, with the gaze of anxiety, just to look at the doctor's expression was to be reassured, and he said to himself, there was after all nothing universal about this letter: it pertains to me alone: there is no importance in it, no importance at all, I can stand that: if the doctor can look at it and hardly trouble himself to see what it means there is no colossal importance to it, nothing as regards humanity: only a little limited importance, for a brief span before being forgotten, as is shown by the fact that it concerns only myself, whom the doctor does not know and in whom the doctor has no interest, only a little curiosity: I have only to examine it with his eyes and, just as the universality I so feared receded from it when I saw him reading it, so will the specificity recede: perhaps it will be neither universal nor specific when I see what is written with my own eyes. He stood in the street, looking at the letter, which he says he did not read, at least not immediately, the doctor having begun to talk upon another topic, some other concern which was for the moment at the forefront of his attention and which for the last few days had between other domestic matters engaged his interest: as it happens, the impending closure of the branch railway: in fact the doctor, so he said, had entertained an assumption that my husband's letter would be a communication on that matter; indeed, my husband said, he seemed to retain that assumption while reading it, and, furthermore, even after he had handed it back, he still retained that assumption. Perhaps, he said, my husband had been a signatory to some small local petition in his civil parish which might later be used to augment the mayor's petition in the confluence town itself. How valuable your signature would be, the doctor had said. My husband, holding the envelope of his letter in both hands, hardly heard him, for the doctor had turned away from him so that he might see the stone chimney-stacks of the station building as he spoke, as though the act of beholding them would aid his speech. My husband, during that brief meeting with the doctor (from the moment he had raised his hand in greeting to the moment when the doctor had turned away), had, on thinking of all the other communications he had received, become aware that his own stay in post must end, and that it was inevitable that he must leave the valley, and that no redress was possible, and that the letter pertained, if it pertained to anyone, only to himself and that beyond himself it was of no interest, not even of local interest, not even at the level of gossip. He had begun, even while the doctor was still speaking about the railway, to cast his mind forward to the circumstances of his departure, at what season, on what day, at what time, whether by night or by day, when the carrier's van would arrive, and, while the doctor was still talking he heard as he had heard before the sound of the wheels of the van on the gravel at the front of the house, perhaps drawing him out of sleep, perhaps making him raise his face from some task he might have undertaken to pass the time in the office (looking down from the desk to the office floor to see as always an image of his predecessor's pallet), some little problem set as it were in a metaphor of self-punishment, now uncompleted: the meal unfinished, the night unslept through, the sun sinking with the day unlived through, the essay half written, the challenge seen at last as having been taken up in ignorance. He said, "I shall look forward now to that time: a night no different from that of my arrival, squalling rain, nothing clear, as dark as night but starless, a bell ringing down, altered from the first only by the summation of experiene which lies between the two, the bell recording a taking back of what once had been given, not, as I once thought (the idea springing from nowhere and invading my mind and, filling it, driving out the reasoning which might once have been brought to bear) the crassness of purpose, of ability, of dedication: when I arrived, and heard the first

135

sound, and watched the destruction of my belongings by the waters of the rising flood, I was asked to give what I had: I offered my substance, my loyalty, my mind, my years; but the sum of these things was not enough."

'I have been wanting to speak to you for some days; I have been trying to find an opportunity; they say that you are an approachable man, even the proprietor says that, much as he dislikes you and wishes you gone: not that I want to take any advantage of *that* fact.' Her voice was determined and strong, and her words were well enunciated; she and the traveller might have been speaking alone in a drawing room and not in a cave. 'When you were first brought down from the mountain we had no thought for anything above your recovery; that goes without saying; it didn't matter that your arrival brought difficulties for my husband, who has his order of set duties; it did not matter that you, above all else a sick man, might or might not have been in a position of authority. The sudden fear of the night and the crisis of the illness changed all sense of order.

'Later, it was different. My husband has his own position to think of.

'There remains only the fact of these letters! Since your arrival he has been turning the matter over and over in his mind. He's been preoccupied with them: he says himself that the worry over them must by itself affect the efficiency with which he carries out his duties. It is quite clear that he wants to discuss the subject with you. That was clear by the preparations he made before each of the visits he made to you. It has crossed my mind—a thought I have kept to myself —that you might be connected with the authority in which these letters have their origins.' She turned her head. 'You deny this: I can see your expression,' she said.

Colver found it difficult to know whether she was looking at him or staring past him into the depths of the cave: her last statement surely indicated that she had been staring directly at him. 'I shouldn't be saying this.' Her voice was softer than it had been. 'I ought to be continuing in my day-to-day life. I don't even know what a woman like myself should do on her husband's behalf: I cannot do his work for him. He's changed in the last five years.' Her voice had an appeal in it. 'The letters are symptomatic of change, surely, and not its cause.'

'You are very faithful,' said Colver, intending the statement to be no more than an expression of speech, a phrase to show that he had been listening. He heard the echoes of his own voice: apart from the echo, and the subdued murmur of the stream, there was no sound in the cave. The echo itself, before it faded, was distinct, but so distorted by the walls of the cave that it gave back the impression that one had been speaking in a language which one did not understand: whatever one might have said would be returned as a sharp glossolalia. The sounds of the world were absent. The outer world itself, an image half overlain by the dark shadow of the cliffs above, was without movement; a striped blanket on which lay the small and foreshortened figure of the magistrate and the shapes of the children playing amongst the scree at the precipice's edge.

'I am faithful! My husband is my husband, and I must see for myself which way to turn!'

'Your husband is a provincial magistrate. He is a fortunate man. I find it difficult to believe these rumours of the letters: one moment he has read them, the next he hasn't; sometimes he knows what is in them, sometimes he doesn't. Your husband is fortunate to be where he is. There is no more to be said than that.'

'Well, that is quite true, in a sense, but it's erroneous to make judgments as easily as that. My brother came to stay with us once and certainly it wasn't long before he lost his patience. He isn't the most tolerant of men. He said to me that he found it impossible to see how my husband's work could be in any way difficult. He would repeatedly look out through the window, indicating the valley with a sweep of his hand, and he would point to the magistrate's house, which is as you know a massive building which because of its position dominates the rest of the village. For all his intolerance he is given to using flowery phrases, a habit which all his life has given rise to misunderstanding because he is often thought to

137

be joking when he is not. He made his judgment with the question: "How can any work be difficult here in the order of this arcadia?" Perhaps generalization is the forerunner of such judgment. My brother called my husband "a weak man", and I was angry at that; it was unnecessary. My brother said, "Any man may fall beneath another's burden, but it is the weak man who cannot lift the burden he has made for his own back." That was one of the things my brother said, and it was all very well for him to speak: he's a single-minded man who is forever judging people because his judgment allows him to dismiss what they say. It is easy for blinkered and single-minded people to call others weak. When I put that to my brother, he said that if my husband wasn't weak, then he was a fool for trying to stand in two boats. He brings out these heavy aphorisms when it suits him to do so.'

'What was it like here when you first arrived?'

'You don't want to be doing with listening to me,' said the magistrate's wife, with a little laugh, but the way she said this suggested that she wished nothing further out of life than the opportunity to continue speaking to him. The outer world might have been concealed by more than the rock of the cave-walls. Looking at the magistrate's wife, it was easy to see that her expression was compounded of both anxiety and humour; which emotion predominated depended for the moment on what she was thinking. Her eyes caught the light entering the cave's mouth, and the movement of the stream and the darkness of the interior of the cave were reflected in her pupils and her dark irises.

'What did you see when you first came to this valley?' asked the traveller.

'Artificiality,' she said, prosaically. 'It was all artificial. My husband had been here for some time before I arrived. He had his own ideas as to what he thought I might wish to see. There was nothing that hadn't been dressed up for my looking at. He would become distressed if, while standing on the top of some hill or other, I looked away from the direction in which he pointed.

'I wish for nothing beyond a simple life: I wish for nothing

138

more. I have put aside without much regret the thought of those social opportunities I might once have learned to expect. I don't want unnecessary difficulties; they present themselves without the necessity of a search: but, for all that, every household must rest on domestic principles. I used to look out of the windows, down into the valley then, and sense my isolation keenly, as though I had imposed it upon myself. He would be in his office staring at the ceiling or out of the window. It struck me that as we often used to stare out of the windows, albeit of different rooms, we might sometimes by chance have looked together at the same object.

'Is there a falsity to the complexity which surrounds not only his accession to the post of secular agent but also his magistrate's appointment? Does even that humble authority rest on a web of false premises? Until his accession to the post of secular agent his civil appointment was taken on trust. Or is the complexity honest? He is my husband, after all, but even so I've never trusted what people say about "self-examination" when they lose their standards of personal hygiene. It was a difficult time for me. You can guess that. Perhaps I was thinking selfishly, for myself and the children, but then it is a mother's place to do that. What is the use of going miserably from one room to the next, from one day to the next, sighing, sending letters to friends who have changed from the memory one holds of them? None of that does any good. Yet I was in a foreign place with two babies and a husband who seemed hardly able to lift his head and see a yard in front of his face. I continually asked myself the question, in those early days: "Is his behaviour reasonable?" and the answer would always be that, looked at in a certain light and with a certain amount of compassion and understanding, his behaviour was always reasonable.'

'Did you ever consider that he had lost touch with reality?'

'The expected question! But: never.'

'Did you ever suspect that he might have been unfaithful to you?'

'What do you take me for?' said the magistrate's wife. 'I dismissed that idea the second after I had thought of it.'

'Did you ever sense that you shared the house with a stranger?'

'How familiar that question is! It's one asked by others—my brother one of them—not by oneself. He's never been a stranger to me; he's altered too gradually for that; he has altered gradually through life as perhaps we all alter. On the other hand his change has not been one of compromise. He once told me that he thought the adaptation of compromise a wasteful process and erosive of the individuality which had been built up since childhood, "turning those of character into staters of the bland obvious, causing those with spontaneous humour to laugh only in response to the unconscious signal". Those were his words. Why they come to mind now I don't know, perhaps for the sound of the words: "The code of acquiescence is tapped out by the stereotyped gesture, the unremarkable expression and phrase, the expected movement of the eye."

'As for a movement of the eye: I cannot put myself in possession of that frame of mind which occupied you when you first saw him. Perhaps—my imaginative eye—you saw in him at that first glance a man with a certain position, with certain standards to uphold by virtue of and for the sake of that position. I have no pointer to that attitude of a first sight: I do not remember the moment of my first seeing him, and perhaps it is with the fondness of familiar retrospection that I believe I saw him as holding, despite the possession of only a prospect of authority, he being a youth on the day I first saw him, the qualities one associates, as it were by kinship, with one who, for all that stands against him, occupies such a position as he now holds by right: but who, for one reason or another, has never until the moment of his formal appointment held the wish or the ambition to place his own character outwards for such consideration: nor has sought by any means to allow himself to be considered: not by the slightest flaw in his character has he ever put himself thus forward. Such was his privacy of mind in these matters that without a conscious burial of his talents—or so it now seems to me—he made it apparent that he was not to be considered; no functionary might find him; no other person might say of him "by his dignity is he worthy": no-one might see, nor would he allow them to see, that guarded behind the silence of the private habit of the downturned eyes, so to speak, he has all the qualities one associates, and generations have come to associate, not only within the little towns such as the one at the confluence of the rivers, but in greater towns, in less provincial places—all the qualities of a provincial administrator and a member of the Bench. Indeed, as he says himself, now he holds that position, there is no difference between a member of the Bench and any other man of high-minded and moral outlook: no difference, beyond a certain ratification, a certain qualification, a certain limitation, as it were, of his qualities. Indeed, looking back on those changes which overcame him when first he saw the material post before him, these changes occurring simultaneously, related or not, perhaps only related because of the simultaneity of their happening and his age being what it was when they occurred: the transition from an upright man to a magistrate occurred at the same time as the transition of the last and least noticeable changes between the states of youth and manhood: by no means could one state the moment at which he changed, from being a man of moral persuasion to being a man of moral persuasion with magisterial duties; from being a man of inner certainties to being a man who by his elevation and breadth of thought must lose those certainties. Perhaps the moment might well be best judged, as he says himself, by a dream which overcame him then, and which he told me of but has not mentioned since, not even during the daylight disposal of other dreams: a dream of a traveller on a road, origin unstated, destination unstated, a grey day, a voice saying, sounding in his ear, or perhaps in the head and attributed to the ear, as though from a premonitory desire that it be external, the simple statement, "The lamp will now be turned out." He said, he awoke; as he awoke he began to reason aloud the one spoken phrase; "The light you mistake for daylight is the light of a lamp: that lamp will now be turned out." For all that he has left the road of the dream and lies looking out of the window and into the mists, his temple heavy against the pillow, the room indistinct about him, the thought comes back to him; the lamp has been turned out but for the traveller nothing has changed: he still walks along the road, in the grey light, origin unknown, destination unknown, for all that the voice has done, internal or external, sounding in head or ear, is to make him aware at least in part, at least a little, of the extent of a blindncss so long suspected but so long unproven, for it has spoken of the extinguishing of a lamp which he has never seen. The feeble light which makes a half-light of the night is seen at last, at long last, as being internal: the greater light has never been seen and its extinction for all its importance has produced no alteration: the traveller continues with his progression, one day's progress allowing him no wider and no more elevated a prospect than the progress of the day before. As for the dream: it is, as I now see it, the dream of a high-minded man who examines his surroundings as with a moral purview, and to whom the thing at the limits of jurisdiction and at the edge of the power of right is as distinct in his sight as is that which lies directly under the power of his right hand. Ah! he says, that turmoil in the stomach on the knowledge that the net cast out in earlier days was spread too wide for these restricted hands to gather in: how cold now to see that the imposed jurisdiction is less than that more real jurisdiction once previsaged, and how cold to see that all that lies between, once comprised perhaps of interests and concerns perhaps once pertinent, is not now to be brought to mind. This reduction, this loss, was one of change: as he himself says, it was a change simultaneous with his acquisition of magisterial authority. By what measure did his knowledge of his lack of certainty balance those certainties which without his foreknowledge had been imposed upon him? What was this change? By what mechanism did it occur? There is no moment, as I have heard it said— and my husband quoting the words of others, which words I ought myself to know—at which one might state that a righteous man has assumed magisterial authority: to give an analogy of my husband's making: an opinion given by a man before assuming magisterial authority differs from that given by the same man after such assumption: both opinions are given by a high-minded man of moral outlook: there is from that point of view no difference in the standing of the two opinions, both being given from a position of honesty and integrity for they are both the thought statements of the working of the mind. In the differences of meaning between the two opinions, I am given to understand, by the sources he brings half to mind (as though they lay unsummonable between the expanse once seen and the expanse now imposed) lies the whole mechanism and procedure by which such magisterial authority is placed upon the shoulders. Further, he says, giving this time no source, as though it had never lain within his understanding, in a like manner might the mechanism of his second appointment, that of the secular agent—a prosaic enough term in its outward appearance— be explained.

'Was his changing behaviour due to an inner alteration which had nothing to do with the appointment he had so recently taken up? He had grown to dislike the intrusion of the monastery, particularly when he was at home; I felt that he regarded the monastery as an institution for which he worked but for which he felt no particular loyalty. How could one have any loyalty to such a place? Have you ever been into the arch of the gatehouse?' She looked at the traveller but she expected no answer. 'He became increasingly intolerant of the sound of the bells, particularly the night-bells, and he found distasteful the idea that, when he woke up at night, he might look up and see the silhouette of the monastery, blurred, beyond the condensation of the window-glass.

'Shortly after his accession he said that it would be better if we were to sleep in a room at the back of the house: he said that it was one thing working for the monastery, he was pleased to do so, but it was another to be forced to put up with the sounds of the bells. The intrusion into his home was an abuse of his loyalty; not only the unpredictable sounds of the night-bell, but even the glow of the moonlight on the walls were intrusions which affected his night's rest. Even after the back room was cleaned out, and while he slept there, he always demanded that the casement and shutters be closed at night, summer and winter. He kept the passage door open to allow some air into the room. I have never liked the back of the house myself, the bedrooms being immediately above the public rooms and filled with an animal taint which rises through the floorboards. The smell of the public rooms rises up the well of the backstairs and one can hear the water overflowing from the cistern in the public cloakroom. In the end, I slept with the babies in the bedroom at the front of the house while he slept above the public rooms at the back. Sometimes I would wake up and hear him shouting in his sleep; when I went to him he would be sitting in bed, all of a sweat, saying that some bell or other was about to sound, or had sounded, or had paused in its sounding. Sometimes he would say that the premonition had come while he had been lying awake: indeed he protested that he could not have been asleep; he had lain awake all night and had heard every hour chime from the waiting-room clock. Sometimes he would say that he had been on the brink of sleep, and had not been aware that he had cried out and that he was sorry that he had disturbed me, and that he hoped he had not disturbed the children: he would grow maudlin and remorseful about the fact that they would have to be sent away to school, and I would have to say to him, what sort of place is this in which to bring up children? His voice would always be half coherent as though he were still half asleep. Sometimes he would wake. If he woke I would bring him something, a drink perhaps, hot water, milk, and the night for the moment would take on a more cheerful look.

'He had always stressed the fact that the monastery was a good and considerate employer. He had frequently told me that he had long since learned to accept the monastery's silence as being thanks enough, and he would often add that its very lack of communication was in itself a manifestation of gratitude. If one supposes that he was telling the truth, and not hiding something from me, then why, if it was to be taken for granted that the monastery was a considerate employer, should the sound of its bells so trouble him at night? Why should they disturb his sleep and give his mind an unwhole-some slant? I could never understand that. He certainly did sleep badly. I used to go and look at him in the night. He would lie in the stillness—the magistrate's house is a profoundly silent place in the daytime, not to mention the night—asleep, but trembling, breathing stertorously as though something oppressed his chest. The mists would lie levelly on the half-way step of the backstairs, like water in a well, coming up from the courtroom. He would wake up as though choking: at first I thought that his tongue had fallen back in his mouth because he was lying on his back. Could it have been only nightmare? Once he shouted out as he woke, and his words were very clear. "One is qualified to ask, but not permitted to assume the authority to question!", and once he shouted out the old phrase (a common enough phrase to rebuke a child) which he almost certainly remembered from his childhood: "Meddle not with things too high for thee!", and once, "The lamp, ray never lit, light never comprehended, is extinguished!" These three occasions, when he shouted so loudly that the whole house was disturbed, did not coincide with the sounding of any bell. Why should he have had such nightmares, unless he brought them upon himself by denying himself the fresh air which he might have obtained by leaving one of the windows at least partially open?'

The traveller, while he had been listening to this, and thinking to himself what a singularly unpleasant house the magistrate's house must be, had looked up again (while the magistrate's wife had been speaking) at the chiselled lines which ran across the surface of the rock.

'It is surprising,' said the magistrate's wife, 'how much one keeps to oneself, even in marriage. I have stored up memories of things seen out of the corner of an eye: they are as important as the great events of one's life. Below all the loyalties, one is very much alone. I don't think I wished to speak to my husband about the things which had so changed him; I would only have put questions to him, and when I myself considered those questions I would have asked him they seemed unim-portant and at a tangent. All that remained were the small things, and they were not worth talking about. He would at that time eat anything, wear anything, sleep between any kind of bed linen, accept the dirt and the inconvenience of the house—it is an impossible house to keep clean. There was a time when he was unable to wash and dress on his own, a few years ago, and I cannot begin to tell you the difficulties which went with that: when the auditors came he might as well have been out in the mowing-field standing in the long grass amongst the poppies for the attention he gave them: I had to engage a man from the village to attend to him, and it was not the easiest of tasks to find someone who was discreet. I asked the priest for his advice; I never told my husband about that; he didn't see eye to eye with the priest on the day of his arrival, and, without any particular event being worthy to call to mind, the rift between them has steadily grown, so that when they have cause to speak to each other they can hardly follow each other's train of thought. In the end I could not speak to my husband at all; one evening, when I went upstairs to his room to close the windows, I began to talk to him, telling him the day's events, and who I had seen: he told me to be quiet; he said that every word has within it a common ulterior purpose and that the deep purpose of each question is hidden: that being so, what would be the purpose of any answer?' She looked at the traveller. 'What do you find so interesting about the walls?'

'I was looking at those marks,' said the traveller. The sun had fallen in the sky, and, as its beam approached more nearly the level, so it penetrated further into the cave, revealing long stretches of the scalloped walls. Far inside, beyond the range of the available light, one could see the coruscation of cascading water. The increased light allowed him to look more closely at the marks. He could see now that they were not the work of man; like the larger scallops themselves they were the result of erosion by water.

'It's like that, is it,' said the magistrate's wife, thinking that the traveller had not been listening to her. 'I thought when I first saw you that you might be in a position to help me. You are the first person I could speak to for a long time.'

'How can I help you? What would you have me do? I am only a traveller: I shall be gone tomorrow. How do you wish me to reply?' Colver held up his arms as though to show his lack of power, an inappropriate gesture because he was a tall and well-built man. 'I can't understand your contradictions. You say that you wish to speak to me because you are anxious for your husband and because you imagine that I might have some authority: when you do speak to me you don't withhold the least detail of your husband's predicament.' He looked down to the stream, and then out to where the magistrate was sleeping on the blanket, which was now in shadow. 'I am only a chance traveller.' He paused. He wondered if he had offended her. 'Is this post of "secular agent" imaginary?'

'No. It would be unreasonable to think that.'

'Has your husband read any of the letters which were sent him by the civil authorities?'

'How persistent you are with that one question,' said the magistrate's wife, as though she had at last grown tired of being alone with the traveller. 'In continuing to ask it you show that you are, as you say, no different to anyone else. About the letters: it was quite clear that the thing which distressed him was not within the reading of the wording: as I have said before, I have no reason to believe that he did not open others of them after the first, and if he did open them, I have no reason to believe that he did not read whatever happened to be within: no: he was distressed by the very fact of their arrival when he first saw that his position was about to undergo an alteration: he was distressed by the circumstances in which he received them, as though they pointed to matters which once had an existence but which were hardly now to be brought to mind.

'My husband,' she said, 'has a strong character. He told me that he had once looked up from the table at which he had been sitting one hot afternoon—he had been staring down at the surface of this table—during a business meeting of the provincial council: on looking up he saw that every face had an expression of temporizing placidity, while the droning voice of the speaker, content nothing, intent all, a speech of circumlocution and generality, might have said, in finer language: There is no talk of the axe suspended above the head lest the tremor in the voice disturb the equilibrium. Perhaps my husband was gently mocking my brother (who was staying with us at the time), for the expression was so like one of my brother's, which to be truthful are as often as not brought out as generalities. "One must not waste time in shouting when one is in difficulties!" my husband said, though when he says things like that, particularly when they are to do with events he attends as a magistrate, one is never sure whether he is serious. Since he has recovered from his illness his sense of humour has returned.'

'He is better, then, than he was?'

'I think so,' said the magistrate's wife after an oddly impartial period of consideration. 'I keep on hoping so.'

The air in the cave was cold and the draught had unexpectedly increased; it would be a pleasure to go outside into the warmer air of the valley.

IX

The bell sounded in the early morning before the light had grown strong enough to give colour to anything in the valley. The mist lay heavily over the valley-floor, shrouding the houses and making a dark and indistinct presence of the wood. Everything beyond the window was grey and indefinite, blurry-edged and seen at an uncertain distance. In a small room near the roof of a house not far from the inn a crying baby had been suckled by lamplight; the mother had opened the shutters to give entrance to the expectation of a dawn. In the street outside the rats chased over the rubbish-heap in which the night-dampness had quenched the fire. The sounds from the nearer houses of the village were heightened against the silence of the cloaking mists. In the upstairs room of the inn the first light gave a solidity to the uncurtained window. The plaster walls were not seen as being discoloured and uneven; the cross by the door was not seen as being tarnished: the washstand and the chair were as insubstantial as though they had been painted upon the wall. The door, recesssed in its frame, might have been open or closed. The floor, stained with a dark varnish, might have been bare or covered. The bell sounded between sleep and outward vision: it was a wakening bell which tolled through the mists; the sound, as though reduced in the manner of everything else in the valley, was devoid of colour.

All down the street the shutters were being thrown open, the woodwork of the shutters' edges banging the plaster walls of the houses. The hands which pushed the shutter-leaves were jerky with sleep; the wide-eyed faces which appeared at the dark rectangles of the windows stared at each other across the streets as though the expressionlessness of sleep precluded any sign of recognition.

Outside, in the street, under the sound of the bell, the opened doorways were thronged with people who, eyes wide and pupils dilated with the empty wakefulness which follows solid sleep, put their hands to their downturned faces to hide those yawns which had not yet begun to form. The air was cold and the dew lay heavily on anything which had been left outside; a scythe laid against the wall last night, forgotten during talk, was red with rust at the sharpened and unoiled edge of its blade; a few garments on a string line dripped with moisture.

The sound of the few words which were spoken indicated above all else a dry and sparse good nature. Colver, looking downwards, dampening his hands and his chest in leaning over the sill, saw those in the street shaking their heads and lifting their faces upwards, calling to each other, pointing, as though to indicate that, their rest having been irretrievably disturbed, they might as well make the most of their wakefulness, though this was largely imagination: the mists were thick beyond the casement of the window and only the indistinct outlines of those who stood directly beneath the window could be made out: had he not heard the sound of their voices in the lengthy silences between the beats of the bell he would hardly have been able to tell whether the moving shapes were those of the villagers or of their animals: though, as far as he could see, in the vacillation of the light, bearing in his mind that the sound of the bell had for some reason altered, perhaps to become a shade more or a shade less confident, a small group of people, grey and indifferent, still for the most part in their night-clothes, as though this early congregation were a gathering made familiar only by its regularity, began to press down the street in the shadow of the oak-wood towards the taller houses in the centre of the village.

In the side streets the mist was dense enough to force anyone pressing forward and haltingly feeling his way by touching the wall to grasp out for the back of the coat of the person who shuffled in front; in the alley itself it was as though the dawn had not yet arrived; the air itself was still dark: one was forced to look down at the uneven ground and to feel the way across the larger stones: one was forced to be mindful of the central gutter which was full of the water which had dripped, overnight, from the roofs of the overarching houses. The caution implicit in the sound of the dragging footfalls was enough to sound a caution in the laying of one's own step: the silences between the beats of the bell were filled with the sound of shuffling, as if those who walked (by common consent stretching their hands out in front of themselves to feel their way) had been reduced to common blindness. Momentarily a back would straighten as the need for caution was lifted at the recognition of a familiar archway, but within a dozen steps this familiarity had been lost. It is not uncommon, in mists like this, to get lost in your own village, and what a fool you can make of yourself while trying to explain your presence in someone else's courtyard! It is easy to enter the wrong door-way, the wrong arch, to tap at the wrong window: the mists do not excuse anything. 'Who are you? Get out of here.' 'Leave go of my cuff: I know where I am.' 'Upon my word, you don't know where you are. This is a private yard,' is the shout of the householder: 'Your voice is foreign to me: if I knew it there would be no difference: you are a foreigner here: how much longer do we have to put up with the offence of your presence? Who are you to trespass? Do you know what time it is? Why are you purposefully disturbing my family? I'll have the magistrate on to you: you see if I do not. He has a reputation for severity with people like you; and do you wonder at it?' The householder speaks in phrases of a length which coincide with the silences between each beat of the bell. He turns his head to make sure that the indistinct rectangle of the lamp-lit doorway of his house is still visible: he does not want to lose sight of it. He is in his own yard, certainly, but in this mist he might be anywhere. All he can recognize are the well-known echoes of his voice from the familiar angles and salients of the walls and from the hollowness of the open stables where the horses are stamping about, caring nothing for the ringing of a bell, but curious themselves as to the nature of the mists and the reason for the late arrival of the daylight.

The door of the parishioner's house was open. The interior, until a moment ago a blackness, was now lit by two lamps which had been thrust in at the door. The old man was sitting in his bed, his back resting heavily against an arrangement of hard-looking bolsters, as though he had passed the night without sleep in that same position. His face, staring at the light of the lamps and looking from one lamp to the other, had the indiscriminate and falsely watchful stare of someone who has only that moment been awakened.

Colver, out in the alley, turned away from the open door. Behind him there were hoarse shouts from those who stumbled further away in the mist.

Inside the dark room, which, being unheated, was filled with a mist as thick as that which lay in the alley, two men looking at each other as though for a cue began to lift the heavy table and to carry it outside: it was plain from the skilful manner in which they coordinated their movements and the way in which they turned the table to avoid the other furniture in the room, the way in which they tilted the table to carry it through the narrow doorway, the manner in which they selected without looking the one place in the alley, fifty yards from the door, where the table might stand level on the cobbles and the gutter-stones, that they had done this many times before, and at more unusual hours. The table itself was laden with the parishioner's books and divinatory apparatus. The two porters had moved the table with such skill and evidence of practice that nothing on its surface had been disturbed. One of the two men brought out a wooden-backed chair from another house. The parishioner himself, watching from his bed the movement of his own and other people's property into the alley outside, submitted to having a cloak wrapped round his thin shoulders. His eyes were searching. He was fully awake. The person who had placed the cloak about his shoulders put a pair of shoes on his feet. The two porters leaned, or, rather, half knelt at the head of the bed. They lifted him up, looking across him to indicate their readiness, communicating with each other by means of simple nods and shakings of their heads and by rolling their eyes in the direction of the door. While he was being carried the parishioner was silent; his only action being to look from side to side in a silent appeal, probably an unconscious gesture, as though he did not trust the competence of the porters, and was afraid that, in the rapidity of the move, his feet or legs or arms might strike the doorposts.

When he was in the chair he lay back to regain his breath, as though he had been through an exhausting ordeal; one could see, in the yellow light of the two lamps which had been brought out of the house, his chest moving up and down with his rapid breathing, the skin of his neck round his wind-pipe being drawn in with each inspiration.

Colver looked at the faces of the men and the women who stood in the alley. For some reason the identity of the women was more prominent: he could not see why this should be so: several surmises quickly passed through his mind: their faces might have been more individual than those of the men though he could not see why this was; perhaps they had been more easily aroused by the sound of the bell; perhaps he had been looking for someone in particular: did he expect to see the magistrate's wife here? Though he had not thought of the past night since the moment he had been awakened, he had dreamed of the magistrate's wife all night, wakening at many untold hours to see her in his mind. Now, in truth, it was difficult to distinguish any of the faces in the mist. The two lamps, even though their wicks were turned higher than might have been necessary for the illumination of a small room, gave almost no light; because of the mist they served only to dazzle the eye; the mist lay round each flaring wick in concentric globes of translucent yellow vapour. The men and women in the alley were silent; the only sounds heard between the beats of the bell were those of breathing. Some of those who looked towards the table were already visibly shivering, their eyes staring forward as though fixed in their direction as though by the effort of fending off the cold. There was a wash of water as someone stood in the full gutter which ran down the centre of the alley. The parishioner began to turn the pages of one of the books on the table in front of him, the action of his tremulous hand silent; the turning page, its paper already damp, lay over the fingers of his right hand so limply that the shape of the hand could be made out beneath it. All the time the bell continued to toll overhead. 'So you have come to this, have you?' The priest's voice was close; the man must have manoeuvred his position so that he stood beside the traveller, though when Colver first turned on hearing his distinct voice he had seemed to be some distance away, the mists rolling between them like a river in an established water-course. Of this uncertain effect the priest seemed unaware: he had spoken between the beats of the bell without looking at the traveller, as though he had recognized the traveller's likeness in another, a chance association which had for some reason caused him to speak aloud. 'It is,' he continued, looking squarely at Colver now, 'an opportunity not seized by every visitor.' The traveller said nothing. The parishioner, on hearing the oblique voice, looked up from the pages of his book. It was impossible to know what he was thinking: that indeed depended on the reason for his sitting here. His face bore an expression of uncomfortable concentration. Despite the cloak he surely felt the coldness of this wet atmosphere. His expression elicited the traveller's compassion: why had they dragged him from his sick-bed? Why was he willing to sit in a chair in a back-alley in this darkness? He looked up, as though through his mind passed for a little while the speculation that the mists might only be head-high and that beyond them might be regions of clear skies lit with the ever changing colours of the dawn. The parishioner began to speak. 'Shall I translate for you?' The priest's voice was slow and full of irony; he had moved much closer to Colver; he made it clear from his tone that anything that might be said would be hardly worth the effort of translation.

The old man, perceived more clearly now, though the mists had become no thinner (indeed, the air was less clear than it had been even a few minutes previously), looked down at the pages of the book in front of him. There was in his eyes the sense of a need for haste. The bell continued to beat overhead. One might have thought that, after this length of time, the pauses between the beats would no longer have seemed so prolonged but this was not so: the periods of silence had an unnatural length to them, as though the beating of the bell were not as predictable as had been thought in the confidence of the waking moment: perhaps the bell was indeed slowing in its sounding. The old man, his head in comparative darkness as he lowered his face to look at the pages of the book, reached for the watch and wiped the wetness from the glass face. It was beginning to drizzle. The old man raised a hand and held it briefly above the surface of the table. He said something in a distinct voice courageous in its ringing distinctness. The priest translated, his voice heavy and impartial, but at the moment of his speaking he lowered his face to the black cloth of his sleeve, at the elbow, to wipe his brow, and Colver was only able to deduce what he had said by conjectural guesses which carried no weight even as he made them. 'He seems to think that the bell will stop in eight more strokes.'

Once the information had been given with authority that the bell would stop in eight strokes it was no longer possible to avoid counting them: these final eight began to take on a significance which had been denied to every stroke in the past, even the first, beyond recall and having sounded in sleep; now those strokes about to sound were named and, being named, were removed from anonymity. The villagers began to mutter words which might have signified the number of strokes, though it was not necessary to believe this; the traveller did not understand their language. On the contrary, those uttered names might be real names, peculiar to each stroke itself and given to none other. The traveller, watching them, was reminded of the simple man who used to go down to the sea and stand on the beach naming the pebbles. He would go down to the sea at seven o'clock in the morning and begin at the place he had marked out yesterday evening. He would hold each pebble in his cupped hands in order to name it. By midday he would begin to feel the monotony of what he had set out to do, and would be amenable to distraction. Visitors used to ask him questions. One day, he and the traveller had begun to talk about the different questions he had been asked over the years. The questions depended on the cast of the questioner's mind. Every question except for one implied a judgment on the futility of what he was doing. All these questions were of no importance. The single question, the one which had implied no judgment, had been the one which had sowed the seeds of a dissatisfaction in his work. His one worry for a long time had been that someone in the past might have given each pebble the same name as he had given it. That would indeed have made his work futile.

The last stroke sounded and the echo died away in the streets of the village. The dawn had progressed to the point where objects were acquiring colour and depth. As though regulated by the process of the sounding of the bell the morning mists began to clear and it was possible, from the configuration of the diffuse light, to tell in which direction the east lay.

Colver felt a compassion for the villagers who stood, looking up at the blankness of the mists, their faces without any expression in the coldness.

All this was seen quickly and only for a brief measure of time. The bell, unexpectedly and with a frightening irrationality, beat out twice as rapidly as before. Halving the pauses between its beats the sound of the bell leapt down from the air above the valley. The air was filled with the noise, an undying vibrant drone, echo compounding sound. Colver, feeling the hair on his head beginning to rise, was separated from the priest and was drawn back to the table. The bell redoubled yet again the tempo of its beating. The sound was beyond frenzy, beyond a call to arms, beyond a summons or a tocsin. It was impossible to be heard above the noise. It was impossible to know how many bells were sounding out: the deepest of the droning overtones produced a tremulousness in the pit of the stomach. Of all things, the sound had a reason; there was no doubt of that. Who was being called, and for what purpose? The bell was a tocsin, but against which eventuality did it warn? The sound was a call to arms, but to which conflict? Colver did not notice the pain in his thighs where the brass edge of the table pressed into them. He had been forced involuntarily forward. There was a pressure at his back, but he did not notice it: the sound was disabling. He closed his eyes and the source of the sound dropped from its height and rang through the alley. It roared through his head like the beat of a fever's pulse: he stood with his eyes closed. The unseen people around him moved with a motion periodic with the sound. This sense of motion caught him; he opened his eyes but he could not see. He saw nothing but motes and daggers of imaginary light. His outstretched left hand was touched by a dozen others, each different in its texture. The bell stopped ringing.

In the silence, only the memory of the bell raced through the head. He looked out into the mist and saw only the table, the two lamps, and the parishioner.

The priest caught his arm. 'What did you mean by that?' he said in a voice which because of his anger was no more than a whisper. He took a little wooden snuff box from the pocket of his cassock. For all his anger he held the snuff box upright as though he had, during some wakeful hour of the night before, filled it to the brim. His voice was extraordinarily loud in the silence left by the vanished sound from above. He grasped the traveller by the wrists as though he would drag him away from the table. 'Make no explanation now! Wait for that until you are away from this place! Look how much damage you have caused!'

When they were alone, further up the alley, the priest said: 'Are you still so ill?'

'Why are you pulling at me like this?'

'You shouldn't enter into things of which you have no understanding: you're the foreigner here. Leave the parody to the villagers.'

'What do you mean?'

'Very much what I say. You shouldn't have stood before the table. Why did you join in their mockery? Or did you think

157

you were being serious? What interpretation do you expect them to put into your motives?'

'I still do not understand you: what do you mean?'

The priest said, 'Do you not?' He paused. 'You closed your eyes and stood with your arm out.' He unfolded his arms; perhaps he would have held out his hand, but he did not do this; perhaps he thought the action would be seen despite the mists and although they seemed to be truly alone, in a wider street, where not even the walls of the houses were visible.

'I did not lift my hand.'

'That's enough of this hysteria! Who do you think you are? No-one touched you.' When they reached the inn he began to walk past, expecting the traveller to follow him, but then, looking up and down the street, he paused as though intending to go no further. He put a hand in one of his pockets and again took out the wooden snuff box. He stood at the inn door. 'You are shaking,' he said, in a voice which had a quietness which until now it had lacked.

The interior of the inn was dark and cavernous. The flagstones of the floor were wet as though they had just been washed. The contrast between the misty opalescence of the dawn alley and the darkness of the room forced him to feel his way. He stood amongst the tables and chairs. The proprietor's wife, though she could not be seen, could be heard scrubbing the floor in a further room as though she had recommenced the routine of her daily work with vigour. The building itself was filled with the sound of people walking up and down the stairs and across the boards of the upper floors. The street outside was noisy with the voices of those who were returning from the alley. The whole village had been stirred up by the sound of the bell. The tall windows of the magistrate's house were marked by vague and floating patches of lamplight through the darkness of the trees.

'I must go back upstairs,' said Colver.

'Your voice is unsteady. You are still feverish.' The priest began to make is way back towards the door shaking his head as though, beneath his quietness, he was still angry. 'Yes, you should go back upstairs. It was a foolish thing to do, to go

158

outside on such a wet morning so soon after your recovery.' His voice had regained its previous rigidity. 'I saw you,' he said, raising his voice, seeing that Colver was about to grasp the stair rail, and as though he wished to delay him no further, 'I saw you call out the word "stop" the instant before the bell stopped sounding.' His view of the traveller was interrupted by people who had just walked in through the door, and who, their eyes not being accustomed to the darkness, felt their way across the room, exactly as the priest and the traveller had done a few seconds earlier. 'They understand that word. It is one of the few they understand. There are no coincidences for the superstitious.'

In the upstairs room, Colver sat on the bed with his head supported by his fingers. His hands were still tremulous with sleep. He raised his head and looked about the bare room. He was unmistakably feverish again. It was impossible for him to go downstairs—he was still shaking—and the room he was in had the atmosphere of an unfamiliar room, one which he had never seen or entered before.

X

Colver stood looking out of the window into the mists which filled the streets. The day was as dull and as overcast as it had been at the moment of his first opening his eyes: in the mists outside there was no longer an intimation of direction. He closed the window. Inside, the shape of the room and its furniture were indistinct and their true nature would have been unknown to him had he not been able to recall it from memory. He sat on the bed and closed his eyes. He would have remained in the room, sitting on the bed, looking at the uncertain walls, as though he had never left it, as if night were about to fall, but two voices suddenly commenced speaking loudly in the room below; he was unable to put them out of his mind; their irregular alternation caused him to rise to his feet and to pace the room, from one end to the other, until, unable to dispel the sound of the voices from his mind even by this physical activity (for there seemed to be no other thing in the room to fix the mind upon), he opened the door and put his hand on the newel post and stared down the stairwell.

The room below was empty and the front door was open. The two speakers must have gone outside the moment before. From his place on the landing Colver could see that a letter rested on the counter. Perhaps it had been lying there for some time, neither the runner who had presumably brought it nor the landlord considering it of sufficient importance to be taken up to him.

On descending the stairs Colver looked round the empty room and walked to the counter. He took the message in his hands. The envelope was unremarkable and was sealed with mucilage. The room was silent as Colver opened it. He found that he was eager to read the message it contained: as though to demonstrate his own sense of wellbeing, he unfolded the page with a certain amount of exaggeration and held the paper to his eyes with brisk and emphatic movements.

He began to read the letter. It was brief. It ordered him, without preamble, to present himself at the magistrate's office on the instant. This tone was so unexpected that Colver saw that he must have done something to offend the magistrate; had the magistrate come to hear of the events in the alley that morning? Colver began to run through them in his mind, so far as the recollection of the bell would allow him to do, for he seemed to hear the monotonous beat of the bell sounding out concurrently with the tocsin. Had he overstepped an unseen mark? Had he abused some little act of hospitality, or taken it as a right?

Following the bailiff (who had been standing in the yard talking to the proprietor and looking in at the traveller with a certain amount of curiosity), he left the inn, and walked across the yard and through the gate into the wood. The mist lay about the river as heavily as in the streets of the village; the sounds of the one were as yet too distant to be heard, while the sounds of the other were long gone. In this short walk, less than half a mile, neither origin nor destination visible, he could only follow the bailiff, though in fact the two men walked abreast; occasionally he and the bailiff looked at each other, as though perhaps one and perhaps the other were about to speak, but they did not speak; they even seemed to find embarrassment in each other's attempts, and after a time, as though by an unspoken agreement, they turned aside from each other and continued walking in silence, some yards apart, where each to the other was only an indistinct and silent shape in the mists. Colver stood still. He paused beneath a tree, one of the tallest in this meagre wood, looking first ahead of himself and then at the bailiff, who walked with his head deeply bowed, a silent figure, hardly perceptible through the mists. Then, too, this further figure stopped in his walk, and turned towards him, as though looking at him, his hand raised, pointing ahead, fixedly, for a minute, before the mist thickened and he was gone.

With the direction of that guiding hand in his mind, Colver walked on, finding at last the metalled road beneath his feet. When he reached the house the only sounds were those of his own progress. He paused under the portico. The wide wooden door was open, propped by a flat-iron, and a cold air blew outwards, dispelling the mists a little, so that the door and the entablature above it appeared more substantial than the windows or the cellar-gratings or the high eaves.

The magistrate's wife stood in the corridor. She was dressed formally as though for an important afternoon social engagement; her dress was black, with long skirts, and her white cuffs and her collar were plain; so formally was she dressed that she might easily have been mistaken at a distance for the housekeeper. She was standing still as if she had been doing nothing except to look down the passage and to stare out of the open door, pausing while walking from one place to another, perhaps from the public rooms to the domestic quarters, in order to look at the brightness of the day. She carried nothing in either of her hands.

She told Colver that the magistrate was out and that he was not expected to return for a little while. Turning to face Colver directly for the first time, she asked him if he was prepared to wait for her husband; her voice was lively and animated. If he did wish to wait, she said, perhaps he might prefer to wait in the drawing room rather than in the corridor or the waiting room. After she had mentioned the waiting room she smiled, perhaps involuntarily, and said (in a low voice) that the thought of the waiting room was hardly to be entertained; no-one had ever waited in it, not at least during her husband's tenure, and a leaking roof some years ago had caused the collapse of some of the plaster-work of the ceiling. It had been, she said, an unpleasant enough room even before it had decayed, being disproportionately tall with windows very high in the walls; it put one in mind of a hospital side room; its overbearing interior was very typical of the age in which the magistracy had been founded. He would be very much better off waiting in the drawing room. By her tone she made it clear that it was only because of Colver's status that she had suggested the drawing room; the inflection with which she had said the very words *drawing room* indicated the privilege conferred by the suggestion, and that, as with all privileges, this would be reconsidered and speedily withdrawn if it were ever abused or taken to be a right. She led the way down the high-ceilinged passage to the door which lay at its otherwise blind end. She did not open this door, however, but, pausing in front of it, she suddenly asked, 'When do you expect to leave?'

'I must leave as soon as possible.'

'Why are you suddenly in so much of a hurry? Have you done something to be ashamed of?' said the magistrate's wife. 'When are you going? Tomorrow? The day after?'

'Tomorrow, if that is convenient.'

The magistrate's wife stood looking at him. 'I see. I suppose you acted as you did this morning in the knowledge that you would soon be gone.'

Colver, seeing that the magistrate's wife had been told an incomplete and probably malicious untruth, was at the same time unsure how he might explain the events. He had found in the past that protestations of innocence often conclude with an admission of guilt. It might after all be true that he had wished to make light of the magistrate's connection with the monastery. He said nothing. He wondered why the magistrate's wife made no effort to open the drawing room door. She appeared to be thinking to herself rather than waiting for the traveller to explain himself; there was certainly nothing indecisive in the way in which she stood, her hand resting on the brass handle of the door.

Colver laid his hands on the surface of a tall couch which stood against the dado of the wall of the broad corridor. Now that he had touched its greenish sticky oilcloth he was forced to look at it to see what he had touched. It had no arms and no back; it resembled a medical examination couch; this appearance was heightened by its hard surface and its substantial mahogany legs between which was a screw mechanism for raising and lowering the head. The magistrate's wife watched him as he examined the couch, but she made no comment on what he was doing, even when he started to turn the crank which raised and lowered the head. 'My husband,' she said, 'spends most of his working day outside. There is no mistaking that he is pleased when his duties call him out of the house. It only needs someone to come to the door, or to call on the telephone, and he tells me that he must go out on some urgent business. The next thing is that he's taking his coat off the stand and closing the door behind him.' She levered herself up on to the couch with her hands; the horsehair stuffing creaked under her slight weight. Her long and newly combed hair was still wet as though she had recently taken a bath; it hung in little tails down the back of her neck; her skin had the odour of unscented soap, far stronger for the moment than the dry and musty smell of the corridor and the damp horsehair of the couch.

'Do you know why your husband sent for me?' asked Colver.

'No, I don't.'

'Did he leave any message? He must have known that I would arrive while he was out,' said Colver, taking the letter from his pocket. 'He indicated that he wished to see me at once.'

'Well, he sometimes exaggerates the importance of things,' said the magistrate's wife. 'He makes a point of dealing with problems immediately he sees them: in that way he doesn't have them hanging over his head. He hates procrastination; he hates it above all things and as a result he sometimes acts precipitately. It would not do to suppose that he tells me his business, but it seems obvious enough to me that he wants to see you about what happened in the village this morning.' She looked down the corridor without any apparent purpose. 'He's heard about it, even the way in which you opened that letter, flourishing it about in the inn; that resigned him in his anger. There are the rumours about you in the village: you can guess many of them for yourself. They say that you can forecast the sounding of the bells, and when they will stop sounding; all the common rumours. There was even a rumour that you

had—' she smiled slightly '—received what they call a vocation. My husband, though he tries not to show it, very
naturally resents interference in these things; that's natural
when you consider his position apropos either the village or
the monastery.'

The magistrate's wife looked down the corridor; possibly
she had spoken to the traveller because she had considered it
her duty to do so; this was her house; the visitor had been
forced to wait for his appointment: Colver felt very strongly
that she had no particular wish to speak at all; if he had not
arrived she would have continued her way either to or from
the domestic part of the house. At the same time, her manner
suggested that she had no desire to hear what the traveller
might have had to say: it was as if she had made a tacit
admission that anything which they might talk about, no matter
how trivial, could only end by their talking at cross purposes.
Her voice had been without emphasis. Colver had the idea
that anything he might say would be altered, in time to come,
to suit various of her motives as they arose. He wondered how
much would be laid at his door when he had gone. He was
aware of the peculiar sense of pointless ennui which ran
throughout the magistrate's house, which, now that the magistrate was away, seemed to be insulated from the rest of the
valley. Colver wondered why the magistrate's wife remained
in the corridor: surely the easiest course for her would be to
admit the visitor to one of the rooms off the passage and to
instruct him to wait.

'I can fully sympathize with his attitude,' said the magistrate's wife, speaking after some minutes of silence, during
which they had been waiting without looking at each other.
'It is difficult to grasp the explanation of things such as the
nature of one's employer when one's own position is unclear.

'He once said, when he first became the secular agent, that
his predicament could be likened to that of a man in a small
boat. He often throws out these metaphors without thinking.
He is playing with words, not being serious at all; he is trying
to be neither lighthearted nor serious. To come back to that

165

one: he said that he was aware of the insecurity of his own stance only intermittently, in the same way that the boatman is aware of his own insecurity only when standing and reaching out for something which floats on the water. His own position becomes increasingly precarious as he reaches out to grasp the floating object; in the face of that instability the more shaky and imprecise his grip becomes. The examination of anything new must endanger one's own standpoint. On the other hand, the more unstable the stance, the more the real worth of the object is perceived. Instability, by causing an alteration of that stance, allows as though by parallax a more complete examination of objects which had previously been seen to have an unalterable conformity with each other.' She lay half-reclining on the couch. She looked at the traveller. She must have seen something in his expression, for she began to laugh, silently—in fact her expression was more of a grin—and she said, 'I thought it rather pointless when he said it. Perhaps he was trying to be amusing; he must have been, or else he would have said, straight off, "things appear to move when you change your position".' She still continued to grin, though one could not help wondering where the origins of her humour lay. 'I can't speak for my husband. One can't speak for any other person even in marriage. The way ahead has to be felt, I suppose. I don't expect the conclusions matter very much.'

'I can understand that, even after all these years, your husband would continue to be as interested in the monastery as when he first arrived,' said Colver.

'You think that, do you? Well, you're entitled to think what you like. I know that he's a hard-working man and that he has a right to play with ideas, even if they don't add up to anything much. He says that when you first view a thing such as the monastery you quickly make an impression of it; later that impression fashions a body of knowledge from all kinds of extraneous memories, all drawn from a past experience which has nothing to do with the place at all. He said that he had looked at the monastery in that light for many years without understanding what he was looking at; only recently

166

has he gained a true impression of the reality of the monastery; and, not only a true impression of the monastery, but of his own relationship to it: I say (as it were for him, for he would not say it; he would hardly mention it at all except in a manner which lacks any seriousness) that the only duties of a man in his position should be the serene planning of those forward strategies towards which every jot and gloss of his training has befitted him, the drafting of the policies for the future by his very entitlement, and not—as is unluckily the case at present —the day-to-day fighting of fires at the door. He has his future to think of and that of his family. I don't mean to talk about him behind his back; that's something I will never do. But the analogy he drew has (and bear in mind that he knows what he's about; he is as hard-headed as anyone else) a certain truthful simplicity. It is childish enough, and I am not sure that he meant it to be taken seriously, but he told me not long ago, when his own analogy must have been forgotten for many years, that, in reaching for his position as secular agent to the monastery, he has by even a consideration of that acquisition relinquished any security he might once have held in the tenure of the magistracy.'

'Has he neglected you here?' asked Colver, perhaps for no other reason than that of an uncertain idea that this question had been expected of him.

'Of course he's neglected me!' Her voice was very sharp; she had shouted. Her lips were curled in anger. The echo of her voice returned from the end of the corridor, and this seemed to anger her the more, as though the echo had been a fabrication of the house and not the result of her own voice: her humour had gone entirely, and the severity of her manner perhaps showed that what Colver had taken for humour had been due only to an inner frustration. 'Do you think I always talk like this? Who do you think I talk to day by day? What would you be like if you had no-one to talk to except those bailiffs and their wooden wives who bother about nothing other than what is going on in the village? I can't be expected to stare out of the window all day long waiting for the magistrate to come back. What sort of education do you think the children will get? What do you expect me to say?' Her anger began to subside. 'What can I do? His post is all-consuming. Not all-consuming, perhaps; it is wrong to say that, but as you know he has an exacting task in the burden he has undertaken. His duties are not light.' She suddenly looked at Colver. 'I don't know whether you know the meaning of the word "duty". Perhaps you confuse it with ambition. Do you know the tasks and the thankless problems which face someone with his responsibilities? How can you have any idea of what he has to look forward to every day? He's told me many times that, with the passing of the years, he has seen no progress at all in what he has set out to do; no progress; it is as much as he can do, to use his own expression, to prevent the affairs of both the monastery and the civil powers from slipping. He says himself that he cannot make headway in what he undertakes: he is no longer a young man; he admits to himself that he can no longer switch his mind, at a moment's notice, from the concerns of one authority to another without obvious dissimulation: how could one expect him to? It's quite clear that these things grow more difficult with time; experience is less of an asset and more of a hindrance. For all that, he is a good magistrate. He is a conscientious agent. He is a fair man. What else can he do but to attempt to hold the standards which he had once set for himself? He knows when he can afford to let them take advantage of him (and they would if they could) and when he must shout "hold!". They think that he is in an enviable position. I remember telling you about his sleeplessness, and about the fact that he has chosen, for his bedroom, one of the worst rooms in the house, above the waiting room and the corridor which leads out of it. How many of those who wait in the corridor know that? Everything, even comfort, has been sacrificed to duty! And there is that man Thibault who is always here at weekends, looking over his shoulder, perhaps with an eye to his own advancement. He has to be tolerated; what else can one do?

'You once said that you were a chance traveller. At first I thought that you were being modest, commendably so, trying in a foreign place to divert attention from yourself. I said to

168

myself: "That's the way a stranger should behave!" I'm not sure what to think now. It doesn't matter who you are.

'I had a certain respect for you. I thought that I had found something in common with you; like myself, you seemed to be someone who had just chanced to be here, but someone with enough self-control, enough diffidence, enough knowledge of local matters, to remain unobtrusive. You seemed to have enough sense to take things as they are, without reading meanings and reasons into them. You were very different from the demographers and anthropologists, whatever they were, who came here last year with their language-dictionaries and their calipers for measuring skulls. *I* couldn't understand them, so I can't think what the villagers made of them. I don't want to mistrust you—I know that my husband has a kind of faith in you—but after your behaviour in the middle of the village this morning I don't know what to think.'

'What do they say about my behaviour this morning?' asked Colver, who wished to hear the full extent of the partiality of the version which had reached the ears of the magistrate's wife.

'How dare you question me like that! Who do you think you are? You owe my husband at least the favour of standing by him when he is abused in the village: he did all that he could for you, and that is how you repay his efforts! You have shown your true colours. You would be dead if he hadn't used the telephone on your behalf. No-one of any character would let his restraint go like that the moment he decides to leave.

'And where did you learn the villagers' language? How dared you to intrude on my husband's authority?' She sat with a straight back on the couch and she pressed the palms of her hands alternately against the green oilcloth, kneading it until the horsehair creaked. 'I didn't intend to talk to you about this: it is my husband's place to speak to you. But what do you expect me to do when they come up from the village, shouting: "The sick man has a vocation!" and such things! "The sick man is guided by the monastery!", "The sick man says that the magistrate is a fraud!" Those were the words which I heard, believe me, even making allowances for the translation of what the villagers said, because they use the same words for "the sick man" as "the stranger".' She looked at him as though she knew that she had overstated her case. 'I know that these are empty rumours; I've lived here long enough to know that rumours are full of local exaggerations that take an unexpected turn when considered: all that being said, even the most unlikely of the village-rumours usually has its basis in events which have been honestly observed; I've lived here long enough to have seen that for myself.'

'I've said nothing against your husband.'

'Well, I know what I believe; you must have said enough for the implication to have been made.'

'I implied nothing against your husband,' said Colver, although he had begun to be ashamed of himself; he was well aware that his very stance was that of a truthful man caught out in telling a lie. 'You know that I can't speak the language,' he said, defending himself as best he could.

The magistrate's wife gesticulated with her hands as though to brush this aside. 'You're the fool, then, if you think that I will believe that. Haven't I seen you looking at him and obviously thinking to yourself: "if this monastery is a closed institution, then how can a man put himself forward to be its secular agent?" You thought so little of him that you didn't even try to hide the fact. Isn't that so? Why didn't you have the humility of thought to accept things in the way in which they were presented to you without this need to make superficial deductions from them? When you were climbing that hillside on the day you were invited to our picnic I could see plainly that you felt my husband to be a man looking complacently out from a fraudulent position, even while you climbed the steepest slopes. You had to say nothing. I could see it in your expression; I could tell that you were thinking, "Let me humour this man, this stutterer. Let me go along with him because he has a certain amount of parochial power." You haven't been here long enough to know anything which would let you make any kind of judgment. Who are you to divorce yourself from your own circumstances and thereby to ask questions of others? My husband demonstrated his

170

authority by his willingness to put up with your questioning and by his willingness to answer all the questions which you might have put to him. Don't you understand that it must take some courage to lay oneself open to the questions of someone unknown who passes himself off as a traveller? You must allow my husband a certain maturity: he has never asked questions of you even though it was his right and, some might argue, his duty to have done so. Why did he not question you? Perhaps he looked at you with a certain tolerance; he said to me that he thought such questions might be unwelcome to you. You never showed such reservation with even the most obvious of your traveller's questions.

'My husband was chosen for his work. He is a complicated man; his task is not an easy one and you have no authority to question it. You have been here for a few days and you seem to think you have seen enough to be able to sum the matter up in your own mind. The reality is that the magistrate has been here, in post, for years, never acting on such a precipitate urge; his position has given him something of an insight: even he, an intelligent and perceptive man in his own right, has difficulty in discerning the limits of his own authority.'

'I implied no slur upon your husband,' said Colver, who had at first been astonished at the things the magistrate's wife had accused him of, wishing only to defend himself so that he might at least leave the valley not ill-remembered; only later had he found the truth of what she had said: he had had no inkling that he had given such continued offence even from the first moment of his arrival.

'Sometimes it's possible to cast a slur on someone you have never seen by means of a wink or a raised finger,' she said. 'That kind of slyness only makes such behaviour the more despicable.' She looked directly at him. 'It's difficult enough to make a life here and to plan for the future without such interference.'

Colver, seeing at last that his good name might never be extricated from the incoherence of his illness, had, in the silence which followed her words, fallen to wondering whether isolation bred touchiness or touchiness isolation, when he was distracted by a movement amongst the hairs on the back of his hand. He looked down and saw that a insect, a lacewing, had settled on his skin; it was making its way with difficulty towards the light. He made no attempt to shake the small insect from his hand: the very transparency of its wings, the paleness of its body and the dark lustrousness of its dark eyes, each the colour of light reflected and re-reflected from gold leaf; each one of these things revealed its frailty and its lack of venom. He held up his hand towards the light. Why had this creature found its way here, to spend so much of its short life in the still air and the dust of this household? He looked back down the broad corridor and saw for the first time that the door of the magistrate's office was open. Perhaps the wind had pushed the door ajar; Colver, the last time he had looked at it, remembered remarking to himself that it had been closed, as though he had for some reason found this unexpected. Now, through the half open door he saw a fireplace, original to the house and with a cast-iron grate and a slate mantel, and above that a mirror in a rectangular frame. On the mantelpiece stood a slate-cased clock with a white enamelled dial and clear roman numerals. He imagined that he heard the ticking of this clock, though its sound could not possibly have been heard at such a distance. In the mirror behind the clock the magistrate's desk and chair and a number of wooden and green steel cabinets were reflected; on the wall was a calendar with the name of a provincial paper manufacturer on it, and a line-drawing of a paper-mill. Also reflected in the mirror was a round-arched french window, the glass of which had been recently cleaned, for the glass itself was invisible; beyond the window was the garden, prominent in which was a terraced lawn bounded by box hedges. To the side of the lawn stood four yew trees which might have been of the same age as the house itself, while beyond the lawn there was a field of mowing-grass, red with poppies; in the further hedge of this field stood a row of cypresses, the distances between them uneven: in the heat-haze which had followed the dispersal of the morning mist their foliage was a smoky blue in colour. Beyond was a reflection of the mountains. It was a hot day, and the reflected peaks were cast into an erratic wavering motion against the cold specked glass above the mantel.

The lacewing, attracted by the stream of reflected light which flooded out into the corridor from the half-open door of the magistrate's office, still made its way across Colver's hand as it struggled to reach the light's source.

'The bells are sometimes so unexpected that they can shock you into doing something which is out of character,' said the magistrate's wife, who had also been looking at Colver's hand. 'How far have they governed your behaviour, in all that you have done since your arrival? How much have you achieved by the power of your own will?'

'I don't know. I am a newcomer here, as you yourself have said. I can see how the monastery would occupy the thoughts of someone who lived here continually.'

'One's attitude to it constantly changes,' said the magistrate's wife.

A framed print hung from the picture rail in the corridor. It depicted a colonnaded square seen by afternoon sunlight. A white statue on a tall plinth stood in the square. The hands of a public clock pointed without any ambiguity to a certain hour. The sky above the clock-tower was featureless and olive-green and declined to a yellow horizon. It was a curiously empty scene, at once dream-like and impermanent, and yet claustral, confined, and pitilessly harsh, allowing no place for rest or concealment, not even for the eye of the observer, neither within the shadows of the colonnades nor in the shadow of the statue's plinth.

Colver, who had seen this print reproduced many times and in many places, looked at it as though surprised to find it hanging here, for at one time he had considered it personal to himself as though it had a peculiar and direct reference to some undepicted search of his own imagination only now brought back to mind. When the magistrate's wife saw that he was looking at the print (though he was looking at it only because he felt that he would compromise his own position by continuing to look at the magistrate's wife) she began to talk about it immediately, saying that her husband had brought the print back from his home town; a few years ago there had been an unexpected death in his family and he had been granted compassionate leave. He had seen the print hanging in the window of an art shop. He had, she said, been walking along an unfamiliar street, narrow and without pavements, and he had looked across it, mindful of the traffic: he had been trying to read the street name on the cast-iron sign: he had seen instead the print, through the windows of a slowly moving bus, a fleeting glance lacking any detail and constantly interrupted; the windows of the bus had been spattered with diagonal streaks of rain and were misty with the condensed breath of its passengers. That first sight of the print had summarized, she said, his view of the monastery. Just one view, through the traffic, had been enough to convince him of the association of the two. He had waited for a space in the traffic, and had crossed the street, entering the shop and paying for a copy of the print. He had bought it without looking at it further, and admitted afterwards that he had been embarrassed by his purchase. Later he said that he would never have acted in so precipitate a manner back in the village, excusing himself by saying 'one might be allowed to behave a little out of character occasionally, while on holiday'. He had not paid much for it; on unrolling it later he found that the reproduction was poor, the inks being imperfectly superimposed. Later he said that the superimposition of the colours in the print displayed in the shop had been poorer: when he had first seen the print from across the street, through the bus windows, the edges of the objects (he had been too distant to tell what they were) had appeared fringed with colour, like the fortification spectra of an aura. He had left the shop without inquiring the name of the artist, and, as he had no cause to go back, he never discovered it. On returning to the village he had the print framed, and had it hung for some months on the wall of his office, where he might examine it during any pause in his duties.

'How does this print remind your husband of the monastery?' asked Colver. Looking down the corridor he saw for the first time that there was a chair standing at the foot of the couch, its back against the wall. He lifted the chair by the topmost rail of its back, intending to place it where he might sit and talk to the magistrate's wife and look at the print at the same time. How light the chair was! It belonged to a woman's dressing room, for its seat and back were upholstered with purple velvet; its guard-hairs were more faded than those of the deeper pile of the fabric; this gave the chair the appearance that it had just been brought inside after being left out all night in a sharp frost. He was not sure whether it would take his weight, and he sat in it with deliberate care, ready to stand again should any of its joints show signs of instability. Because it was expected of him, he looked up at the picture again. He wondered why the magistrate, who of all men seemed to dislike uncertainties, should wish to hang it on the wall of his office. Colver repeated the question: 'Why should this print remind your husband of the monastery?'

'All this was some time ago,' said the magistrate's wife dismissively. 'He hung it in his office only for a few days. I think it got on his nerves very quickly: he's a man who likes harmony in his surroundings. I suppose we all do. He had the print taken down and put in this corridor where it would be out of the way. The drawing room—' she pointed to the door at the end of the corridor '—isn't used very much.

'I remember his mood at the time. His mood fluctuated, but he was withdrawn, and one couldn't help but notice that he was becoming preoccupied with the monastery; he would seize on all kinds of things with which to compare it; some of them seemed to me to be quite irrelevant. The print was one of the first of these comparisons. He used to say, looking at it, "Has the thought passed through your mind that it might not be a monastery at all?"'

'I know what I have been told,' said Colver, thinking that the question had been put to himself. He was anxious to leave, but could not see how this could be done without giving offence to the magistrate's wife. Besides, he perceived quite clearly that the magistrate's wife would misrepresent him to her husband on his return, and the only way he could see of forestalling this was to wait outside the house in order to be present at his arrival. 'What else could it be but a monastery? Why should anyone have thought otherwise? It is easy to see that the building of its nature could have no other purpose. Enclosure does not make for an enigma. I see no association between the monastery and this print. What other building would have a precinct wall, a gatehouse and a bell-tower, and, above all, a voluntary isolation?'

The magistrate's wife sighed as though she had listened to someone who had kept her waiting by saying something which at first had a ring of importance to it, but which after all turned out to be a worn recapitulation of an old and self-obvious theme. 'I wasn't talking about the monastery,' she said, 'I was talking about my husband's attitude to it at the time when he brought back that print.' She looked down the corridor. 'Then the print was most valuable; now he says that the print is all a contrivance, and that he doesn't wish to see it again. When he first had it framed it was the thing of the moment and all absorbing. I saw him carrying that roll of cardboard under his arm: I wondered what it was. He said that this one thing, found apparently by chance, had "as though in a blinding revelation" solved the questions which had burdened his mind. I say this to give you an idea of his preoccupations at the time. I also know that I am not behaving as I ought by telling you these things, but when one is forced to live an isolated life, one has to take advantage of circumstances when one can.'

'Why should he have found this print of any particular importance?' asked Colver, crossing his arms. He was aware that he and the magistrate's wife were playing a game, and that she knew it as well: indeed, she might have initiated it as a way of passing the time until her husband returned. Colver, for his part, recalled how successive questions had been devalued, a fact of which he had been unaware at the time he had asked them: 'How does this print remind your husband of the monastery?' 'Why should this print remind your husband of the monastery?' 'Why should he have found this print of any particular importance?' Colver sat on the frail chair, trying not to move, forced by the very chair in which he had chosen to sit to look straight ahead of him at the framed print; he dared not stand; he might have no opportunity to rest again and he felt exhausted. The magistrate's wife, tired of waiting, had begun to recline on the couch, her eyes half closed. Her hair had dried and no longer hung in strands round her delicate neck, but in bouncy coils each of which supported its own weight; she put a hand to her neck as though she wished to do nothing more than to comb her hair, alone and in the privacy of her own dressing room, and that she was only putting up with the traveller's presence because he happened to be waiting there.

'The print isn't unpleasant,' she said, looking at it as though through tired eyes. Her tone of voice suggested that even now she was unsure of the truth of what she was saying. 'He once told me that one could look at it for hours: at the time when he first had it framed, he said that, were he not busy with plans for the future, he could have conducted a debate with himself as to its meaning. "Every picture tells a story!" he said when he first watched the bailiffs hanging it in the corridor to the court-room (he had it hanging there first). Later, when it was in the office, he said that one could have conducted a debate with oneself as to why the objects are grouped as they are in the square, and why the square is as it is, and why it seems to be a certain time of day, and why the clock face tells the hour it does. One is given only the facts of the colonnaded square, the statue on its plinth, the clock, the incident light. He said, many times, that it was a picture which could be examined from many viewpoints.

'I think he had read a paragraph from an exhibition catalogue he had found in the house. The catalogue had been lent to me by the doctor's wife. When he said that this particular painting "was painted not from the viewpoint of one observer, but from the varied viewpoints of many" I knew that he was not stating his own mind: the phrase came word for word from the catalogue; I remember the very sequence of words. On balance I think he was being playful at the time, only remarking on the overuse of this phrase; he might have

177

been making gentle fun of the doctor's wife and the doctor himself. When I placed the phrase I looked for it in the catalogue and found that it referred to some picture or other in a school very different from this man's work—' she briefly glanced upward at the print '—I wish I could remember his name. One must acquire, without the realization of doing so, any explanation for one's behaviour when isolation is forced round one's life. The house was intolerable to me during the working day; even at the weekend there was no-one in the house except for myself and the servants; they of course came from the village, and it is quite natural that they would be in the habit of talking about domestic circumstances from the point of view in which I saw them. I used to paint then as a part of the daily routine; they used to take a pleasure in stretching the paper for me, and, in the mornings, they used to put out the boards in the corridor ready for the day's work. Sometimes I went out into the garden; occasionally, when it was raining, I used to take shelter in the old stone barn near the cypresses. I think that I only wished to be able to record what I felt. I think perhaps my painting was an alternative to conversation. I don't think my husband thought very much of what I produced, and certainly he was quite right: I don't think much of it myself: it is all a long time ago. He used to say that I relied too much on the exhibition catalogues which the doctor's wife sent up, and he used to read the most hackneyed phrases out aloud. He would use the print which hung in his office (when he had grown tired of it) to exaggerate his meaning. To give an example of this, I remember him once saying that if one were to draw lines along the axes of the prominent shadows of the statue and the pillars of the colonnades, one might only draw the conclusion that the square itself is lit, not by the sun, as one would naturally think at first examination, but by a luminary which, though outside the picture, is only a few hundred yards from the very canvas. What we see in the painting is an instantaneous scene, a frame of film which has been arbitrarily stopped as it has passed through the gate of a projector. We are left to consider the nature of the film which has preceded and which follows this

178

one frame, but we have only this frame to help us interpret the rest of the film. In previous frames the statue might not have been there: only the walls would have stood: the statue would have been standing, veiled in canvas: the grey shadowiness would have given way to brightness as the luminary was lit: the statue would have been liberated from its blindness by the unveiling. Only then (and these were his words) would the statue (were it alive) have seen the nature of the place it was now in. The clock tower, being behind the statue, would be invisible to it; the statue would know nothing of it except by making an examination of the faces of those, who, in travelling across the square, happened to look up at it. The statue would not associate the change in the travellers' expressions with a regular temporal progression. The statue has no idea of time: the square is lit by a single unmoving luminary. The statue, being observant, sees that the object behind him gives information welcome to some and unwelcome to others. Given the constraints imposed upon the statue, no other conclusion could have been reached had the clock-face been directly in front of it. One thinks of a statue as being a statue: this is a painted representation, and perhaps not of a statue at all; perhaps because its solitariness makes it a representation of an embodiment of self, any individuality being (as such things are perceived) a statuesque pose and a statuesque permanence. That is fair: no-one cares to deny the use of the words "dignity" and "permanence" about himself. The statue has with time become rigid and inarticulate and uniformly coloured because it dare not be otherwise: it is always in the public eye. It has its eyes open because it would be unimaginably indecorous for a memorial statue in a public place to stand with its eyes closed. It holds its hands, one of them clasping the spine of a book, in front of its body because it would be inconceivable for a statue in a public place to stand with its hands covering its face. This statue is uniquely visible: it cannot hide its face, which is doubtless what it would wish to do. The stance of the statue is moulded from two things: a sense of dignity and a sense of permanence. To assert the first its makers make a show of its victorious stance: to assert

179

the second, its makers have placed it so that its back is to the clock. To either side of the statue the colonnaded walls, seen at first as being enclaustral surroundings, become the defenders of the statue from the outer world. The statue, thus protected, adopts its statuesque pose and its statuesque dignity, standing as though it were unseen, never knowing that from the viewpoint of the observer the walls are deficient and that the statue is, after all, only the more visible if only because it is white and the shadows of the colonnade behind it are dark. Where is the corpse to which this statue is the memorial? This whited stone is unprotected even by the patina of time.'

Colver, who was about to say that he had never listened to so much nonsense before, stopped himself only because he did not want the magistrate's wife to give a bad report of him to her husband. While she had been speaking, Colver had been looking down the corridor to where the half-open door of the magistrate's office allowed the view, through the mirror, of the room within, and beyond the room the garden with the box hedges and the yew trees, amongst which the magistrate's children were playing. It was difficult to guess their game; they crouched at the top of a small bank or terrace, looking down at the earth with engrossed faces. Behind them the trees with their blue foliage were stirring in the same slight wind which now blew the office door closed again. The traveller wondered why he and the magistrate's wife had been forced to wait in this dim and unpleasant corridor, breathing the dust of the badly cleaned house, when they could equally well have been standing outside in the sunlight, or sitting in the shade of one of the yew trees, beneath which one could, until the door had closed, see a white-painted table and chairs by the side of a sundial; all these things had been clearly reflected in the mantel mirror above the fireplace of the magistrate's office.

'What are you looking at?' asked the magistrate's wife, her voice considerably more animated than when she had been talking about the hanging print.

'I was looking down the corridor,' said Colver. As he rose from the chair he felt a sudden compassion for the magistrate's

180

wife: he heard again in his mind the spiritless way in which she had chosen to describe her surroundings. As for the print, which her eyes now ignored, why had she talked about it for so long if it was of so little importance?

Perhaps she understood what he was thinking, for she said something to the effect that she had not thought about that particular picture for some time, and that it was only the fact that she had, by her present circumstances, been forced to look at it, rather than just seeing it as she had walked past it once or twice a month to see that the servant had cleaned the drawing room properly, that she remembered that it had once been one of her husband's obsessions. Colver had not heard her properly; she had been speaking in a low voice, as though she had been thinking of something else that she ought to have been doing. She followed his gaze down the corridor. 'I longed to see this place after it had been described to me: but since my arrival I have wished only to leave it,' she said, without any particular emphasis, so that Colver did not know whether she meant this stretch of corridor, this house, or this province.

'Why do you impute all your thoughts to your husband?' asked Colver. When he received no reply he hoped that she might have misheard him. He had spoken in a low voice, almost as if arranging his own thoughts by speaking aloud. He looked again at the print. He still could see no way in which its subject could be likened to the monastery. He wondered how the magistrate and his wife passed their days in winter.

On looking at the profile of the magistrate's wife—and her profile, now that her hair was dry but still uncombed gave her a girlish appearance—it was easy to see the choices which had once been open to her but which she had voluntarily put aside. 'Do you wish to stay here?'

'What do you think I would do with myself anywhere else? It's a mistake to return to any place when one has left it.' She phrased her reply deliberately, perhaps to give no reply to the question.

Colver began to speak, but coincidentally a heavy bell began

181

to toll: the sound flooded out from all the open doors in the corridor. 'This is enough,' said the magistrate's wife, in a preoccupied voice, as though the sound of the bell had put her in mind of a domestic duty which would stand no further delay. 'I can entertain you no longer.' She slid off the couch and walked down the corridor, pausing at a junction of the corridor with the opening of another passage. This opening had been hardly noticeable before, set as it was obliquely and covered by a green arras of heavy woollen material, the purpose of which might have been to separate the domestic from the public parts of the house. She turned briefly back to Colver. 'You might as well go to the waiting room if you intend to stay until my husband arrives.'

Colver felt in his pocket for the envelope which still held the letter. How ever had he the conceit to imagine, when he had first held it in his hands, before he had opened it, that the magistrate's wife had sent it? He had reached the green arras; he turned back a fold of the heavy material so that he might see along the length of passage which led to the private rooms. The corridor he looked out on was, apart from its orientation, very little different from the public passage in which he stood. The magistrate's wife was so distant that it was difficult to make out anything of her except that she was a receding figure: one could see that she was walking as though in time with the periodicity of the tolling bell, but that was in itself not surprising: whenever a bell sounded, everyone in the village fell into step with it after a time.

The next day, having obtained permission from the magistrate, he left the village.

PART TWO

XI

Colver, the magistrate, the right arm of his coat empty, stood in the corridor which ran from the side of the magistrate's house to the public rooms. He stood in front of the heavy arras which separated the public from the private rooms of the house. The air in the corridor was faintly smoky, as though someone within the private part of the house had not long lit a fire in a grate with a poor draught. The corridor was silent. He saw (he had not noticed this on his one previous visit) that the floor of this passage was flagged with wide bluish-white stones joined together in an irregular bonding. The stones of the corridor had become guttered by the tread of those who had walked over them, as though they were memorial stones with effaced inscriptions. Now the corridor was a dead and empty place. The only sounds were those of the driver and the guard as they carried the magistrate's belongings into the house. It was early in the evening and the sun was on the point of the mountain. The passage door was open and the rays of the sun fell at a slant through the open rectangle to strike the floor obliquely. The light, cast back to the ceiling by the smoothness of the flagstones, was reflected in various ways by the hollows and scallops, its rays converging to form two irregular curves which met at a ragged point, the lines of light being seen clearly in the thin coal-smoke which hung in the air.

The warm pleasure of standing in a silent place overcame Colver. Until a moment ago the irregular lateral motion of the conveyance had still made him distrust his sense of balance: the ceaseless sound of the conveyance's onward progress had still sounded in his head. On a moment and without reason the sensation of movement and the sound of phantom travel stopped, though why at that moment he did not know; he had put himself to nothing of any importance; he had diverted his mind into no particular channel: and when he looked up, the vertigo of travel gone, he found himself alone in the silent corridor. There was no need to shout to make himself overheard, and no need to grasp the strap continually with his single hand to keep a sense of balance.

He had followed the advice of wearing old clothes for the important journey and he still wore these travelling clothes. Now, in the silence of the corridor, he was for the first time certain that the journey was over. He looked along the corridor, first in one direction and then in the other, pleased to be in a stationary place. The inns at which they had stopped, the names curiously repetitive, a succession of lamp-lit rooms alike only in conceding the need for a temporary halt to travel, had each imparted a sense of movement so uneasy that every lamp-lit dawn, following a night in half-sleep, had been a relief in that there was the certainty that, after an uneaten breakfast, a meal in name only, uneaten and probably unprepared, the hands of the black-cased regulator clock would signal a return to the conveyance and a return to the onward commission of the journey.

He took a deeper breath on recalling the jolt of departure and was aware for the first time of the scent of the rarefied coal smoke.

He stood with his back to the green arras and looked down the corridor towards the magistrate's room and the public parts of the house, and then, drawing aside the curtain with the fingers of his left hand, he looked along the length of the other empty corridor which led towards the private rooms. There was no difficulty in choosing which part of the house should be visited first: the private quarters were, after all, only there for domestic purposes, while the offices were certainly more important. On the other hand, so much had been left in the house by every previous occupant that perhaps the best thing to do would be to walk round the house, opening the door of each of the residential rooms in order to seek an impression of their state. He walked down the corridor to the magistrate's office. This did not have his predecessor's name on its panels, only the two words 'The Magistrate' in roman print. Inside the room, which gave the appearance of being smaller than it had been when he had last seen it, the slanting sunlight entered the windows and fell upon the polished linoleum floor. The room was, apart from the diminution of its size, very much as he remembered it. There was a fire burning in the grate: it must have been this which had earlier produced the smoke which had blown out into the corridor; the fire had not long been lit, for the coal had hardly quickened. Colver thought at first that the housekeeper must have lit it; the fire looked like a housekeeper's fire, efficient but economical of kindling: on the other hand, the house-keeper would hardly have jurisdiction beyond the domestic quarters. Perhaps one or other of the bailiffs had lit this fire. He had called it economical but in fact it was nearly out: the coal had not caught but the wood had burned away. The cast-iron surround was stone cold to the touch. All living flame left the grate but for another more minute diminishing amounts of smoke continued to rise sluggishly over the fire-back and into the flue. The magistrate looked across the air of the room, through the faint haze of coal smoke to the window.

Various dates on the paper-merchant's calendar were circled in a brownish-red ink, all dates in the past and signify-ing nothing for the future. The desk was still covered by a mass of papers.

Of all things he was grateful that the motion and the sound of travel had stopped. He looked down at the fire: it gave the false impression, although all the kindling had been burned beneath it, that the grate had been newly laid, and that only a match would be required to bring it into life.

The driver's footsteps, which he now recognized from hearing their sound on the many inn yards at which they had stopped on the journey, sounded on the flagstones of the

185

corridor. He heard the hesitancy of the man as he paused at each doorway to look briefly into each of the rooms, and he heard the sound of the arras being pulled back. The driver continued his walk down the corridor: he had seen the half-open door of the magistrate's office and his walk was direct.

The magistrate stood in front of the fire, the tired attitude of someone who has travelled a long way clinging to him as though it were a garment, the manner of someone who has no need to shake off the beginnings of sleep and certain fatigue.

'We have finished, sir, I think.' The driver stood at the threshold of the room. His voice had a downward inflection. He paused in the corridor.

'I am grateful to you,' said the magistrate, remembering as if by the driver's presence the many halts and interruptions on the journey. 'Will you have a drink?'

'No, I don't think so, sir.'

'I can't dismiss you like that! Come and have a drink!'

'The guard's already gone to the inn.'

'You'll be staying the night there?'

'It seems as if we must.' The driver still stood at the door. His face was perceptibly less lined than it had been during the halts of the journey, but certainly he, too, was exhausted by the ordeal of past travel. 'I've met the housekeeper,' he said. 'In the house.'

Colver felt his gratitude from his heart, but he could do no more than repeat himself. 'I'm grateful to you!' He began to feel with his left hand in a right-hand pocket for money: he had reckoned, at each drawback in the journey, each hesitation at a fork, how much he might give the driver when the destination was reached without appearing to be either nig-gardly or over-generous, but that sum seemed insufficient now that the journey was accomplished. He stood in the room, still with his back to the fireplace, and he looked at the money in his hand.

The driver, seen as a shadow in the corridor, held up his hand, perhaps seeing the awkwardness of the magistrate trying to reach his own pocket. 'None of that, sir! The journey was

186

more difficult than I might have imagined! That is all there is to be said, The road—' He had been leaning against the back wall of the corridor, but now he stood in the middle of the passage, looking towards the open side door; his face was illuminated with the reflected light. '—the road was all too frequently decayed and often the metalling was half gone. That's all there is to it.'

The magistrate listened to his tread as he walked down the corridor and out through the door, and then out along the path which ran by the side of the house. He still stood in front of the grate which had never caught fire. The room was not cold. Perhaps the fire had been made not so much to give out heat to the room as to give a welcome, the first thing that a newcomer would see on entering the room—and why should this office be heated? Surely there were no matters in the civil parish which pressed to be started tonight.

The public end of the building, which was sequestered in the wood of small thorn oak trees, retained the damp of the mists of the night. The corridor, empty of furnishings, had the atmosphere of a stable. When the driver had coughed the sound echoed. For some reason the echoes were the echoes heard in bare outbuildings and farm offices, or other rooms which are always damp and which retain throughout the whole year the cold temperature of the winter season and where the breath always smokes.

He stood in silence, looking round the room. When he had seen it for the first time, from the corridor, he had thought what a friendly and welcoming room it had been, with its fireplace, its mirror set in an overmantel, its slate clock, the reflections of the desk, the cabinet, the calendar on the wall even, the reflected view through the window: all that had been pleasant. Then he had been in the company of the magistrate's wife. When he had first seen the magistrate's house he had thought that there must be a harmony between the atmosphere of the house and the individuality of her character: he had thought it wonderful that this should have been so: he had been pleased to stand in the corridor of the house, talking to her and looking down the corridor at the closed doors which led to rooms whose interiors had been closed to him. He now knew that he had only associated her with the house because she had by chance happened to live there. There was nothing more than that. The stretch of the corridor was damp and empty. This room, which he had never truly seen before, and then only as a reflection in the mirror, was no more than a cold room seen by the light of the end of the day.

He saw on the desk a broad paper marked out in columns familiar to him: even the feel of the paper's texture was familiar. He knew the document well without the need to read the heavily printed words; the weight of the print on the paper was enough to enable him to recognize it. The columns towards the right-hand margin were too broad for their purpose while the columns to the left, the earlier ones, were too narrow: those required to complete the form, unquestioningly following its construction, might in their obedience fill the broader columns with unasked for detail which clouded their intention, while, on crowding the narrower columns, they might truncate the information they set down and so destroy its sense. The writing on this form consisted of several lines which, although they were related to them in no way, kept to the compartments of the original printing as though the writer's wish had been altered at every point by the nature and the appearance of what he had chosen to write upon. Colver, seeing that he was wasting time, was equally well aware that there was no firm starting place in the examination of his duties, only a place where he might say to himself 'It is reasonable to begin here', just as, in the future, in the absence of a firm place at which to finish, he might say to himself 'It is reasonable to end here'. He studied the paper, which he might so easily have taken for granted. The corners of the sheet of paper were as dog-eared and as rounded as the page of a valued book which has been bound and re-bound many times, constantly read and constantly referred to; often quoted and read out: there was dried spit and dried ink from brief pen-marks on the page and the pressure of a thumb-nail, where the sheet had been held in the hand; the page itself was creased and recreased and the surface was roughened with fingerprints. There were uneven circular spots on its surface, as though someone had stood outside with it while rain had been falling. Yet, for all that, the surface of the page was not dirty: the person or persons who had looked upon it as being of importance had had clean hands. The columns of figures had clearly meant something to them, but now the information was beyond interpretation. He allowed the sheet to fall to the surface of the desk. For some reason the shape and texture of the paper, when seen from a distance, reminded him of the peculiar dimensions of those papers which had required him to submit his appraisal of his own character and which had instructed him on the tenure of his present and final post; in fact this paper was in almost all respects identical with those. He looked up at the shelves, searching the grey spines of the books for something he could recognize. The books had not been touched for many years, though the volume numbers were disordered. By the window, where the light was greatest, the titles on the spines had faded, while by the door the titles were seen but could not be read because of the shadows and the bad light. Someone working regularly in this room would learn to recognize the contents of each book by the act of looking up from the desk, knowing where to find a particular book by the length and width of its spine, its colour, the roundedness of its binding. He saw himself as the magistrate, at some time during the intermediate years of his tenure, wishing for guidance and looking up towards the book which for the moment had taken on a certain salience of meaning, bringing the required information to mind only by the act of looking up at the spine: just to imagine it would be enough, just the fact of bringing the spine to the forefront of the mind: it is impossible to be cognizant of anything except by a continual jolting of memory and all that is to provide an aid to memory: on reading an arbitrarily chosen section from one of these books, so the thought passed through his mind, one can be easily led to think that one has read it before, and, indeed, that one is its author: the more familiar the juxtaposition of familiar words, the more one's own authorship is seen in each phrase. A moment of vague abstraction, and there it is! The swiftly chosen page is untruthfully drawn before the forefront of the mind to stand comparison with events of the present to which it has no real point of correspondence, only a resemblance which is constructed to seem more certain than it is: the similarities which allow events to slide one into another without shock are not produced by informedness, but by the deft exercise of an unseen sleight of hand in the swift choosing of the page: there is a moulding of both memory and perception as though each would be forced to answer to the other and to be so recognized: one would only have to look at the spines in order to know how cramping and inappropriate would be the examination of such guides.

He sat at the desk and laid his arm on the leather surface. Beyond the sleeves of the magistrate's coat the cuff of his white shirt was stained and grey with travel. His hand was dirty: he looked from his hand to the paper: he had, in touching it, out of curiosity, made indelible marks upon it, seen now as the marks of a hand acting from curiosity rather than one acting with purpose from a sense of utility. He looked down at his hand. The indented scar on the first finger had grime in it. He had no idea where there might be a washbasin. There were cloakrooms in this, the public part of the house, but the magistrate's wife had said that these cloakrooms were disused, and that the water had been turned off because of the danger of burst pipes in winter.

He looked towards the door and the vacant passage beyond it. He had left his case of travelling documents in the hallway at the front of the house: all these things, he surmised, should be together in the office. He left the office and walked down the corridor and out of the house by the side door. It was almost night outside. The front door was open, as it had been left by the driver and guard. He closed the door, bolting it behind him. His case stood where he had left it on the hall floor. As he bent to grasp the handle of the case he saw a letter lying on the tiles beside the case; the address and the stamp were facing downwards. The tiles on which it lay, as though it had been dropped, were squares, rectangles and triangles of deep blue, red, and ochre, laid to form a weaving pattern which possessed within itself a movement which suggested that the floor was uneven. The envelope, lying on the floor, was white: had it been of one of the colours of the tiles he would not have seen it: its shape and its dimensions, the chance position in which it had happened to fall, had matched exactly those of the tile which lay beneath it. When he stooped to grasp the letter he wished that he had left the door open: he had seen the envelope lying by the side of his case before he had closed the door, and at first he had taken it to be a tile, perhaps a recent replacement of a cracked tile, lighter in colour and less worn than the original, a fragment of the house itself: when he had closed the door the diminished light had allowed him to see only the patch of lighter colour which he remembered being in a certain position. When he stooped he was almost assured in his own mind that his fingers would encounter nothing but the smooth surface of a light-coloured tile set into the floor.

At the moment he entered the office, which was now in almost complete darkness, he heard the sound of footsteps in the hall. Someone, walking up the passage, carried a storm-lantern which, as it swung, cast a fluctuating circle of yellowish light across the walls. This newcomer wore heavy rubber-soled boots and walked with an unsteady tread. 'Did I see you with a letter?' he called, hardly before he was seen, his voice hoarse and anxious as though he had spoken the first words which had come into his mind on a sudden impulse. Colver, the magistrate, finding such a sense of familiarity in the sound of the stumbling, heavy tread in the corridor, and the echo of the sound, and the splash of water in which the newcomer trod as he made his progress, his hand touching the painted wall, his fingers running over the paint, as though in places the plaster work was solid but in parts hollow, though the solidities and hollowness could not be told apart other than by listening to the sound: he found such a sense of familiarity in the swinging of the lantern, a shepherd's lantern, which was reflected from the painted walls up and down the corridor, now momently hidden behind the newcomer's body, now glowing in front of him, illuminating with its red light the buttons of his coat: Colver was so struck by a sense of familiarity that he imagined himself to be in the presence of his father or of his uncle, or in the presence of one of his uncle's friends: even the voice was familiar: but, as the newcomer continued ever more slowly to press his way along the corridor towards the door, that sense of the familiar fled, until the man regained the attributes of one who has never been seen before. The newcomer, as though sensing this, paused: in his walking his gait had been fumbling and slow, not, as Colver had first thought, because he was infirm, but rather as though he were unfamiliar with the clothes on his back and the boots on his feet, the sound of which Colver had found familiar a moment ago; now the man, who stood in the centre of the corridor in an attitude of silent titubation, as though from long travel, seemed in his uncertainty to find even his own presence unfamiliar to himself, for the light of the lamp was yet redder than it had been and the air was filled with the smell of a wick burning without oil.

'Who are you?' asked the magistrate, quite startled out of his introspection; he had thought himself to be alone in the house.

'Did I not see you with a letter?' said the newcomer again, ignoring the demand for identification, his voice louder and more assured than might have been expected from a man who seemed to find difficulty in standing upright. He hid as though for warmth the dying lantern beneath his long coat, or pluvial, which might once have belonged to a priest or to a magistrate: perhaps it was he who had brought the water into the corridor.

The magistrate looked at the letter in his hand and saw that he had made a foolish mistake: he had never looked at the address, his mind being at the time filled with cloudy and contradicting thoughts. 'I cannot continue making these foolish mistakes!' he said to himself. 'So you are the demographer, are you?' he said, standing at the door of the office. 'I never knew of your existence.' He held out the letter: each turn in this brief chain of events might have been designed to illustrate a point not to be readily apprehended but which lay behind the forefront of his mind.

'If you wish to call me a demographer,' said the man, the tone of his coarse voice amused as he looked round the room behind Colver as though he found its type familiar. His hair and the shoulders of his raincoat were wet and beads of moisture clung to the glass of his lantern. For the first time the rain was heard against the glass of the dark window. 'What are you doing with my letter?'

'This is the first day of my appointment,' said the magistrate, holding out the letter.

The old man looked at the letter as though suspicious of its having been opened and then resealed.

'So you are the magistrate!' said the old man, as though connecting two unrelated facts for the first time. 'Surely as a magistrate you can recognize your own name.' He raised the lantern to the level of his face and held the letter to it as though to see through the envelope at whatever was within. He looked at Colver, his face cast in shadow by the letter although the lantern was so close to his face. He put the letter in his pocket and lowered the lightless lantern. He stood in the doorway and looked down at the dead fire in the grate. 'The housekeeper hid away the coals I'd been saving up.' He looked at Colver as though he might later say that he had never begrudged the coals for the fire, or as though he might bring the subject up again with a remonstrative eye; his look at the dead fire had been one of someone who views a breach of trust with a certain forgiving indulgence. 'The housekeeper said that she would get you something to eat an hour after you arrived.' He looked at Colver. 'She said that to me. I suppose she means what she says.' He looked at the grate again, and then at Colver's face, as though to fix as best he could his features in his mind's eye, and then turned away, sorrowfully, and began to walk down the corridor, continuing into the building, the light from his lantern extinguished.

Colver, on thinking over this encounter, in his office, was unsure of whether it had taken place, or whether he had ever held a letter in his hands. He stood in the passage. His own

193

voice made echoes indistinguishable from those which had been raised by the demographer's voice: when he ran his fingers over the plaster of the wall, as the old man had done, he heard the same little sequence of solidities and hollownesses. He closed the door, locked it, put the heavy key in his pocket, and left the building, with the intention fixed in his mind that he must go to the inn to ask where the housekeeper was and who this unsteady man had been.

XII

The inn yard was dark. A widening wedge of lamplight, cast from the half-open door, fled across the yard, magnifying the unevenness of its surface. The wedge of light lost its colour and its intensity as it widened. The inn's silence enhanced the gentle and periodic breathing of the noises of the wood. The muted sound of the river, heard on a long and intermittent front, dominated the other sounds of the night by its distant persistence.

The magistrate pushed open the door of the inn and stood at the threshold. The room was empty. It had been recently cleaned; a broom stood propped against one of the tables, the three lamps casting shadows of its irregular handle. Someone was walking about across the boards of the floor above, pausing and retracing his steps as though even at this hour he was occupied in moving furniture from one place to another. The counter was bare. The empty trays which earlier in the day had stood propped on the counter were stacked in the corner by the door. The air was moist as though every item of furniture had been cleaned only a few minutes before with a wet cloth.

The sound of people sitting at supper came from the curtained door behind the counter; it must be the proprietor's family; the magistrate, remembering that the proprietor and his wife took their evening meal at this hour, opened the flap of the counter and pulled aside the curtain which hung in the doorway.

The driver and the guard, alone in the room, stopped eating

and turned to look at him; both held their knives in their hands as though they had a moment before not been eating but comparing the provenance of their eating irons. Colver, who had never seen this inner room before, looked from the door to the table, standing in the doorway, beneath the lintel, still holding the curtain in his hand, looking at the familiar domestic furniture. The small framed photographs which were fastened in groups on the wall, the plaster reliefs of two horses, their heads facing away from each other across the width of the room, the high open-fronted dresser with dinner-plates, all of them having in common the reproduced picture of a saltmarsh seen by a clear evening light in which could still be seen the tails of a recent storm; all these things told more about the circumstances of the proprietor and his wife than anything Colver had yet seen. The centre of the room was filled by a long trestle table. The driver and the guard had put down their knives. Their hands almost touched as they bent over their meal, a thick-crusted pie in an oval dish. A single oil lamp hung over the table; the pie-dish had been placed directly beneath it and stood in the shadow of its receiver. A spoon stuck up out of the dish, half-turned in the substance of the pie, as though one man after another had used it to load his plate. The two men, both becoming aware of the presence of a third person at the same moment, looked to see who was standing in the shadows by the curtain, and the guard, recognizing the magistrate, began to stand.

'You must not get up,' said Colver, looking into this room which he had never seen before.

The driver, still chewing his mouthful, sat at ease in his chair, his legs apart, his hands resting on his knees. The guard, looking at the door and then at his meal, caught the driver's glance and sat down again and resumed his eating. He ate as if he were very hungry and as though someone were about to come and take the plate away; he held the side of the enamel plate forcefully with the fingers of his left hand. The shadow of his head was stationary against the pattern of the paper on the wall of the room.

'Did you find the housekeeper?' The driver's voice, drowsy

and replete, still had its heavy humour and its welcome familiarity.

'I was told about her. I was told to expect dinner in an hour.'

'What did I tell you?' The driver looked under the lamp at the guard. He began to eat again. 'You won't want to eat a last meal with us, then.'

'Where's the proprietor?'

'The landlord and his wife have gone to bed. They was here with us until half an hour ago. His wife looked exhausted. She was almost asleep. She excused herself; one could see that she was very tired; the landlord, who livened slightly at first, became almost equally as exhausted and took himself off to bed. He looked as though he were about to fall asleep with his head on the table.' The driver stretched himself in an attitude of one who is content with what he has eaten. 'They work very hard here.' The affability in his voice suggested that, in the company of his fellows, he might have been regarded as something of a wit. 'Did you see the housekeeper?'

'No.'

'Come into the room, sir, come in.' He shifted himself so that he could look round the lamp at Colver. 'Close the door, sir.' The lamp chimney, not far from his face, was reproduced as a vertical image in each of his eyes. 'She'll be there. Small. Oldish. Dressed in black. They always are. That kind of housekeeper is always unpopular in her own village. She will have worked out her time under many an official.'

The magistrate stood at the end of the table, leaning forward, his hand grasping the back of a kitchen chair. All the chairs round the table were different. There was no sound in the room except for the creak of the driver's and the guard's chairs as they leaned forward to resume their eating. 'Are these housekeepers so alike that you can make generalizations about them?' said the magistrate, speaking out of form, as if for something to say, for he was very tired himself, though he had only recognized his own tiredness when the driver had spoken of the exhaustion of the proprietor and his wife.

'So you think you can't make generalizations about them?

197

Well, that's as may be, but there is no more to making generalizations about such things than travelling with your eyes open and looking for clues and pointers which others would miss; the observant are, I put this to you for your comment, allowed to make generalizations.' He sighed a drowsy sigh of counterfeit exasperation. 'Where do you find farsighted drivers nowadays? How do they recruit the men you see in the service now?' He looked at the guard, who was watching the magistrate, and raised his eyes briefly. 'What do you find nowadays but drivers and couriers who have a bored look, and who treat each journey as though it led nowhere but to those places with names already familiar to them: I tell you this,' he said, looking at the tines of the fork, worn down to the brass, which he held in his own hand. 'Such men are increasingly common: one can tell the vehicles which are in the charge of such drivers: it is as though they as well as the horses were blinkered: the journey to them is nothing more than bad weather between the doors of staging-posts.' He looked up at the magistrate. 'You are a rarity! You—I couldn't fail to notice this; I mentioned it to the guard—you took an interest in your journey, for all your disability. It's a pleasure to drive for a passenger who looks out of the window to see the things that pass him by. It is when I do the driving for those who talk amongst themselves, as though they were not travelling, that I wish I were at the end of the journey. One waits outside the doors of the building and they appear singly in the darkness of the corridor. From the driver's seat one is on the same level as the top of the steps of the building, and, on looking in, it is possible to see the passenger walking down the corridor a long time before he stands beneath the portico. The vehicle is one in a line of many—sometimes there are as many as twenty under the portico—and the porter on looking at the destination-board indicates the correct one to the passenger. The porter only wears a light suit to show that he is a porter: the old porters have grown used to this; they are sturdy, red-faced men, usually, with thick silver hair: they eat and drink a great deal to make themselves fat and to keep themselves warm in winter when they are on this particular duty.

The younger ones, new to it, thin rakes of men, blow on their hands when they think no-one is watching them, and, standing in the snow and almost crying in the cold, putting their fingers in their mouths, they are hardly able to articulate their voices when the passenger asks which is his.

'These passengers may travel singly; they may travel together in groups. Sometimes one never knows how many passengers one has until one's first stop. The first thing they do when the porter closes the door on them is to pull the blinds down.

'I am a different man when I am on the road. The ways are open; one looks to the left to see the plain and the ribbon of the river; as the streets of the town are left there is acre after acre of market gardens. The glasshouses rise from the fields in long terraces; then, over the flat land, where to either side are field after field of brussels sprouts or cabbage, the fields so long that, even when seen from the position of the driver's elevation, the further fences are lost in distance. All this is lost on the passenger who hardly perceives his journey. He has drawn down the blinds, and he can see nothing of the country through which he passes: he wouldn't know where he was, were he not able to smell the sprout fields at either side of the road. Often, in fact, at the same moment that I first smell the fields, there is a rattle as the passenger pushes up the windows as though he preferred the fustiness of the carriage to the smell of the cabbage-fields, and would keep the smell out. They have no patience. They act precipitately over everything. They make no allowances for anything. The sound of the closing windows and the rattle of the blinds are reminders of their presence, and I feel a disquiet. And I look ahead—ahead there is a glorious transition. We climb up out of the river valley, up the broad road which climbs slowly along the shoulders of a sandy ridge to an open plain where the hills stretch for further than the eye can see; the road ahead is seen at each summit: the road is straight and there is no deviation in it. I do not know why that country should always take me like that. Perhaps it is just the straightness of the road. When I am on it I have no wish to stop.'

'How old are you?' said the magistrate.

'Nearly fifty,' said the driver, who had to think about the question as though his age were of no importance to him.

'Have you always felt an exhilaration about that stretch of road?' asked the magistrate, who associated the peculiar ecstasy of travel with the years of his own youth.

'Always. Ever since I stood beside the road as a child.'

'How long have you been a driver?'

'Since I was given the opportunity to leave the stables.'

'You say that when the passenger closes the blinds and the windows you feel a disquiet. Why is that?' asked the magistrate, still leaning forwards with his hand resting on the back of the chair.

'The sense of dragging a blind weight,' said the driver. 'In the drawing of the blinds and the closing of the windows there is a denial of sight. The behaviour of such a passenger shows that he believes that vision is a distraction. As he draws the blinds I can look behind and catch a sight of his gloved hands. As for the vehicle: the very vehicle draws as though it were overburdened; at the moment when one sees the nature of the passengers the vehicle slows as though a brake were being applied; it is like driving up a perpetual incline. That's all. You get used to it. There is nothing as pleasurable as fast journeying in solitude, where there is nothing to interrupt sight or hearing.' He looked at the magistrate. 'You showed a considerable interest in your surroundings.' He transferred his gaze to his colleague, who was still sitting silently while looking at the magistrate.

'Do you often carry people like myself?'

'Very often.'

'This is the first time I have taken up such an appointment.'

'And you are not above looking for advice!' said the driver with a genuine expression of approval. 'That's very good! You say you were told that your dinner would be ready for you in an hour, but at the same time you haven't seen your house-keeper. Who told you? Was a note left, or something like that? I wouldn't be surprised. People take unusual stances in the provinces after a few years; what might have once passed as

200

slight eccentricities become ingrained. I once knew of a housekeeper who would communicate with the official she worked for only by notes left in a certain place, drawn upon slates: she had lost her voice altogether, and would bark like a dog when spoken to.' He fixed the magistrate with his peculiarly candid eyes. 'It's quite true,' he said, as though accusing the magistrate of doubting his word, 'I saw it for myself: the housekeeper stood at the side-door with a piece of hessian in her hand, barking like a dog.

'That's of no matter. It's only a good story. It might, this barking, have been a joke between them. How did you discover that dinner would be ready in an hour's time? Was it something like that? Was it written down somewhere?'

'No,' said the magistrate. 'I was told in the house.' He found that he was most reluctant to mention the unsteady man, who had appeared so suddenly, and had spoken so discordantly, and had gone as suddenly as he had come, that the magistrate could easily have believed him to have been no more than a phantom, the result of the stress of travel, an apparition which had arisen in his own mind.

'So, someone in the house told you. What else did he say to you?'

'Nothing very much,' said Colver, falling into the driver's manner of speech. 'He told me that a letter I held was his property, that my dinner would be ready in an hour, and that the coals which were burning in the grate were his own.' The magistrate was still reluctant to bring himself to describe the unsteady man or to mention his initial familiarity and his final strangeness. The more he thought about his meeting with him, the more unreal this meeting seemed: if he were to continue to think about it, the more unreasonable his own behaviour would seem.

The driver, who had been watching every nuance of the magistrate's expression with great care, began to laugh, and turned to the guard. 'What do you think of that?' he cried, as though neither of them had ever heard of such a thing before.

Colver wondered what the driver and the guard had been talking about before he had entered the room.

'I know what I read in the papers,' said the driver, the beginnings of indignation in his voice. 'I don't believe half of what they say, but they must have their basis in fact: they say that you only recognize the crudest of imposters for what they are,' said the driver.

'Where did you find this idea of the imposter?' asked the magistrate, expecting either the driver or the guard to take a newspaper from a coat-pocket.

'From my sister. She used to tell me about them when I was a child. I didn't disbelieve her then,' said the driver, 'and what she said is confirmed by the things one reads daily in the papers. Listen to this.' He took a newspaper from under the pie dish, where it had been placed to prevent the heat from damaging the table. In the steady lamplight he turned the pages. He began to read out in a loud sonorous voice: '"Imposture wishes a metamorphosis; its only wish is to become its subject: it copies and emulates it tirelessly, imitating it as far as it can until no-one can tell the difference between the subject and itself, except that the imposter acts blindly and without apperception." That is only what my sister said in simpler language; she used to frighten me with such stories.' He ignored the echoes of his own voice and looked at the page again, shaking it with his hand to remove the creases which the heat of the dish had made in it. '"The imposter within,"' he shouted in the same loud voice, without regard for those who might have been asleep upstairs, '"makes demands loudly, appealing to whatever seems the strongest argument of the moment; the arguments of duty are particularly likely to be chosen."

'Don't you see the truth of this?' The driver looked at the magistrate, who for the first time saw that his opinion was being sought as if to settle an argument between the driver and the guard. 'When I am travelling along a straight road, at speed, without any principle or emotion dictating my travelling, without orders, without duty, in a solitary onrushing, I feel and I recognize the feeling as likely to be spurious, for the moment of travel, that the inner imposter has been purged from me, and, for the moment, has been left behind. And what am I? I am only a driver of no importance—I am not a fool; I know that I am never sent to places of importance—I have no belief in the importance of what I do. Within me I know only that I must reach the end of the journey, and that a staleness will overcome me; there are limits to all straight roads. That's what I believe.

'When, during this last few days, you journeyed with me, I thought to myself, "there is a man who will not give in easily"; now you tell me that you have been challenged on your own doorstep by someone who claims your property for his own.'

The magistrate was aware that he had not told the driver the whole truth. He had regarded the driver (and had from time to time so addressed him) as a servant for the extent of the journey, though he had not recognized this at the time. The driver, who throughout the journey had acted with a practical stolidity, obeying such commands as had been given him, inasmuch as they did not impede the course of the journey, and hiding his feelings, now, at the end of the journey, unable to restrain himself any longer, expressed these feelings in an oblique way, giving vent to indignation without apportioning blame. Colver saw the extent to which he had misjudged the driver; what a valuable man he had been; even now that the journey was finished and he was no longer responsible to the magistrate, he still held dear to himself— perhaps because of the very difficulties of the journey—a wish to help his former master: but, because the magistrate had spoken of the unsteady man as though he were an allegorical figure, he had told his tale in such a way as to communicate nothing; indeed, as he spoke and while he paused and as he continued speaking again he seemed to be well aware that he was making himself appear more foolish with every word he uttered and every pause in which he stood silent: the magistrate's lack of forthrightness had caused him to speak sincerely but indirectly to a man who did not exist, but who might have been, as it were, a base and preremptory man who stood looking (so to speak) over Colver's shoulder.

'I want no misconception of what I say,' said the driver, no longer looking at the guard but referring to him from time to time as though he might later require corroboration of his statements. 'I like to speak baldly and to the point; I'm an experienced man in my duties. Otherwise I would rather not speak at all: I would rather go my own way and take a meal if it is offered, or forgo and imagine it if it is not: it's all one to me: I find what I want to eat somewhere.' He smiled as though at himself and looked down at the dish which contained the remainder of the meal, and his look conveyed the renewed pleasure of satiated appetite.

Colver looked round the room. When he had left the village, after his illness, he had taken his journey with the knowledge, now seen to be quite spurious, that he had grown during his sojourn to understand the valley well: he had thought he had looked beyond himself as if to judge whether this was so. Now he saw that there was no such easy conclusion; the valley was as remote from him as it had ever been. This room, which he had never seen before, even though the slant of the stairs, up and down which he had constantly passed, occupied a corner of it, had never existed even in his imagination while he had lain upstairs in his sick-bed saying to himself that he knew every view from the window, every distortion of which the window-glass was capable, every crack and bulge in the glass: that, of all people, by reason of the heightening experiences of his illness, he knew at least the circumstances under which he was confined.

'What are you thinking of?' asked the driver, speaking to the magistrate but looking at the tall dresser which held the differently patterned plates. One plate in particular caught his eye, a plate with a broad patterned rim, and which depicted in its bowl a flat marsh on which was built a windmill with broad, sweeping sails. His manner was affable and indulgent; the way in which he looked at the things in the room showed that he was familiar with them, or, if not with them, as he appeared not to be, then with their type. He looked at the magistrate. 'What does one imposter say to another? What can one say to that?'

'The words "imposter" and "it" are yours; that's a fact,' said the magistrate, feeling that a familiar game had been played on him, and feeling also that the driver had after all been a more dependable and reliable man when he had been treated as a servant. 'The man in the house who demanded his property: I was unsure of him: I took him to be a demographer.'

'Ah! You never said that,' said the driver, looking away from the magistrate as though embarrassed by this admission, staring again at the plate on the dresser. 'A demographer would be a likely enough person to be found in the house of a provincial magistrate. I thought you were talking in parables.' He put his hands on the surface of the table, and looked at them with a moment's silence as he saw at last that he and Colver had been talking at cross purposes. 'I remember an official in a village in this neighbourhood,' he said, speaking as though to hide his embarrassment. 'I shall not name him: indeed I do not remember his name, though I recall his household well; the very fact of bringing it to mind sets before me the sight of the brick walls of the estate offices and puts the dust of the stable-yard beneath my feet: I can see the approach to his household, in my mind's eye, as it was first seen from the shoulder of the hill. I do not remember his name, but the approach to his household is in my mind's eye. I was so well known there, at one time, that a little dog, a little stable-dog, a bitch as I recall, lying in the dust between the stable gates with a vigilant brown eye, on seeing I suppose it would have been my shadow on the shoulder of the hill, amongst the stones, would raise her head, then stand, head cocked, one forepaw raised, then would run towards me, first along the level ground before the house and then through the woods and up the hill to meet me. I began to look for this little dog immediately I stood upon the shoulder of the hill, the extent of the valley disposed to my eye. She was a little dog with a small head and large trusting brown eyes: her master in conversation called her Brachet, and, as I cannot remember his own name—if I ever knew it—I shall for present purposes apply the name to him.

'I was carrying out various mail duties at the time—this was a few years ago—and I had cause to drive through his village about twice a week. He was a man whose good nature immediately drew me to him; his openness was unfeigned and he was generous. He treated all those he met as though he had the ability to see matters through their eyes. I shall say little more than that. This Mr Brachet grew used to seeing my face. I shall not embarrass myself by saying that he used to seek my opinion on various matters. He knew that I liked to read a good newspaper, as he himself did, not the usual partisan thing foisted on you at staging inns, such as this,' he said, pointing to the paper which he had replaced on the table beneath the pie-dish.

'Once a driver or a messenger is a regular caller at a house it is natural that he should be looked upon as a source of knowledge about the place in which the newly-arrived magistrate finds himself: in some ways it's a true assumption, and in some ways it's a false one.'

'I can understand that,' said the magistrate.

'Well, then, perhaps you do,' said the driver, 'and you are fortunate to be able to do so. Most newcomers, and I have to say that Magistrate Brachet fell into this category, look at the driver as though he spent every second of his time in acquiring knowledge about his surroundings, which is in a manner of speaking far from the truth; the driver knows less about the place as time goes on; it's not the driver's place to get himself tangled up in local matters; he goes out of his way to avoid acquiring too much knowledge about these things; he works best from a position of ignorance because no-one can then accuse him of partisanship and he is not forced to feign a neutrality which he does not feel. He can just shrug his shoulders. He has his old age and his children to think of. All he knows is the geography of the region.

'Magistrate Brachet's first question was asked as though the answer were of no particular importance,' continued the driver. 'He wished to know how he might best learn the language of the place to which he had been sent.' The driver turned to the guard, smiling, as though this was the beginning of a joke of which he had only to speak the last line in order for its full extent to be brought to mind. He pushed aside his plate and rested his elbows on the table, leaning forward, looking with a comfortable familiarity from the magistrate's face to the guard's and then at the row of plates on the dresser. 'Make no mistake about it. Language in a village such as this is far from stable. It changes constantly: a man, even if he has lived here from birth, has only to walk away from his village —perhaps with no intention of leaving; perhaps with every intention of returning—and, even while he is boasting that he understands the language and can speak it fluently, all the time he is quite deceived: the language has begun to change from the moment he first entertained the thought that he might leave his village; his own surroundings had begun to be foreign as he lifted his gaze to look out at broader horizons. It is because of the fear of this isolation that the wise amongst the villagers rarely leave; it is as if they were certain, without ever finding the need to voice the thought, that to leave would be to make foreigners of themselves. I frequently call to mind the proverb which runs "Leaving is difficult, sojourning distantly is difficult, returning is difficult, staying is difficult". It is change which makes the difficulty in all four states. In the light of the changing language, Magistrate Brachet quite reasonably asked: how was he to learn it? I have no idea why he asked me: I get along in these places by making signs and gestures and acting the part of the foreigner: that works well enough for my subsistence and my requirement for an impartial ignorance of local matters. It is easy too for someone like myself to forget that he, too, was once a child in a village, long before he gained his various honours, and had grown through his childhood, from conception to adolescence, in a village, and that he now acted as though he might draw on his past experience to help him where he now found himself, having, as he said himself, seen the path to this magistracy at the moment he was able to write his own name: a false supposition from the best of motives. Sometimes a newcomer is tempted to believe that he will be able to learn the language from the priest, but that isn't so at all; the priest as likely as not is a newcomer himself, unable to speak a word of the language beyond the common words of the liturgy's office. That is why, when a newcomer relies on the priest to teach

207

him the language, everything he says has what one might call an intercessionary nuance to it: it used to be said that any dialogue with the people from the village was by way of justification: the villagers used to think what supplicatory people the official travellers were because they believed that they appealed to superior powers in everything they did, while the travellers used to consider the villagers stiff-necked because they found unbearable any impression that they might be in the wrong, even on a single point, because in all their actions they justified themselves by reason of their own stance and by the authority of such limited things as they had seen with their own eyes: but of course that was all untruth: the sense of any mutual understanding—and sometimes we felt a powerful sense of mutual understanding—came entirely from within one's own party; sometimes the officials thought the dialogue had gone well when in fact the reverse was true; sometimes the villagers rejoiced on the very eve of the official abandonment of the dialogue. One cannot attempt to use a language of mediation for the purposes of dialogue. If the truth be known, the dialogue was even at its beginning no more than a series of supplications for justification.

'Magistrate Brachet—' (he struggled in an effort of recall as though he found it difficult to remember even the name he himself had chosen) '—saw that when he left there would be no-one to take his place, and that he would not be succeeded, and that within a few years all his efforts would be undone. He had sufficient strength of mind to be able to understand that nothing, nothing at all, would remain of his work. He knew, furthermore, that the decay would begin at the moment of his death, and that it would be doubtful if anyone would trouble themselves to bury his body, and that even the initial of his name would be lost: in fact I in my speaking have chosen it at random, an initial which as I speak I shall try to remember the reason for my choosing it; perhaps I did so only for the sake of euphony. He saw full well that his work would be continued in a travesty of his intentions. Perhaps (though he never said this) he believed that even in his decline his intentions would be taken for granted and thus his duties taken from him. He once said: "I am dead now to the matters of importance more often than not." I saw that he looked forward to my arrival, though in fairness that may be a conceit on my part. "Samuel," he would say, not bothering to speak confidentially, "something has been troubling me for the best part of a week. Tell me what you would do were you in my position." He would ask his question.

'But I was going to tell you about his housekeeper.

'One fine day in winter, with snow already fallen deep and a frosty wind and a low, weak sun above the pine-woods, I made the long journey by foot from the staging post to the place where he resides. It was a journey which needed some preparation: when my grandson is old enough I would wish to still have the strength to take him on such a journey, to plan it, to embark on it, to continue in it and to return from it. The journey was mapped out in my mind's eye. At midday I sheltered from the wind on a hillside amongst a clump of scrub oaks—' he pointed through the solid wall of the inn '—such as these, contemplating the pleasure of arrival. The signs of the end of the journey are before you in the evening; the familiar signs, the sudden familiarity of the perspective of the hills; the sight of the valley, the smudge of smoke over the village; then, the massing of the houses and the lights in the windows. I feel as though I were returning to a place I love; nothing mitigates that pleasure. Afterwards, the message is delivered and that is all there is to it. The door closes, and the warmth is gone, the message is gone, and all that remains to face is the night and there is no longer anything to do except to make a way back to the shelter, such as it is, of the staging post: you have yourself, sir, grown in this last journey to know these places well, but I have known them all my life, having, so they tell me, been born in one. When I arrived at Magistrate Brachet's house I stood by the side-door and rang the bell. The housekeeper answered the door. Instead of handing over the message immediately, as would normally be the case, I asked: "Is the magistrate in?" "No," she replied, opening the door only a crack, keeping out the flurries of snow and the cold wind. "The magistrate is not at home."'

While the driver said this he elaborated upon his story with vivid gesticulations, as though he held the journey still clear in his mind. 'Condescension! She had been fighting with someone; she was still furious. I might hardly have existed, for all my journeying, only as a hand in the darkness with a letter for the magistrate in it. She was dressed in a black overcoat, one of the magistrate's, over her house-clothes, and that increased the righteousness of her anger; the expression on her face was frozen as though with cold and anger. She held out her hand for the letter, and who amongst us could have told how important or unimportant it might have been? She held out the flat of her gloved hand, in the crack of the door, willing to admit no-one; only to keep out the gale. At that moment there was a brighter light in the passage behind the door, and the sound of an interior door opening. Mr Brachet's voice called, he having heard the sound of the bell: "Who is that?" "It's only a driver; not even one of the familiar ones, a strange one we have never seen before," said the housekeeper. "If there is anyone at the door," said the magistrate, "send him in: what do you think you are doing, keeping someone standing outside?" The housekeeper opened the door wider. Her face was white with a cold rage. The magistrate's voice continued: "What do you mean by denying your love of giving charity?"

'The housekeeper turned her head to dart back a look along the passage towards the office door. She shouted, "What do you want, seeing a driver you have never seen before?" Her voice was full of fear on his behalf, as though she saw the worst in the letter and the effects it would have on her own life. "You, Mr Brachet, ought to remember your position." I, a driver, had never heard anything like this! The night was so bitterly cold that there was a presentiment of warmth about even the look of the stone floor of the passage: by comparison with the outer world, even the housekeeper's rage was understandable. "Which one of us is able to remember his position with the roof half blown down and an outbreak of fever in the village?" cried out Mr Brachet, his voice hardly to be heard over the howling of the wind; he was at the end of the corridor, beating his hands together in the cold air, struggling to keep the papers under his arm and out of the grip of the turbulent air: he had just come from his office: he wore nothing over his white shirt except a black waistcoat and his teeth were beginning to chatter. On hearing him speak, the housekeeper seized my arm and pulled me across the threshold and along the passage and into the office. She flung the office door shut behind me. The letter was still in my hand. I could hear her footsteps as she walked down the passage again.

'Mr Brachet said, after a time, "What am I to do with her? She has been the housekeeper to more of my predecessors than I can name." I asked him how she first became a housekeeper, and what were the qualities which recommended her. He replied in a very general way, his voice that which he had used earlier, out in the corridor: "How do any of us do anything? How do any of us come to be what we are?"

'I told him that it was almost certainly the case that the housekeeper had had the ambition of becoming a magistrate's housekeeper when she had been a young girl in the village; she had looked away from what she was doing for only a moment and in that moment the beginnings of an alteration overcame her. She resolved to become a magistrate's housekeeper.' The driver spoke with the loud voice of someone who speaks ironically, affecting to be blind to the fact that the sonority of his speech makes its content ridiculous. 'By reason of her very ambition she knew what to expect of the interview; she learned how she might best influence the magistrate and convince him of her diligence. When she gained admittance to the house she lost her identity in the village and, after a few years, she no longer knew even how to speak its language. I asked him: "What happened to the housekeeper who preceded her?" "I do not know," he answered, "She has never talked about her predecessor. The life of a housekeeper is her life; she has chosen it." He said that the housekeeper was ill and could not be expected to continue her duties indefinitely; as it was, she had grown to live by standards which she would never have countenanced in the past; her eyesight had deteriorated; she was no longer able to see the dust and the dirt in the shadier and more remote rooms of the house; her steps had become more slow—her voice was low and husky, and one could, he said, see a slow pulse beating in her neck; her eyes had lost all their enthusiasm and she stared dully about her, her upper eyelids always halfway down the irises of her eyes. She was tired. I would see her sitting down; she would be sitting, looking at her swollen legs. It was difficult to be reasonable with her, so the magistrate said: she would not listen to anything he said; her dark eyes had become opaque and lustreless. She could not be made to accept that a house-keeper cannot maintain herself in her duties forever, especially now that the budget of the civil parish had been reduced. One cannot expect, he said, a woman of her age to rise at dawn and to undertake such duties as had once formed the stable routine of her life. How standards had slipped! He was embarrassed to ask his neighbours and his colleagues into his own house. As for the housekeeper, all she wanted to do was put her fingers in her ears every time the magistrate spoke, and to contradict everything he said, lest he turn the subject to criticism of her work and even of her appearance. She acted as though she could hear, even through her closed ears, his hints of her dismissal. The result of all this was that she spoke to no-one all day; when spoken to she did not reply; she talked to herself in a vituperative voice, sparing herself nothing over the least of her neglects even though to others she pretended that nothing was neglected. When I had cause to see her, standing outside at the back of the house near the magistrate's mounting-block outside the stable gates, I saw that her anger towards me was not directed to myself: she was afraid that I might bring the state of the house to the notice of the magis-trate. "Had I not noticed the state of the room?" he asked. He was still shivering with cold. He had put the letter I had given him on the table as if he would open it later. How could he have expected me to notice the state of the room? The only thing to see in it was the fire: there was nothing else of any importance in the room. I sat by the side of the fire, looking out of the window and wondering who else might have cause to travel on such a night. Perhaps he expected no answer. I stared into the coals. What could I feel but gratitude, that I was out of the searching wind and sitting in peace by the side of the fire, listening to the ticking of the mantel clock and thawing the ice from my clothes?'

The driver sat back in his chair, the open newspaper lying across his legs. He stared steadily across the room, at no particular object, as though the act of staring by itself assisted his concentration. 'The housekeeper saw the direction which events were taking: she foresaw the hour of the day when she would find herself no longer able to work in the house. She would look out of the windows, fearful of leaving the surroundings which the years had made so familiar to her. She had, of her own free will, stopped to listen long ago to the imposter as he had painted the events of a glorious life for her.' He looked down at the paper. 'This,' he said, tapping the page, 'would say that she was living a life intended for someone else. Well, perhaps that's the case, or perhaps it isn't; I can only speak for what I saw. She did not see eye to eye with this new magistrate, Mr Brachet, as I have called him. She had overheard him (she was, I know for a fact, never beyond the next corner when he was speaking to someone in his office), and she must have imputed things to him which he never said. There was nowhere for her to go: she had of her own free will left the village which was her home and she could not go back to it, her life having altered so much. Therefore she continued in her course, remaining inside the house, denying the importance of her relatives, not allowing him to speak to her lest he draw even accidentally on to the subject of her leaving, while at the same time she became attached to him, hiding from herself the less pleasant facets of his character in order that she might never have to believe that he would so much as consider whether he might be able to dispense with her: she would watch him from the windows of the upper storeys as he walked in the garden; she would praise to herself his work on the reconstruction of the house; she would mutter to herself her concern as to whether he was or was not damaging himself by his hard work; she would remonstrate with him over his working through the night.

'Once, when her nephew visited her, she took the child to see the magistrate's office, the magistrate's bedroom, the stall in which the magistrate's horse was stabled; the dogs in the yard which the stablemen had called by names they considered the magistrate might deem appropriate. She allowed the child the opportunity of inspecting these things in silence, even to the examination of his name—which as I have said I now forget—as it appeared on the door. She stood behind him as he traced with his finger the name in white on the dark varnished wood: she stood at the open door and watched him as from his position in the centre of the floor he slowly examined the room, looking first at one thing which attracted his eye, and then another, in the manner of a child, examining each of his appurtenances. She was unaware, was she not, of what she was doing: a question I still ask myself. Did she wish the boy to copy the sense which lay beyond the ownership of these dead things? Did she praise him for drawing them in his school rough-book? Under the education of the house-keeper, the magistrate's belongings were beyond being prop-erty, as are the trivial objects in a museum dedicated to the memory of one man, balls of wool, gloves, waistcoats, fire-irons, objects laid out as though they were more than the transient property of the dead man who in the past has touched them. The boy said, in my hearing, "Once N was like me: one day I shall be N." What do you suppose he is now but a foreigner in the place where circumstances have put him? In his way perhaps even now, because of those words once uttered so thoughtlessly, he shares his solitude and his anonymity.

'And why do I now remember—at last—that the boy called him N, an arbitrary initial since I do not recall if I ever knew his name? What might that initial designate?'—the driver's voice was loud and monotonous: it was difficult to think of the proprietor and his wife lying asleep through it—'What else should the boy have traced with his finger on the woodwork of the door?

'As for the housekeeper: towards the end she would do everything for him except to clean the house or to prepare his meals for a set time. She became angry when he began to take his dinner in the back room of the inn, a little room hardly much different from the one in which we now sit: indeed, his chair might be the very chair against which you, sir, now rest your hands, each leg different on the provincial lathe. The housekeeper asked him, phrasing the question to suit her appeal: what kind of advertisement in the villages was such behaviour for her? He was as thin as a lath: why hadn't he told her that he was hungry? "Say nothing! I know about these things!", she said, making her point from round a corner of the newel near the passage which led to her room, so that she might turn and flee in order to avoid hearing his reply. What hope had she for the future? At one time she had thought that hope in childhood might be treasured up as though in a store for use in the bleaker years, being beguiled by the nature of hope as it is seen during the extent of a tranquil life; perhaps she saw hope as an extension of that sensibility which has developed for the purpose of establishing a general fortification against any dull pain. As for her, there was nothing to hope for, surely; there was about her circumstances no pain to be dulled: she lived more deeply within the confines of her principles with each day. As for the magistrate, in post now for some time: initial ardour cooled, initial enthusiasms gone, grand strategies forsaken, she knew his one fear; the fear that she would do nothing all day but follow him about the house. She knew that he suspected her of sleeping in the corridor outside his door; every morning when he opened his door she was there, standing by the passage window, ready dressed and with her hair brushed back, looking at him with her suppliant eyes, waiting for him to walk either towards her or away from her. She knew that the magistrate could hardly bear to look at her, not because the sight of her uncritical gaze was in itself repugnant to him, but because there was in her face the look of a material and an emotional searching which she saw he found pitiful to see. What was passing through her mind? What passed through her mind when she was asleep? She gave up all use of language, in very much the same way as she would have done had she left that employ and gone back to the village where she had been brought up, and as she gave up the use of language she was overcome by, not deafness, but an inability, which might have been feigned or unfeigned, to interpret any words spoken to her, recognizing his voice alone, even when he had not spoken, listening to its tone rather than to its sense. She lived her life in a contemplation of her chosen object, that is, the magistrate, and I still cannot remember his name, in a silence that was hard even for her to bear.

'He, outwardly living a life of routine and order, did not know what he might do to act for the best. His housekeeper sat in her kitchen, looking out of the window, her slow eyes taking in what was happening outside, her eyes following as though by reflex any moving thing. The door would be left open. When I entered she would look at me, and, irrespective of anything I said, she would look from me to the passage which led to the magistrate's office, as if to say "I expect he is somewhere, I have just seen him, he was in this room with me not one minute ago", and she would move her head as though following in her mind the various floors of the house. The staircases were by this time beyond her. Perhaps she saw those upper floors as she had once cleaned them.

'He said to me, on one occasion, "Unless circumstances change, one day I shall open the door of my room and find her lying dead on the landing, looking up the stairs with open eyes." He said: "She is ill. She is not old; her illness is not that which accompanies age." I said, ignoring his last remark: "You must put her away." It was careful advice. The only thing she wanted was peace: on the other hand, the last thing she wished for was the peace of solitude: no-one who has borne the imposter's voice for a life wants the peace of solitude. In the end all imposture is put away.

'He was persuaded to find a new housekeeper, a woman of his own age, I was going to say, it seemed more proper, but in fact she was much younger, hardly more than a girl; she was one of the village girls, good at her work. When she became a housekeeper she settled herself in a certain routine. She was always very correct in her behaviour. She had her hair tied back and plaited; she always reminded me of a schoolgirl: that was an idea he had planted in my mind because when she wasn't there he used to call her "the head-girl". She used to show me to the door of the waiting room and keep me there, near the stove in winter, until the magistrate had seen the letter and had written any reply which might have been necessary; she had sense enough to know that all new provincial magistrates underrate themselves—that's been a consistent observation of mine—and she found and retained his affections. I suppose she wondered about what would happen in the future. Who doesn't?

'It was not often that I was called within the house. Magistrate Brachet's new housekeeper kept me waiting outside with the door closed and nothing to occupy myself with for hours on end except an examination of a pair of doorscrapers; the door was at the inner end of a covered alley as dark as a cell and, whatever the season, filled with an incessant turbulence of the air. The letters were taken from me at the door, and I was left to wait in all weathers. When the housekeeper returned with the reply she would give me a small sum of money in a screw of paper: "Here. The magistrate asks me to give you this for your dinner at the inn and asks you not to get drunk on it." The man himself would look at me as if he saw me at the end of the passage, or, if it were summer, should he happen to hear me walking towards the cell of the alley, over the slabs of the path, he would glance in my direction. It was no concern to me that I was no longer of any value in his eyes. I knew full well that the magistrate had only befriended me during the first days of his arrival because he wished for my opinion, because he did not know how to act in certain matters of his new appointment. He was, by his own understanding, no longer a newcomer. Now he had found his way he had no need to be observant of the viewpoints of others. It would have been pointless for me to have taken upset because of the ending of what had only been a friendship of circumstance. Even when he first asked for my opinion— me, a person of no importance at all, hardly qualified as a driver—even when he first summoned me to his office and allowed me to warm myself at his office fire, I knew that familiarity between those so unequal is offered for a purpose and is withdrawn immediately that purpose has been fulfilled. "One day," I said to myself, as I sat in the heat from the fire, looking down at my boots, "this man will see the dignity of his position, and keep me waiting at the door." Sometimes I came near to saying this to him. It would have been impertinent of me to have said it, or perhaps, on the other hand, it would not have been impertinent. What do you think?' Here he kicked the guard's feet beneath the table. 'Keep awake,' he said in a studied undertone, though the guard had been very much awake and the remark had been pointless.

Colver, still leaning on the back of the chair, looked across the room at the hanging lamp above the table. It swayed almost imperceptibly as though in an invisible current of air which ran through the room despite the closed door at one end and the hanging curtain at the other; its movement was only seen because the movement of its shadows caused one to look up to the lamp itself. The driver and the guard, lifting their arms simultaneously, began to drink from their glasses. For the second time the magistrate looked round the room. The shutters at the one tall window had not been fastened, but beyond the glass nothing was visible save the darkness of the night, rendered all the more impalpable and insubstantial by the sharp reflections of the lamp and the room it lit.

The floor of the room was paved with uneven flagstones. Unlike the other walls in the inn the walls of this room had been papered. Dampness had pushed the paper from the walls; the arsenical patterns, once florid and vigorous, had been dulled into the general smoky colour of the room by age and by the salts in the mortar of the wall; some strips of the paper were markedly brighter than the others; in the places where the paper had bulged it had been tacked back to the plaster by little nails or brads with rusty heads.

During the driver's talk the guard had looked covertly at the magistrate, possibly judging his response to the inconsistencies in the driver's speech: he had paid no attention to what the driver had said; he seemed familiar enough with his monologue. 'This is a strange room,' he said in a tolerant voice.

'I have stayed in this village before,' said Colver.

'You are a wise man.' The driver sat back at his ease.

'Who is this demographer?' asked the magistrate.

'I don't know. I've never heard of such a thing before,' the driver said, perhaps wishing to dismiss the subject. He began to stand. He looked at the guard. 'We have been told to sleep in the stable-block,' he said. 'The landlord,' he said to Colver, as though he thought the fact might interest him, 'told us that he would be going to bed early. He said to lock the door and to put the key in through the letterbox.' He looked at his watch. 'Your hour will be up! This watch keeps accurate time!' He felt the surface of the table in the shadow of the pie-dish and lifted up a large iron key; it had been resting in the middle of the table directly beneath the metal receiver of the hanging lamp, in the centre of the shadow it cast; it had been lying invisibly in the deepest part, the bull's eye, of the shadow; the magistrate saw it for the first time when the driver put his hand on it. 'I suppose you can be trusted with it,' said the driver, looking at the key, turning it over and over in his hands.

Colver, incessantly aware since the first moment of his entering this room that the inn had once been the guesthouse, looked at the key as though it had undergone a change: in it he saw for the first time an object which without doubt had once belonged to the monastery. In his eagerness to hold the key in his hand he leaned across the table and his shadow, now that he was close to the lamp, had become huge behind his back so that even he was aware of it, while his sudden forward movement had caused the driver and the guard to look, not so much at him, as at his moving shadow.

'I suppose that we can trust him with it,' said the driver again, looking at the guard and holding the key in his hand.

The repetition of the remark made Colver angry. 'Do you know what that key is?' he said.

'It was only a joke!' said the driver, hastily, putting the key down on the table and pushing it towards the magistrate in one movement, and making out that he might sit down again.

'As if anyone could be more trusted with a key than a magistrate!'

'I can do with no more of this,' said the guard, pressing the table as he stood up, and speaking only for the second time, his voice loud and flat in the narrow room.

Colver, alone in the room, holding the key in his hands and looking at its wards, heard their voices in the stable at the back as they shouted to each other. Their voices were very distinct; every syllable could be heard. The village was asleep. The two men were talking, not of the journey which they had undertaken, nor of the journey ahead, but of a debate they had heard or been taking part in at a hall in the confluence town; the motion of this debate, so he gathered from their alternate sentences, touched upon the universal nature of dissimulation; one of the speakers, in a short proposition, had mentioned a character invoked for the purpose of a parable who imputed ulterior purposes to two other parties who discussed his next move between themselves as though he had no free-will of his own, least of all in an exercise of his suspicions. They read too much into the meaning; this is where their idea of the imposter came from: that and the newspaper, said Colver to himself. This seemed quite likely: the speaker's parable seemed to have made a deep impression upon the driver, so much so that doubtless Magistrate Brachet had been a character in it: indeed, Colver could not help but wonder which of the three characters he had been.

When the driver had finished a ringing monologue in imitation of the proposer's speech, or perhaps remembering it verbatim, the yard was silent. The magistrate put the key through the letterbox of the inn door. He was uncertain whether or not the driver and the guard had after all left the village; they had certainly spent some time out in the stables talking to each other. The night was cold; the layer of mist was thin. Only the brightest of the stars still shone overhead, each the centre of an indefinite silver halo. The reddish moon had gone and there was nothing by which the time might be judged, for unseen variations in the density of the mists altered the constellations until the eye might ache in looking for a familiar pattern.

He walked through the wood to the magistrate's house. The oak trees were silent. The air was still. The mist had consolidated itself in the hollows and gullies, and the shadows of the trees lay across it in the moonlight. He stood in the centre of the wood; ahead he could see a glimmer of light from the windows of the hall at either side of the door of the house. He stood still and looked across his shoulder. The noise of the river was louder than it had been earlier in the evening. He followed with his eye the ridge of the mountains. He looked upwards towards the monastery as a heavy bell began to move. 'What do they want now?' he said, aloud.

He saw the tower amongst the shadows of the mountains. The single window was no more than a shadow of deeper darkness. He looked up: above him the bell, ill-seen but swiftly moving, swung in its arc and rang out. The single stroke sounded and the bell drew to its rest.

Inside the hall a lamp had been lit in preparation for the night. The light cast by the lamp, passing through the coloured globe, gave a peculiar aqueous quality to the still air of the hall, and further, up the stairs, as though it would, as if by the will of whoever had lit it, illuminate every room with its altered light.

Colver, standing in the hall, looking at the tongue of flame within the lamp, and seeing in its wavering a small echo of the bell which had so recently sounded, resolved himself at last to find the housekeeper. He lifted the lamp, holding the stem beneath the receiver, surprised at its unexpected lightness, for it had looked so substantial that he had doubted whether he might lift it with his one hand. He carried the lamp into the house and unlocked the door of his office; on entering he placed the lamp on the desk and drew the curtains across the casement. On sitting in the chair a sleepiness overcame him, and when he closed his eyes he could see no glimmer of light, only a darkness so profound that it seemed that the lamp had been silently extinguished at the moment of his closing his eyes or that his eyelids were as opaque as coins. He leaned forward and looked at the shadow of his head on the wall to his side. He held up a document which lay on the surface of the table, as though for the sake of its familiarity. The green light, which was so easy on the eye, appeared to take the dullness of the prose from the page; it gave the words a mysterious quality as though they were being read for the first time, their meaning becoming speculative and open to question. The magistrate, sitting in the chair with the papers on the table in front of him, on the verge of sleep, had read the same page twice and it had differed substantially with each reading. On the second reading the statement was seen to act only as the vehicle for the meaning. As the magistrate looked at the document in the greenish light the rolling motion of the day's travel resumed in his head.

There was a knock at the door; the housekeeper entered; she was an old woman whom Colver had seen many times in the village. She removed her black headscarf as though she had just returned from the village; her hair was profuse and black and arranged as if only a few moments ago in the parlour of the house she had just left. She looked round the room as though uncertainly aware that something was amiss, but she did not seem to immediately recognize the source of the change. Her face was red and damp, as though she had come from a hot kitchen full of steam. Her look of uncertainty vanished when she saw the green-shaded lamp on the magistrate's desk. She stood quietly for a moment, hardly looking at the magistrate himself; perhaps she found it difficult to begin any kind of introduction. Colver was about to speak— he had already stood, out of deference not only to her presence but also to her age—but she turned abruptly from him and walked to the window, where she lifted her hands and pulled the curtains more closely together, extinguishing the crack of night which lay between them. She took up a smaller lamp which stood on a shelf, and, her movements brisk and fussy with unnecessary activity, she took first the clear shade and then the chimney from the lamp. She lit the wick with a match from a large box which she carried in the wide pocket at the side of her dress, smiling with a fleeting embarrassment at the magistrate while she did this. She replaced the lamp chimney and the shade and put the new lamp on the desk. She took up the green-shaded lamp and made as if to take it back to the place where it belonged. While she was at the door, however, she looked back and saw the dead fire in the grate. Her expression was one of regret and exasperation, not with the magistrate, whom she might have suspected of not wishing for a fire, the weather being so mild; not with damp wood and coals of the fire, but with herself, and the appearance of incompetence which she had presented within the first few minutes of her meeting the magistrate. After all, she had, or so one thought, changed the lamps because she had felt a sense of incorrectness in the hall lamp being used in the office: there is no point in changing things for the sake of it, or in taking, as a child does, the first half-appropriate thing which comes to hand, whatever the purpose and the function which have for good but unremembered reasons been allocated to it. She was angry with herself for the fire going out. She looked down at the hearth as though she might re-light it, but then she looked at the severe face of the mantel clock in the manner of someone seeing that time presses heavily. She paused before lifting the green-shaded lamp again in her two hands, as though she found it weighty, and left the room, ignoring the magistrate, as though she might bypass the moment of introduction; she closed the door gently behind her.

Perhaps her reticence had been due to shyness, particularly when she had decided in her own mind that her first meeting with the magistrate differed from the meeting she had imagined. Perhaps she thought that she had disgraced herself in the first moment: and all that after so much care in preparations which had gone into the evening! There had, her attitude seemed to say, been the constant worry about the presence of the demographer, who would accuse her of taking his things: perhaps he had deliberately wet the firewood: it certainly smelt damp: perhaps he had even come into the room when it had been empty and unlocked. And, of course, she had to clear up after the demographer: he was messy, a person who thinks that order comes naturally, and that rooms clean themselves. Surely the magistrate would not be able to understand the salience of these simple domestic matters. Perhaps she had thought that a smile alone would make her look silly. It is difficult to say, in a foreign language, 'you and I are on the same side: we are all on the same side' without being either familiar or trite, and it is difficult to give a look suggesting understanding which does not imply complicity and underhand connivance. Perhaps she had chosen to behave as she had because she wished to preserve the regularity of her set dignities; in order to do this she must keep herself apart from the magistrate, as he would, no doubt, keep himself apart from her. She might have said to herself: the last thing one must do is to compare past and previous incumbents of such posts: when one begins to do this, one begins to look to the past and dread the future and continue greyly from day to day: certainly, comparison in these matters is always a bad thing. She was old. Her expression had been neutral and absorbed. Perhaps she did not speak to the magistrate because she thought that her own presence might be an interruption. Perhaps she had formed an immediate attachment for him, as a magistrate, admiring him for wasting no time in setting down to work on the first night of his arrival, as though he had walked down the corridor, taking up the first lamp he saw however unsuitable, and leaving the rest of the house in darkness, with nothing but the lofty thought of his work steady in his mind. She might have seen the papers he held as being important things and the perusal of them uninterruptable; sometimes she had looked at them as though she wondered how the magistrate could bear to sit quietly in the discomfort of the office chair while studying such momentous things. She might have regarded the closely written pages with a mood which had within it the utter contempt of superficial familiarity and the profound awe of deep ignorance: though on the other hand perhaps she thought that the attempt at reading the papers by the green light would strain the eyes, even though that light had been far more intense, green as it was, than the

224

feeble and flickering light given out by the ragged wick and the sooty chimney of an ordinary study lamp.

The magistrate, who had allowed her to have her own way during their introduction, sitting down again and beginning to re-read the document by the light of the new lamp, found that the mysterious and allusive meaning had been taken away from the phrases and that the spacing of the paragraphs had become ordinary, of no more importance than the official circulars with the jargon of the moment. Even the touch of the papers had become different, as though he held them under circumstances very different from those which had prevailed only a few moments ago.

The long dining-table was laid with a clean cloth. The room itself was long and narrow with a high ceiling. At the end of the room was a round-arched window which had no curtains but only internal shutters of a dark-painted wood held together by a broad bar and a steel clasp. Now that they were in this room, nearer the housekeeper's territory, she secretively attempted a trial of communication, an upward glance with her eyes, a momentary lingering of her glance indicating that only she knew what a meal had been prepared for him at the end of his journey! She had gone out of her way to astonish him with the amount of cutlery and crockery in the house; the knives and forks (some of silver, some of plate so old that the underlying brass showed through, some of aluminium) were arranged about his place: it was as if a formal meal had been arranged as though for an important event. On the other hand, how could a formal meal be arranged for one person? The table was a narrow board upon two trestles: the room itself was too narrow for comfortable use as a dining room. As to the peculiar dimensions of the room, they were brought about by the division of a larger room which in its original state would have had fine proportions. The room had a smell compounded of long years of neglect and much recent activity. There was a mingling of the fresh scent of cooking food and freshly polished furniture, but no smell of any previous occupant, as though the room had been untenanted and kept shuttered and locked for a long time. He had the sudden wish to stand and to walk to the window and to fling open both leaves of the shutter, as though he had been sitting in a room which was lit by lamplight because the sun has been excluded. So closely did the shutters sit together that it might as well have been clear daylight outside. He looked down at the table. The spoons on the table's surface reflected from their concave bowls the tiny inverted replicas of the wicks of the three lamps. The housekeeper poured him a little glass of plum spirit. After a silence of some fifteen minutes, during which the magistrate examined the room without moving his head, she began to bring in the food. When the housekeeper was in the room he looked at the closed shutters, following the grain of the wood, while, when she was out of it, he sat looking down at the table. The housekeeper brought in the soup before again leaving the room. She served this meal with an air of intense preoccupation, as though she would allow nothing else to distract her, although in her preparing and serving of the meal it was quite clear from her manner that she must have had numerous events and times and sequences bobbing for notice in her mind.

The housekeeper had left the room. Beyond the frame of the door she had left open he could see the light of a small lamp which stood on a narrow table in the passage. When, an hour later, he still sat half-asleep in the chair, the plate of congealing meat pushed across the table in front of him, he still heard the housekeeper moving about near the sideboard behind him. He had fallen forwards in his desire for sleep; his head was crooked in his arm and his cheek was heavy on the coarse black woollen cloth of the sleeve of his coat. The table's surface swayed with the motion of the conveyance. He heard a sharp cry behind him: the housekeeper on turning her head had found something which offended her still further and had exclaimed involuntarily. He raised his head and looked at her and saw that there were tears in her stern eyes, for all that there was not a word in common between them, as though she wept that she had been driven to expressing herself aloud

226

with an inarticulate cry. He tried to push back the chair in order to stand but she was directly behind him and for the moment he could do nothing beyond putting his hand to his face, as though he had cried out himself and would hide his face in the black cloth of the crook of his arm. When he was able to stand, still half awake and still aware of the motion of the table, he stood by the sideboard where the housekeeper had cried out and looked across the length of the table to the open door at the other end of the room. The meal was still on the table before him, and the sideboard was still full of dishes and plates. Two of the three lamps had been taken away, and the one remaining lamp had been turned down to a glimmer. At the other end of the table the round-arched window had been unshuttered and the sash had been partly opened as if to allow the night air to ventilate the room.

He stood in the doorway and looked back at the room, finding difficulty in recognizing it. He was exhausted after the days of travel. The corridor behind him was dark; the lamp on the small table had been extinguished. As he stood in the doorway of the narrow dining room memories of her mannerisms came to his mind. He had seen her frugality: the fire in the office had been built mostly of slack and dust, not that it was that which had prevented it from catching light: the lamps had been turned out in the empty rooms and, even in those which were occupied, they had been turned too low to see anything by.

The housekeeper sat awkwardly on a high wooden stool. She held one of her hands to her breast, tightly clutching a small handkerchief. So tightly did she grasp it that only a little of the lace border was visible. A moment ago she must have been dabbing her eyes with it. Now she sat, aware of the magistrate's presence. She rubbed her hip with her other hand. She turned away from the magistrate and began to climb slowly from the stool. This seemed to cause her pain for she involuntarily grimaced. She made her way over the flagstones, which were wet with condensation, to a corner by a cupboard; she began to lift up, one after another, a few silver knives and forks, breathing on each piece and then polishing it with the carefully hemmed rag which Colver had taken to be a handkerchief. Colver looked round the room and saw the remaining dishes which were to have made up the rest of the meal. 'Nothing has been done for me; only for the holder of a position,' he said, as if that would excuse the waste in his own eyes. He walked round the table, as though to stand at the house-keeper's side, but at his approach she turned away from him, as though he might have been about to make advances to her, and, or so it appeared, having no intention of admitting to him the fact of her pain. She put the silver back in the velvet-lined box and struggled across the room to the central table where she without purpose began to stir, with the precision of long habit, a jug of stewed fruit. The thought passed through the magistrate's mind: how had he, from what he had seen of her, come to form an opinion of her from the sound of her one utterance, articulate or inarticulate, and, from that opinion, an idea of how he himself must appear in her eyes? When she left the kitchen he began to feel the beginnings of a pity brought about on seeing the small do-mestic items, on which, he was certain, she set so much value; small familiar items which she must use day after day, picking them up in sequence for each particular task, gathering them together so that they might be used one after the other, and then returning them to the drawers and the cupboards to which as if in the security of a previous dispensation they had been allocated. He looked round the room. The room and the corridor leading from it were silent as though the house were empty. He drew back the bolts of the door. His own position was impossible: he was certain that he could say nothing to her should she return. He turned the key to unlock the door. Outside, the red moon had gone. He heard the soft splashings of the water on the stones of the river's bed. The mist lay thick about the house. As he stood on the threshold he felt two compelling urges; the first to re-enter the house, and the second to go beyond the threshold and to close the door; he stood in vacillatory thought with his hand on the latch of the door, but at the same time looking outwards towards the unseen river beyond the wood, as though by this vacillation he might assuage the compulsions of the two desires; then, when the position of standing at the threshold of either the house and the wood became intolerable, he turned back to the door.

XIII

The magistrate met the driver and the guard in the stable-yard behind the inn. He had the certain knowledge that they would be reluctant to speak to him, but, as he had come upon them suddenly, turning a corner of the inn, they could hardly avoid him.

'How have you got on?' said the driver, who seemed to be half asleep still; he had the look of one who has been drinking until late. He was one of those people who only flourish in conversation in the late evening. The guard's manner was very much the opposite, for he was brisk and alert, continually looking round at his surroundings, staring past the magistrate's head to follow with his eyes a woman who was walking down the street past the inn.

'How have you got on?' repeated the driver, perhaps thinking that he had not been heard the first time he had spoken. 'Did you meet that demographer?'

'No, I never saw him.'

'So, he wasn't there,' said the driver. 'Perhaps after all he was an imposter.'

The guard began to laugh, as though pleased with the day and the prospect of travel, and as though he had needed only this pleasantry to make his pleasure in the day vocal.

'I took it,' continued the driver, 'that you met the house-keeper?'

'I certainly did,' said the magistrate, briskly, resenting this questioning.

'I expect she prepared a good meal for you,' said the driver.

'What did you do wrong? She was talking about it in the inn this morning.'

'One expects that kind of person to talk in the inn,' said the magistrate, his sympathy for the housekeeper evaporating rapidly.

The driver looked away. 'Well, yes, one does expect that kind of thing to happen.' He paused. 'I don't suppose it matters very much,' he said.

'When do you leave?'

'In an hour.' He turned to the guard. 'There's nothing further to do here.'

'Have you been to this village before?' asked the magistrate.

'No,' said the driver. 'I can,' he said, turning to the guard, 'speak for both of us.'

The magistrate had the momentary conviction that he would have no opportunity to speak to anyone else for a long time after the driver and the guard had left. The thought came to him very suddenly, as though it had been in his mind for some time.

'There is an old man down in the village who listens to the bells from the monastery,' said the driver, accurately divining the magistrate's thoughts.

'I have met him.' The magistrate looked at the driver, embarrassed that his thoughts should have been so obvious to the other man, almost as though he had voiced his mind aloud. He would never have known that his conviction of coming isolation had been so obvious had not the driver spoken as he had. 'It doesn't take you long to look at a village such as this!'

'Well,' said the driver, becoming more reticent now. 'When you constantly travel, you see that some things are universal and others are prone to all kinds of fluxes and variations.' He looked away from the magistrate. 'You develop an eye for these things. That's all there is to it. Remote places such as this are very different when you cannot get away from them easily: it is one thing to visit a place and another to live in it. I have an interest in amateur drama, and perhaps that helps me to understand these things. Some might have argued that

231

you should have made more of an effort in understanding the housekeeper last night. Still, things are what they are. We—' he indicated the guard with his hand, and then pointed to himself, '—went down to this old man's house to see the housekeeper and to see if anything could be done.'

'What made you go down there?'

'As I say, to see if anything could be done about your reconciliation with your housekeeper. The old man speaks your language quite well.'

'You are quite mistaken,' said the magistrate with the certainty of conviction. 'The old man speaks no language but his own. I am sure of that.'

'I must contradict you,' said the driver without raising his voice in the least. 'He speaks fluently, with a command of unusual words. Say what you like: I've spoken to him. He's certainly an impressive speaker; it wouldn't do to underestimate him should one happen to live here; he impressed us. He is a very intelligent man, and not in the least as ill as he looks. I have heard him for myself.' He paused to look round the dusty wall of the stables. Under the shadowy eaves the martins were flying to and from their nests in well-defined paths through the air. The driver peered past the magistrate's shoulder, towards the gate, as though his attention had been caught by something further away on the hillside. 'He has a precise manner of speech. If he hesitates it is to find the correct word; he uses every word in his vocabulary in its proper context,' he said. 'You must have known that. There was nothing of what you might choose to call reticence about his manner. He proved to be quite open and frank. If there was any dissimulation it was on our part.'

'What do you mean by that?' asked the magistrate, who could not understand in the least what the driver was talking about; perhaps he had been making an elaborate joke, though his manner did not suggest this; on the contrary, he looked worn and ill at ease, as though despite his drinking last night he had not slept well. 'What do you mean by "If there was any dissimulation it was on your part"? Here I am: I have seen the old man on a number of occasions, in the past, and he has never uttered a single word which made any sense to me. The only words which had any meaning were the words which he used to describe the building which fascinates him.'

'What building is this?' said the driver, somewhat ingenuously, for the gatehouse of the monastery was directly above the perspective allowed by the gateposts of the stable; the driver had been looking at the building not more than thirty seconds ago; besides, he himself had mentioned the old man's interest in the sounding of the bells. He looked up again to the monastery. 'Oh! That!' He pointed upward with his finger. 'Do you mean that?'

'Certainly I mean that. Did you not hear the bell tolling last night?'

'I heard it, yes. It rang once; it pays to be accurate if one must describe these things. They told me down in the village that you were called to the place at one time. I suppose we all have our vocations. As for the old man, he seemed to have lost his interest in it,' said the driver, turning his back on the building, as though he had never looked at it and had no desire to see it. 'Not that it matters one way or the other. Besides, in the future you have time enough to find out these things for yourself.' He looked at the guard. 'What time is it?' The guard pulled out a watch from the pocket of his coat, a task he found difficult for he was wearing thick leather gloves over his hands, the usual sort of black gauntlets worn in winter by drivers in the provincial mail service. Perhaps the driver had given him this pair of gloves, though if that were so it would have been unusual; a guard was generally thought of as being higher in standing than the driver and it was difficult to know why he might want to wear a pair of the driver's cast-off gloves. Perhaps he wore them out of a sense of humility. They certainly made him look clumsy and ungainly for they magnified the size of his hands. 'Ten-fifteen,' he said, taking off one of the gloves in order to wind up the watch, and then examining his bare hand now that he had taken off the glove, flexing and extending his fingers and inspecting the movement of the tendons as they ran across the back of his hand. 'We must,' he said, as though for the first time exercising

233

his authority as the more senior of the two, 'leave in a quarter of an hour's time.'

The magistrate was very reluctant to see them go. 'Perhaps you'll have a drink before you start on your way,' he said. 'There is some plum spirit in the house.'

The driver and the guard looked at each other. 'That's a hospitable enough request,' said the driver, looking up at the pass of the hills. 'How do we stand for time?'

The guard did not look at his watch again, but he glanced up at the sky as though an examination of the weather would in some way modify his answer.

In the magistrate's office the driver and the guard stood formally, like servants, at either side of the fireplace. Both of them, as though struck by the same thought at the same moment, held their glasses up to the light of the window and examined the light as it passed through the liquid, which, acting as a lens, focused an image of the window across each of their eyes. Then, seeing that they were mimicking each other's actions they put their glasses down on the runner which lay along the top of the mantelpiece. The driver took a step towards the door, and, leaning out, he looked up and down the corridor, as though he found it unusual, or as though the sight of it reminded him of the termination of his journey yesterday. 'You'll always look at that corridor,' he said, 'in a certain light.'

'What do you mean by that?' said the magistrate indulgently, though the last thing he wished to do was to treat the driver and the guard as though they were his two familiars in this village. Besides, they had made it clear that they were used to this hesitancy on the part of local officials who had been set down in remote places in the provinces, and their common desire to keep those who were familiar with them close by them as long as possible. On the other hand, as the driver had said, there must always be a moment at which one must leave. The guard had looked at his watch and then out at the garden, as though thinking what a pleasant place it was, and how much he would have given to have been allowed to have lived with his family in a house like this. One could see him looking from one object in the garden to another, sighing with a kind of envy over each of the prospects which the garden offered; his gaze lingered on each terrace. Once he had walked across to the window and had looked out as though to admire the carp-pool, where the deep orange and black-flecked backs of the fish moved with a calm unpredictability in the world beneath the floating leaves of the water-lilies. He had put his hands up to the window and had clasped the painted glazing bars, as children do when they are intent on watching something beyond the closed casement of a house window. The guard's face was set in an unfeigned expression of quiet pleasure; the expression which the magistrate had taken for envy was not envy at all but rapt enjoyment. The guard looked down at the glass he was holding in his hand, and he looked at the drink within the bowl; he had not tasted it; he looked at it as though he anticipated the pleasure of drinking the spirit.

'You must not think I wish to see you gone,' said the magistrate to them both, speaking to the driver rather than to the childlike guard, though his glance was directed first at one and then at the other, 'but on the other hand I have no wish to keep you from your journey.'

The guard, who had begun to turn round on hearing the magistrate speak, resumed his pleasurable examination of the garden at the moment when he had finished speaking. Certainly he seemed to be familiar enough with the words.

While the guard had been looking out of the window, the driver had been standing at the door. 'It is surprising—or at the bottom of it all perhaps it is not surprising—how many of those who have been taken out to their station in the provinces wish to return at the moment of their arrival. What is it? I have never been able to bring myself to ask this question before. What is this desire?'

The magistrate said nothing; perhaps he thought that the driver had asked the question without expecting any answer.

'No-one answers that,' said the driver to the guard.

The magistrate began to pace up and down the room. 'Did

you know my predecessor?' he asked, looking at the driver. The guard, still staring out of the window, had begun to steam up the pane through which he examined the outside world with his breath.

'I never knew him,' said the driver. 'I never met him.' He took a step back into the room. 'Do you wish us to go?' He looked down at his hands. 'Or what?'

'Certainly you must go.'

The direct way in which the magistrate said this caused the driver to rephrase his question. He looked at the magistrate's coat which hung on the hook behind the door, and then glanced at the bottle of spirit which stood on the desk. 'Do you wish us to stay?'

'I can add nothing to what I have said,' said the magistrate, looking from one man to the other, wondering why they were making such a demonstration of their going. Their manner of staying he found a pretence. The guard, although he was looking out of the window, had signified his readiness to depart, and the driver, even though he had been making a play of standing at the doorway with one hand round the frame of the door, and the other wrapped round the door itself, had heard the guard's signal. This question as to whether they might go or stay was no more than a vacillation at the point of their departure. 'You might employ us,' said the driver.

'You are already employed. You would be of no help to me. I need someone with a knowledge of the locality.'

'So you have met the demolition men already have you? What good do you think they will do you? They look the sort who would take advantage of any leeway they are given.'

The magistrate said nothing.

'What is your plan now?' asked the driver.

'What I may do or may not do is hardly a concern of yours.' The magistrate stood in front of his fireplace, looking out of the window and encompassing the guard with his gaze on one hand, and then turning to the door, and encompassing the driver with his gaze to the other.

'So you wish us to go?' asked the driver.

'Certainly. There is no point in your staying.'

'Well.' The driver looked at the magistrate. 'If that is how you wish it. We stayed here, I think I answer for both of us, largely for your benefit. We had formed the impression that you might have needed us and so we had made up our minds that we should, for the moment at least, be prepared to stay.'

The magistrate had for a moment the conviction, no doubt put into his mind by the driver's constant reiterations, that he had not left the city at all, that the journey here had been a pretence, and that the preparations for his travel had been preparations for a journey which would after all never be undertaken. It seemed to him as though it were he and not the driver and the guard who was about to leave. The very clock on the mantel signalled the imminence of the hour of departure. He cast his mind back along the past of the few hours which had elapsed since he had awoken. He was aware that during his examination of his own surroundings he had taken the viewpoint of a new arrival: in this he had been mistaken: his true viewpoint had been that of someone who pauses while grasping for his own peace of mind a rest from the motion of travel. It certainly seemed to him that he was about to resume his interrupted journey. Was that why the driver and the guard had behaved as they had? If he were due to depart, and not the driver and the guard, then why was he so ill-prepared, and why were the driver and the guard so ready to stay, at a moment's notice, in a rhetorical setting aside of their own lives, as though this talk had become no more than a standard preface to further inconclusive argument? He looked from one man to the other. He picked up the handset of the telephone, and then replaced it; then he pressed the bell to summon the housekeeper.

One of the bells from the monastery began to ring; as far as he could tell (though there was no certainty in this) it was the bell which had rung out not only last night but on every other occasion of its sounding. He sat listening to the sound but the continual pauseless beating blocked his further thought. As he looked down at the floor between his feet, in the attitude of an intent listener, the one thought came into

237

his head, over and over again, that this bell had never ceased in its ringing: he heard it now and at some time in the future he would hear it no longer. With a great effort, which cost him most of his strength, he raised his head from his chest and lifted his gaze to the coat which hung behind the door, to look at every loop and curve of the black braiding on its breast and sleeves and every black button on its cuffs. As for the sound: he thought: how far have I fallen; how dull the sound has become; what for all other hope has this noise ever served but to light me to the place where I am.